BURNING SUSPICION

A fiery mystery set in the Scottish Highlands

JAMES ANDREW

THE
BOOK
FOLKS

Published by The Book Folks

London, 2021

ISBN 978-1-913516-54-3

www.thebookfolks.com

To Eve and to all other friends at The Pen and I.

ONE

Alex

It had been a magical sunrise and they had plundered it, out on the shimmering flat of water opposite Nairn that was their world that June morning. They were side by side, dressed in black wetsuits as they stood on paddleboards and pulled them over the calm surface, grinning at each other. Alex was beside himself with the joy of his young marriage and the optimism of what he later realised was his prime. They had risen early to take advantage of the weather, and here they were, in the bay, looking back at the abundant greenness of the Links with its row of sea-gazing houses, and at the bronze-roofed bandstand in the centre of it, flashing at them in the sun. Heather's balance on her board was easy, and Alex was enthralled by the grace in her movements; her black hair flowed around her face, almost like a frame. Her glance caught at the quick of him, as he took in the jaunty angle of her chin, and the challenge in those eyes.

They had been married only a few months and had not long moved to Nairn. Alex had a job in Inverness with an electronics company, and Heather was sure she would be able to find work in the Health Centre, as she said there was always some for a qualified nurse. They were only renting at the moment but were saving for a deposit on a mortgage. They felt in control of their lives.

Alex loved the seafront at Nairn. When they had been exploring Nairn before the move there, they had luxuriated in strolling by the putting green underneath tall trees that bent their leaves in the breeze. The smell of newly cut grass mingled with the tang of the sea as they sat in an octagonal shelter and looked out over the waves. As he remembered it, their voices had mingled with abandon.

And here they were, as they had planned that day, settled in Nairn, and revelling in it. The early morning light gave an ethereal feeling; the shine of water that stretched out to the horizon drifted into a haze. Below their paddleboards could be seen the different shades of the sea as it stretched over rock, seaweed, and sand. The touch of the breeze was a delicate sweep of fingers over the cheeks.

Alex looked to the west towards the Sutors, the two headlands that guarded the entrance to Cromarty on the opposite coast. A rig reflected sunlight; the sharpness of the structure jarred against the roll of hills behind it. Alex knew he was an intruder here, like the rig. Nature has no need of humans gawping at her. Then Alex became aware of it.

A fin broke the surface of the water with an easy roll. Alex pointed and Heather's eyes followed the direction of his finger. The fin broke again, and, as it did so, Alex became aware of the massive body that was being pulled after it. Its darkness added to the impression of bulk. Then Alex realised what he was looking at, a basking shark. He knew that was nothing to be afraid of and started to paddle towards it.

'Alex!' Heather shrieked.

'Nothing to worry about,' Alex said. 'They're harmless.'

But Heather did not follow him, just watched. Alex did not intend to paddle too close. He was not that bold. Any sort of brush with something that size would topple him from his board. But his wonder at the shark drew him on.

Despite its size, it displayed an elegance as it moved its huge gills through the water to sift for plankton. It turned, then turned again in a circular effect. There was a murmur as it broke the surface, and an impression of a deep breath of water. In. Out. Its fins moved like wings; it was a huge animal in flight even if it was in a different element from sky and air.

Alex stopped paddling. He wished he had brought his phone with him. This was his best photo opportunity in ages. As he glanced over at Heather, he saw she had hers out, and was videoing the whole thing. As the creature moved away, Alex reached out with his paddle to pull himself behind it. He wanted to make the most of this. Heather's fear must have disappeared; she did the same.

But they did need to be careful. This beast was heading out to sea, and, if they followed, they could find themselves too far out.

For the moment though, it was enough to follow this shark, and do what it was doing, bask in the moment. Alex thought he had never felt so relaxed. There was such calm in its movements. And, if it had noticed them at all, it paid them no attention, as if they were flotsam.

There was such togetherness with Heather as they both revelled in this wonder of nature. Alex felt insignificant compared to the shark and humbled by it. It was the luck of a moment for him and Heather – this dawn, this beast, this bond between the two of them as they followed it. Alex never forgot that morning. As the years went by it gathered greater meaning. It symbolised a time when he and Heather were together, young, hopeful, and full of wonder.

* * *

As Alex woke up, there were often dreams thrumming through his head and it had come to feel as if these were sent to nag and worry. He often dreamed of that June morning, but, though the memory of it did not lose its appeal, some of the feelings associated with it had. Both he and the circumstances he was living in were different. This morning, as he woke with it in his head, he groaned, and turned.

Recently, he had taken to doing an early morning run. He had never considered himself a runner and had surprised himself with this; now he was amazed he continued with it. But it did successfully dissipate the depression that dominated first thing. His feet pounded away at it, and, by the end of the run, his mood was lighter. He might be physically tired, but he was mentally refreshed.

He was forty-four now and struggling through middle age. They had lived in Nairn for twenty years and he had achieved certain things, but some of them also weighed him down.

He had risen in the company to become Marketing Director. It had taken a lot of work and he had pride in what he had achieved. Heather was well established in the nursing set-up at the Health Centre, and he was proud of her too. They owned their own house and had even paid up a good chunk of the mortgage. They also had a daughter, Anna, who was in her first year at university. Looked at from the outside, everything in their lives seemed set fair.

But inner grumbles were never far away. For one thing, he had risen as far as he would in his job and there were younger more energetic employees who eyed what he had.

Wasn't what he had as much as he could reasonably have hoped for? Was he expecting too much of life? Perhaps he always had. His thoughts drifted back to that June morning. He knew what emotion spoiled the memory of that idyll: it was bitterness. Where had that come from?

He ran out of the front gate and along Altonburn Road. This was a quiet street with a row of houses on one side and greenery on the other, culminating in a wood. He continued his jog till the turn up at the track by the Muthu Newton Hotel. This was the part of the run he enjoyed the most.

It was early November and leaves littered the path; the variegated reds and browns of beech and horse chestnut trees billowed about. At one moment it felt as if he were ploughing through waves of them, and at the next, as they scrunched under his feet, it felt as if he were running on top of an expanse of water made up of leaves. But it was not the glide over the shimmering calm he remembered from that dream dawn. This was a disgruntled tramp over the bruised endings of the year. More in tune with his middle age?

He denied being in the autumn of his life. Middle age was still touched with the vibrancy of youth, wasn't it? Or not. Something in the faded colours of the leaves did echo where he felt he was. He continued pressing down one foot after the other, pushing away at that incessant dissatisfaction; and hoped it would work.

The November air was cold on his skin, but he felt the warmth of his blood pumping through him as he ran. The run was slightly uphill, and his breathing was deep, but his rhythm held. He wished he had been running for longer. He could be fitter than this. When he had first started on this exercise regime, he had been ashamed to discover how unfit he was. It was easy to assume the stamina of youth was still there – until it was tested.

Where had the motivation come from? Partly it stemmed from what he saw when he looked at himself in the mirror, though he found it easy to fool himself when looking at that.

But this need to cling on to anything that might be left of his youth came from a stronger place. Perhaps it had something to do with the memory of that morning out on the water. It had seemed to hold so much promise. Though now he wondered if he had hoped for more than there was in life.

When Alex reached the summit, he turned back with relief. It was downhill home and would be easier.

Alex took in the smells and colours of autumn as he ran. Trees towered over the path, their branches reaching towards each other from either side of the track. It felt as if he was running through a tunnel. And there was a melancholy feel to this darkness.

He continued to push at his limbs. The rhythm of his running cheered somehow. He felt as if he were becoming movement itself. And it was good to know he could do this running lark at forty-four.

But when he turned into the drive leading to his house, he realised what had been bothering him – he was losing Heather.

TWO

The woman Alex was with was called Jasmine; she was leaning across the hotel lounge table towards him. He couldn't help admiring the grey-green eyes, so open and alluring, the sweep of brown hair – and the lips that teased a smile towards him. Jasmine was petite, elegant, and young, with a softness of skin and femininity of scent that beckoned to him. And he was becoming increasingly annoyed by this.

Alex was at the end of his working day but nowhere near going home. After a diligent day at company headquarters in Inverness he had driven off to Elgin and the conference centre in Fraser Park Hotel where he was due to spend his weekend. Work had gone smoothly. Alex was efficient and focused, his underlying discontent only motivating him the more. But he was feeling a particular dissatisfaction with Jasmine. Or told himself he was.

Jasmine was the dutiful secretary he had come to depend on. She organised appointments, reminded him of things he needed to do and places where he needed to be, and, increasingly, pointed out the things he ought to have done but hadn't, which he was grateful for. He didn't want slovenliness creeping in. As an employee, she had more than justified her presence at this conference, which would help in her development. But, since they had arrived, a certain frisson had entered into the working relationship of boss and secretary.

He had not tried to attract Jasmine. Or had he? He didn't think so. He had only intended to pursue the working relationship, but he was starting to realise how personal Jasmine's feelings for him were becoming. Not that his were. Were they? Why was he so drawn to that turn of head and the quickness of that smile? Was that what was irritating him about her? Jasmine was speaking to him now and it brought him out of his ruminations with a jolt.

'It's good to see you in a place where you can be relaxed.'

'Yes?' he said.

'You're always so stressed out.'

'Am I?' he said. 'Maybe.'

'You work too hard.'

He supposed that was true. When had he started doing that? Things had ramped up a lot at work lately, but then they always did.

'I wouldn't believe all the rumours,' Jasmine said.

'Rumours?' he said.

'About the downsizing. That may never happen. Rumours are always coming out of the CEO's office. That's down to Magda. And she makes up most of them.'

Alex laughed, which surprised him. This was a serious subject.

'Magda always looks the epitome of industry and propriety,' he said.

'She's also the queen of the gossips.'

Alex laughed again. Perhaps he was starting to unwind.

'There are more competitors on the horizon,' he said. 'As always. And we have to keep costs down.'

'If they do get rid of anybody, it'll be someone peripheral. It won't be you.'

Why did Jasmine say that? Did she know he worried about it?

'I do get older every year,' he said. 'Which means I have to be twice as good as the young ones coming up.'

'You don't have any trouble competing with them,' Jasmine said. 'You look fitter and younger than a lot of men ten years younger than you.'

Alex knew that was not true. He had to hope the running would help – if he kept it up. He hadn't even graduated to longer runs. And he didn't suppose they would take as much as ten years from him.

'I have started making an effort,' he said.

He was enjoying his morning exercise and had even begun timing himself. He was as ashamed of that as he was proud of it. Was he chasing after something he would never catch up with? His lost youth? And perhaps it was no wonder things had become distant with Heather. He was too busy being somewhere else doing something else. He sipped his gin and tonic, sat back, and looked around him.

He and Jasmine were not at a table by themselves. The others with them were people also attending their conference. They were not people he knew well. He looked at them. They were mostly sales managers and none of them looked as old as he was. He had felt for some time he was developing into a dinosaur. They laughed and joked and knocked back drinks. Someone cracked a joke in his direction to which he gave a distant smile. Someone else made a remark about his company's latest results. Alex replied with an attempt at effusion but there was something unreal about this – and everybody, as if they were cardboard cut-outs – or holograms, gesturing and miming speech, noiselessly, in some sort of vacuum.

Alex did his best to relate to them. This was work. These relationships mattered. He looked down at his glass. It still looked full. He had taken one sip from it. And he supposed he still had his serious work face on. When had he stopped being able to relax?

'I'm glad you suggested I come along to this conference as well,' Jasmine said. She was leaning forward further as if the words she spoke were so confidential.

There was something magnetic about her. He noticed the lift to her chin and the sparkle in her eyes. He tried to remember why he had been annoyed with her. Oh yes. It was this interest in him, which she was making so obvious. It wasn't something he wanted. Was it? He was a happily married man. Wasn't he? That was what he'd told himself he wanted to be, and it was how he had seen himself for a long time.

He gave her what he hoped was an executive's work smile. She leaned even closer. He supposed she thought he had invited her on this weekend for reasons other than work. He sighed. If she could read something in him that encouraged this, it was his own fault. He had never stopped noticing young women, but he worried he had been developing an obsession with them lately: the lift in their steps, the curve of their breasts under their top. He turned his head at anything. He had never thought middle age would make him like this. He smiled again at Jasmine. As she smiled in return, he realised she had stopped annoying him, and he had a strong idea about what that was going to lead to.

THREE

Alex did not hang about after receiving a phone call like the one he'd received. He was in his car and revving away as soon as he could manage it. He'd had that large gin and tonic and he knew he shouldn't be driving, not in Scotland, but he would have to risk it. This was urgent. It was night-time and there was not a lot of traffic on the road, which helped him keep up his speed, but he did remind himself to drive carefully. As his car powered through the darkness, the headlights gave clarity to the gloom – and to his thoughts which raced almost as fast as his car. His house on fire. Oh God, Heather must be in there. She was probably asleep when it started. Or did she manage to get out in time? He could not bear thinking about any of this.

He kept his foot down, then realised he was taking corners too fast. He had to cut that out. Another car passed going in the other direction, the lights glaring in his eyes. Keep your concentration on the road. Watch the cat's eyes. Keep them in their correct place. Breathe calmly. Don't let things get to you.

He drove on. The road disappeared under his wheels but too slowly. He tried to will the miles behind him, but nothing hurried this journey. He kept his hands firm on the wheel and kept up the pace; he would do this.

When he drove up Altonburn Road he could see the fire raging ahead. There were vehicles at his house, and people round it. A fire engine stood in the drive. And there were two others in the street. Fire crews aimed hoses. Alex brought his car to a shuddering halt, without paying attention to how he parked. He got out and ran towards the house.

A policeman stood in front of him, and he stopped.

'And you are, sir?' The official voice struck him. There was something offensive about that authoritarian neutrality.

'That's my house,' he said. 'It's on fire.'

The stupidity of what he had said struck him. Anyone could see the house was on fire. That was why the fire engine was there. And that was why the flames were surging out of it.

But why had the constable picked him out to ask questions? There were other onlookers. And what were they doing there, staring at his house as it was being destroyed in front of him? But he sensed nothing going to stop the neutral urgency of the policeman's questioning.

'And your name is, sir?'

Alex ignored the question and stared at the fire. How long had that been raging away?

'Is Heather still in there?' he shouted at him.

'Heather?'

'Is my wife still in there?'

He did manage not to call him a numbskull. Alex thought that was good but noticed he was screaming at the man. He supposed that was why there was a flash of anger in the policeman's eyes. Alex had to admire the man's control as the emotion was quickly buried in the official face before a look of heartfelt concern showed itself.

'Your wife might be in there?'

But Alex now stared at him as if he was an idiot.

'She was asleep in bed. Where else is she going to be?'

'Oh God.'

The constable stared, looking as if he did not want to believe this.

'You'd better come along with me, sir.'

'Come along with you? What do you mean? You ought to be in that building getting my wife out.'

'Now calm down, sir.'

'I'm perfectly calm.'

Alex was yelling at him. He was being unreasonable and knew it. He stared at the building. It had been a smart enough bungalow and a decent size. The flames seemed to make it grow larger. His house was an inferno. But it had been blazing a while now and it was obvious Heather must have been burned to a crisp long before this.

'My sergeant will want to speak to you about your wife, sir,' the constable was saying. Alex and he stood and stared at each other for a moment. 'And the fire chief needs to know if there really is a woman in there.'

Someone should have told them about Heather long before this. Perhaps he should have done. It had been a neighbour who had phoned him. Alex didn't know why that was. The confusion of the moment? But Alex had asked his caller about Heather; and he'd told him about her. Had the man not passed any of that on?

He spoke firmly to the policeman beside him.

'Take me to the fire chief.'

'Yes, sir.'

He followed the constable with impatience. The fire chief was standing together with the police sergeant, as they surveyed the response. They were middle-aged men with the bulk of uniform and the solidity of office, but both had a look of alarm on their faces when they were informed that there might be somebody trapped inside.

'Where's the bedroom, sir?' the fire chief asked.

At least he wasn't attempting unemotional tones. Alex pointed as he told him. The fire chief stepped away and towards the men on the hoses. Then he came back to Alex.

'When we arrived, the fire was up too much to enter the building,' he said. 'We looked for indications someone was inside but there were none. Are you sure she was in there?'

'Yes.' Then Alex became exasperated again. 'Instead of standing around talking about it, shouldn't some of you be doing your jobs and going in there to rescue her? Why are you wasting time talking to me?'

The fire chief looked back at Alex. Then he looked across at the sergeant.

'They've been fighting this fire for hours, sir,' the sergeant said.

'But Heather! Why haven't they been in there to get her out?'

The sergeant did not look as if he knew how to reply to that.

'If there had been any sign of life, sir,' the fire chief said.

'Sign of–? Couldn't she have been overcome by the smoke?'

'Of course,' the sergeant said, 'but–'

'It was impossible to go in when we arrived, sir,' the fire chief said.

'Impossible? But Heather was in there. And you just stood and watched it burn?'

'These are firemen, sir,' the sergeant replied. 'They don't stand and watch anything burn.'

Alex turned his gaze on the flames that had been his house.

'Heather,' he said, but he was talking to himself now. He knew the futility of arguing but he was still sure there was something the firemen could have done. 'Heather,' he said again, and found himself starting to run towards the building. Then arms were around him and he was stopped.

'It won't do any good, sir, really it won't. Leave it to us.'

Alex found himself standing with his face turned towards the sergeant. He attempted to pull away, but the sergeant's grip was strong, and Alex could not overcome it.

'You've made your point,' Alex said. 'Now let go of me.'

But the sergeant didn't. His hands still grasped Alex.

'You need to calm down, sir.'

'Calm?' Alex replied. 'How can I be calm? That's my wife in there. Do you think I'm a block of stone or something?'

'You do need to get a grip though, don't you?'

There was a tone of menace in the sergeant's voice.

'And we're not going to let you kill yourself in that fire.'

'Kill?' Alex said.

Then the meaning of what the sergeant had said sank in. Alex turned his head towards the building again. He supposed the sergeant was right. There was nothing he could do. The futility of his situation struck home, and the start of a tear began its way from an eye.

'I can't–' he said. 'There must be something.' Then a sob escaped him. 'No, no, no, no.' Another one retched up and he felt something tearing him apart. 'Heather,' he moaned again.

'I know, sir,' the sergeant said. 'I know.'

His tone was gentle now, and that was worse. Then more sobs were surging through Alex. Shudders engulfed him. 'Heather.' The word escaped again. It rushed towards the flames and joined them, burning and soaring into the air with the sparks.

Alex felt a different arm on his shoulder and looked to see who it was. Jason, his next-door neighbour but one. Jason was a figure only spoken to occasionally, and now his arm was round Alex and his concerned face was in his. Alex became aware of more neighbours drawing close.

'We're so sorry, Alex'. That was Aileen.

'If there's anything we can do, just say.' That was Anne.

Alex should have been glad of this sympathy but all he felt was anger. What right did they have to see him like this? What were they doing feeling sorry for him?

'This is awful, and I feel for you.' Jason again.

He also asked if there was anything he could do to help. What sort of stupid remark was that? What was there anyone could do? But Alex bit back the reply. He knew he ought to take control of himself, as the sergeant had said, and he forced himself not to snap at the man. A perplexed look was on Jason's face. His other neighbours looked puzzled too. Then a reply found its way to Alex's lips.

'Thank you. It's good of you to offer.'

But the fury still surged in him, and Alex turned his face away as Jason stepped back.

'It's a shock, sir,' the sergeant said. 'It's bound to be.'

The patience in the man's voice was welcome if inexplicable. Alex stood up and looked around him. It was a busy scene, with firemen and hoses, and onlookers, not all of them neighbours. Some stared. One or two looked as if they might have liked to say something. There were people he had passed and nodded to as he had gone about his everyday business, often without knowing anything much about them. But everyone knew about this. It occurred to Alex it was the middle of the night. What were all these people doing here? He supposed this would be difficult to sleep through. In any case, there must have been the worry more than just Alex's house might have gone up. The neighbours should be grateful for the size of Alex's garden, not that it looked much of one at the moment. It was a mass of hoses and men with big boots. Shrubs Heather had planted only weeks ago were trodden right down.

A different voice found its way towards him. This one was feminine, soft, and trying to comfort. He recognised it straight away. Elsa's. He turned and looked towards her.

'Alex. Are you OK?'

Of course I'm not OK a voice screamed in his head.

'I suppose,' he said.

Elsa didn't live in this street. What was she doing here? The fire had caused a commotion.

'Heather?' she said.

'I don't know,' he said.

'She's in there?'

Anguish tore through Alex again. He did not speak at first. Then a word forced its way out. 'Yes.'

'God. Surely not?'

'Where else would she be?'

'Oh God.'

There was such sympathy on Elsa's face. She held her arms wide, then hugged him, which he responded to gratefully. The feeling of another human being close at such a time was helpful, as well as natural.

Elsa was someone he and Heather had a lot to do with, though he did not know her well as such, certainly not well enough to have ever been the subject of an embrace from her before. She wasn't a friend. She was their maid. The curly-haired brunette would be seen around their house every Thursday as she busied herself.

'Were you away?' Elsa asked.

'A conference in Elgin,' Alex replied.

Then he turned towards the fire and looked helplessly at it.

'I wish I hadn't been,' he said.

'It's just as well you were,' Elsa said.

Alex didn't reply, just stared at the blaze. He wondered how long it would continue to burn.

'Why is there a police sergeant here?' Elsa asked.

Alex searched for a reply. 'Damage to property, risk to life, I suppose,' Alex said.

Alex felt comforted by Elsa's presence. Everything was bizarre. It was good to speak with someone so familiar. He took in Elsa's lean face again as he glanced at her. She was a middle-aged woman but had a fit and sturdy look to her, from her job, Alex supposed, though Elsa was not just a cleaner. She owned the cleaning company, and had others working for her, though she usually did their house herself. When she visited them, she always carried such a sense of being in control of the things that happened around her.

She was a competent person so that was not surprising. It was good to feel her presence, even though there was now anxiety on her face.

'I got a phone call,' Alex said. 'I don't think I've ever driven that road so fast.'

'I don't suppose you have.'

'The thought that Heather's in there.'

'I know.'

'Oh God. I didn't need to go to that conference. That sort of thing gains kudos at work, but I wasn't learning anything I didn't already know.'

Elsa's look was patient.

'I should have been here,' he continued. 'Maybe I could have done something to stop the fire.'

'Don't torture yourself,' Elsa told him.

'We don't know, do we? Maybe I could.'

'Or perhaps you'd have been caught in it too.'

'If I'd been with her, I'd have preferred that.'

There was a pause as they both stared at the fire.

'Do they know what started it?' Elsa asked.

'They haven't said. I don't suppose they do yet.'

'They're doing everything they can.'

The anxiety built up again in Alex.

'That's not been any help, has it? The house is burning down completely.'

Alex heard his voice becoming frantic.

'Why didn't they get here earlier? Why didn't they get her out?'

Another sob burst out of him. Elsa gave him another hug, which didn't help this time. More sobs built up in him and forced themselves out. Words seemed to fail Elsa.

Alex turned away from her and glared at the fire. They both stood there doing that for some time. Then another voice found its way to him; he recognised it: it was Heather's. Heather? Was he hallucinating now? He whirled round. No. Heather was there. Standing in front of him. Heather, with that upwards tilt to her head, that sweep of black hair, and those hazel eyes, which were holding an appeal in them now, for some sort of sense to all of this, he supposed.

'Alex?' she said. 'Thank God you're here. What's going on?'

'Heather,' he said, then realised he was gaping. 'I thought you were in there. We all thought you were. Thank God you're not.'

Then his arms were round Heather, and he felt he never wanted to stop holding her again. Fearing he might be squeezing her to death, he released her, before stepping back and gazing, and he could feel tears were trying to squeeze their way out of his eyes. 'It's fantastic to see you again,' he said.

'And you,' Heather replied.

She turned her head to look at the building, then turned to Alex. Something seemed to strike her.

'You're right. I could have been in there, couldn't I?' she said.

She stared at the flames again. Then she noticed Elsa.

'Am I glad to see you,' Elsa said. 'We were so worried. We were sure you'd gone up with the fire.' Elsa flashed a smile at Heather that was dazzling in the relief it showed.

'You were somewhere else?' Alex asked. 'Thank God for that. But where were you?'

Heather hesitated for a micro-moment. Or was that his imagination? 'I was at Margaret's,' Heather said.

'Margaret's?' Alex replied.

'Margaret Affleck. You know her.'

'I have met her, I think,' Alex said. 'But why were you over at her place?'

Heather hesitated for another mini-second, then said with what looked like difficulty, 'Her mother's died.'

'How awful,' Elsa said.

'Oh no,' Alex said. 'I'm sorry to hear it. That must have been sudden.'

'Hardly that,' Heather said. 'It was cancer – and it was a few weeks ago. But Margaret hadn't been talking about it. So things boiled up inside her and she needed to talk things through tonight, which was why I was over, and time just passed.'

'It would,' Alex said. 'And you didn't know about the fire till you turned up here?'

'No. Did you?'

'I received a phone call.'

'What happened? How did it start?'

The same question he was wondering about.

'I don't know.'

'They'll investigate it,' Elsa said.

'But it'll take a while,' Alex said.

The sergeant, who must have picked up on the conversation, walked over at this point.

'Heather Ross?' he said.

'That's right,' Heather replied. The smile she attempted to give him didn't work. She was far too anxious about all of this.

'Alex's wife?'

'That's right.'

'We're ever so pleased you're not in there. Alex thought you must be.'

'I was at a friend's. She had an emergency.'

'I see. There's not likely to be another person in your house, is there? Someone's just told us you have a daughter?'

'Anna. Yes. But she's away at university.'

'And there's no likelihood of anyone else being in there?'

Alex and Heather looked at each other.

'No,' Alex said.

'Thank God for that,' the sergeant said. 'The fire's been burning for some time – and will burn for a lot longer. Then we might get in there to work out what happened. Have you any idea how it could have started?'

Funny it should be the sergeant asking that. Alex and Heather looked at each other. 'No,' they replied, almost in unison.

'We'll talk some more about that later on, sir. We've had reports some kids were letting off fireworks in the vicinity. It's a windy night. It's possible one of their rockets was carried onto your building and set the whole thing off. Though that's a guess at the moment.'

'We did have fire alarms, two of them,' Alex said. 'And I checked the batteries only last week.'

'Where will you spend the night?' the sergeant asked. 'Do you have anyone you can stay with?'

'There's my mother – or Heather's parents,' Alex said.

'But they live nowhere near Nairn,' Heather said.

'We'll find you a hotel, sir. Don't worry about that. Stay around here and we'll get it sorted.'

Alex's mind went blank. He hadn't given a thought to where they were going to stay. But then his mind hadn't finished reeling from the thought Heather might be dead. And he was still adjusting to the fact she wasn't. But never mind tonight, he thought. What about afterwards? Alex looked at the burning remnants of his house. He took in again the yellow-clothed figures of firemen, and all those bystanders. It was a cloudless night with a myriad of stars above. The moon was full or nearly so. He could see so clearly the amount of destruction – and everything he owned was in there. He was sloughing off his previous life as a snake sheds a skin. But there was nothing new to replace it, just an emptiness welling up inside him. Then he felt Heather's hand in his, warm and giving. They hugged each other again.

FOUR

Across the river loomed Inverness Castle, a statement of castellated solidity. Its grandeur impressed tourists, but left Alex untouched today. Last night's euphoria – and he had experienced some of that after he realised Heather had survived the conflagration – had evaporated. Their house and everything they owned had been turned to ash, leaving them with what? The clothes they stood up in, the monthly payments on their cars, and the weight of the depression that sat on their shoulders. Everything else was gone: the furniture and possessions they'd built up over the years, the albums of family occasions, the paintings they had bought as remembrances of holidays shared, the presents given and received, and the mementoes of Anna's childhood spent in that house, like the door where her height had been measured and recorded every year. Alex felt he was walking into an overwhelming and empty present with nothing to prop him up but the clothes he stood up in.

Alex put money into the machine at Cathedral Car Park, took the proffered ticket, turned, and walked back to his Audi. Heather stood waiting beside it. He put the ticket on his dashboard, closed the door, and pressed the lock button on his keypad.

'Are you ready?' he said.

The look Heather gave him in return was wry. 'Ready? How could we be for any of this?'

Her gloom matched his own that morning. It was a pity one of them wasn't feeling forward looking, but what could be expected?

'I don't know,' he said. 'But we might as well get started.'

He glanced over at the Cathedral beside them. The old stone building gave familiarity but did not cheer. He didn't think anything could.

They crossed the road onto the path that followed the river into town. In summer, this was a peaceful stroll, but he noted the river was full today. Rain must have fallen in the hills behind Inverness, and the water here was swirling, and encroaching far up the green banks behind the iron fence.

They walked towards Ness Bridge and the city centre. Alex plumbed his mood and tried to define the anxiety at the centre of it. There were enough things to worry about, but what was that eating away at him? He shook his head and tried to dismiss the question.

They had decided to buy the things they needed in Inverness; it would be easier than shopping in Nairn where they would be faced with endless questions from people they knew, and probably people they didn't. They needed to suffer by themselves.

As they walked over the concrete sweep of Ness Bridge, Alex was looking at the modernist architecture ahead of him. Inverness had been developed in the sixties and seventies, brutalised some had said. At one time there had been a stone bridge where Ness Bridge stood now, but it had been deemed too narrow for contemporary city traffic. There were still some traditional buildings further on, but the huge block that was Eastgate Centre, Inverness's mall, when they eventually reached it, dominated its space with concrete, glass, and steel. Alex felt proud of a mall like that in a small place like Inverness, in common with everyone else local who appreciated the convenience of the shopping; yet, when visitors came, they showed little interest in it. They said it made the place the same as everywhere else. Today, Alex and Heather's only interest was in the wares in its shops.

They started off at Boots as they had no toiletries except what their hotel provided. Alex glowered at shelves of shaving gel and razors as Heather wandered off to shelves that supplied her needs. Alex had difficulty concentrating on this. Other shoppers annoyed him as they loitered and picked out items. How could anyone be calm when he was in the turmoil of emotions that he was?

Gloomy thoughts flitted through his head. He felt he no longer recognised himself. Why was that? He realised the extent to which possessions must have defined him. Anyone could have seen he was a successful person because of the house he owned. When that was stripped away from him, what did that leave? Perhaps that was not as silly as it might sound. A roof over a man's head gave a feeling of certainty; it was a place in the world separate from the everyday anxieties of earning a living. He realised he had unknowingly carried something of his home with him even as he drove away in the mornings; that hadn't occurred to him till it was gone.

He was still staring at the same range of gels. He picked one then frowned. He never bought that brand, not that he could remember why. He put it back and grabbed another one. It was probably one he normally said he hated too but he could not bring himself to care or think properly about what he was doing.

After he and Heather had filled a couple of carrier bags each in various shops, they wandered off to Costa's where they queued for coffee and doughnuts, then collapsed in coffee-coloured armchairs by a plate-glass window overlooking the ground court of the mall. The people walking past were strangers and Alex was grateful for the anonymity. They had not yet met anyone from Nairn, or his place of work.

'That was depressing,' Alex said.

'Wasn't it?' Heather replied.

Alex sipped his coffee and looked out. A mother was pushing a pram with an older child walking beside her. The woman's cheerfulness struck Alex. He felt like asking her to join them, but they didn't know her.

He turned to Heather and said, 'I didn't see a single shirt I liked.'

'You did buy some though?' Heather said.

Alex leaned down to a carrier bag and pulled one out. It looked limp and unattractive.

'You never buy black shirts,' Heather said.

'Is that what it is?' Alex said. 'So it is.'

'You must have noticed,' Heather said.

She reached down and looked in one of her own bags.

'Hmm,' she said, and the tone sounded dubious. 'I must have been thinking about something else today too.'

Alex laughed. He wondered if it was hysteria.

Heather continued in a calmer tone. 'I hadn't been considering buying clothes just now, and I don't suppose you had either.'

'Probably not.'

'I thought of that dress I bought last month with those red flowers. Gone. In a puff of smoke. Literally. So I tried to find another one the same. But, do you know, I couldn't remember for the life of me where I'd bought it.'

Alex tried to give thought to the problem, but he didn't suppose he was with Heather when she made the purchase.

'You did buy pyjamas?' Heather asked.

'I got the essentials.' There was confidence in his voice, but he knew there would be something he had forgotten.

'I've no perfume,' Heather said.

'That's an essential?' Alex asked.

'Yes,' Heather replied.

Alex thought of the bottle he'd bought Heather the Christmas before. It had seemed sixty pounds well spent. Heather must have been persuasive.

'But there are more important things to worry about,' he said.

'I can't think what,' Heather replied, and he saw she was now repressing a grin, which was more cheerful.

But neither of them said anything for a while. Alex wondered where Heather's thoughts had wandered to.

'How's Margaret?' he asked Heather.

'Margaret?'

'You were with her last night?'

'Oh, that,' Heather said. 'That was grisly.'

'Was it very difficult with her mother?'

'Ever so. It was cancer. It's like a release when they finally go.'

'I'm sure it is.'

'That's what made it so tough for her. She was glad when her mother finally died, and she felt so guilty about feeling that way.'

'You haven't mentioned Margaret's mother before?'

'I haven't seen Margaret for a while. That's why. She was tied up with looking after her.'

Alex thought of his own mother; she had been on her own for so long since father died.

'I really felt for her.'

'Yes,' Alex said.

'We talked into the small hours,' Heather said, 'and, when I drove home, I discovered I didn't have one.'

'I was quaffing a gin and tonic in a bar with colleagues when the mobile rang,' Alex said.

'Lucky you.'

'I don't feel that now.'

'No.'

'I drove like a madman. And when I got home, there were people and vehicles all over the place, and all those flames. It didn't feel real.'

Alex sipped his coffee. He had forgotten about it, and it was no longer quite hot. There was a sharp taste, and he did like that. It brought concentration to his mind. He became more aware of the bustle in the café: the queue at the counter, and the chatter at the tables. That was what he liked about coffee shops: they were busy. They were often full of complete strangers – as now – leading intimate lives so close but so separate. It suited Alex when he wanted to hold his feelings close, as he did now. He was glad no one from his work frequented Costa.

'Have you any idea how we're going to get through this?' he asked.

'No. But do tell me we will because it doesn't feel like it now.'

Then Alex realised how anxious Heather was – as he would expect her to be. She must have been making a huge effort not to show her feelings more. Alex attempted to sound strong.

'We will get through it.'

What sounded like a snort came from Heather; Alex supposed she was going to get into one of her stews.

'We have our health, our jobs, and our wits. Why wouldn't we?' he said.

But Heather arced questioning eyebrows at him.

'We've got to tell people,' she said. 'We haven't done that yet. Not that I've any idea how we do it. But Anna will have to know. And my parents. And your mother. And all we've been doing is selfishly hiding away.'

That made Alex smart with guilt. That had been his idea – to wait till they'd calmed down a bit and had worked out how to tell them. That was because he was afraid of his mother's reaction. She'd been fragile since father died. Not that he had any idea how to explain this to Anna either.

'It's a good job Anna lives away from home,' he said. 'She has her own life at university separate from all this.'

'It'll be an awful shock. She's lost a lot of things. And there isn't a home for her to come back to.'

Then Heather's face seemed to crumple. Alex reached over to her, but she pulled away. Why would she do that?

Alex looked at her. Heather was struggling with this, as he knew he was too. They sat in silence.

Alex thought back to Heather's friend, Margaret. When had Heather last mentioned her before last night? Yet that was where she had been when their house burned down.

'Are you going to eat that doughnut?' Heather asked.

Alex looked down at it, then across at hers.

'No,' he said. 'Are you?'

Heather took a hesitant nibble then pulled a face and put the doughnut down.

She looked so normal, and so natural, and so… Heather. He dismissed the suspicion that had occurred to him. Of course she had been at Margaret Affleck's.

FIVE

The police had phoned saying they wanted to talk, and Alex and Heather were seated in their hotel lounge, waiting for them to arrive. The place felt insipid to Alex with its beige tones and standard furnishings reflecting a feel for inoffensiveness and geometry rather than taste, though the seats were comfortable enough.

'I wonder what the police want,' Heather said.

Alex's look was questioning. 'Our house burned down?'

'They want to know if we did it?'

'Of course they do. They're the police.'

'This is all we need.'

He looked across at her as she began studying her long pink nails, something she did when anxious, as if the secret to coping with stress lay in carefully tended nails.

'You're right,' Alex said.

When the police did arrive, Alex turned out to be the jumpier one. He found himself facing a police inspector, who introduced himself as Detective Inspector Black and was dressed in plain clothes though the black woollen jacket he wore was not unlike police issue. And Alex saw he had brought a sergeant with him, who Alex learned was Detective Sergeant McPherson.

Alex studied the inspector. He was a tall man in his early fifties, with salt-and-pepper hair. There was a confident if stern look on his face; he had a long nose that hooked out from under luxuriant eyebrows; his eyes were dark, expressive and intimidating; and they were fixed upon Alex.

'You kept us waiting,' Alex said.

Now, why had that blurted from his mouth? Alex wondered what kind of powder keg of emotion he was. He became aware of Heather's frown and attempted to temper the comment.

'Though that's in your favour. It shows how busy you've been.'

The inspector just said, 'I'm sorry we were late.'

Alex tried to think of something else accommodating to say, but all that occurred was another sharp rejoinder. The fire must have upset him even more than he had realised. Why did he have to be so on edge?

'These situations are difficult,' the inspector said as he seated himself opposite. McPherson continued to stand. The sergeant remained no more than an impression of a large man in a crumpled suit to Alex, who could not take his eyes off the inspector. Black settled in his seat and inspected both Alex and Heather.

'How are you coping?' he asked, and the tone was sympathetic.

It was Heather who replied. Alex was biting back another sharp comment.

'With difficulty,' she said, and her look was weary. 'It's been horrendous. Everything we owned up in flames like that. How does anyone deal with that?'

'You've access to enough money?' Black asked.

'Yes,' Heather said. 'We had our cards on us. Which have been in use. We only had the clothes we stood up in.'

'I expect so,' Black said. 'Horrendous. How's the hotel?'

'It's a hotel,' Alex said. 'Hardly a home from home. Comfortless and full of strangers.'

'The management aren't sympathetic?'

'They are. Very,' Heather said. 'Don't pay any attention to Alex. This whole thing has turned him inside out.'

'It would have that effect on me too,' Black said.

'Not that I mean to be snappish,' Alex said.

'What did you want to see us about, Inspector?' Heather asked.

'Just some questions,' Black said. 'And I do have information to give.'

'Information?' Alex asked.

'Not that the investigation has concluded.'

'Do you know how the fire started?' Alex said.

'No.'

'The sergeant said it might have been due to kids playing with fireworks in the area?' Alex asked.

'And we still don't know it wasn't. But we have worked out the area where the fire started.'

'Which was?'

'Your utility.'

'That's separate from the house.'

'But close enough. And you'd electricity in there?'

'Yes.'

'Were there electrical problems that you know of?'

'No,' Alex said. 'There was a circuit problem – but that was in the main building and we had an electrician out to fix that. About six months ago. I don't know of anything else.'

'Who was the electrician?'

'A local man. McGregor. Lives in Tradespark.'

'We know of him. We'll get in touch with him. Thanks.'

'Was it caused by an electrical fault?' Heather asked.

'We don't know, but it's another area for investigation.'

'When will you know?' Alex asked.

'A few days. Do you have house insurance?'

'Yes,' Alex said.

'That'll help you. Is it just buildings?'

'Contents as well.'

'You'll get up and running again – all in good time unfortunately. But you'll get there.'

Black was empathetic. Alex had not expected an interview with a police inspector to be so easy. He was starting to relax and was even beginning to take to Black.

'You don't know anyone who would wish you harm?'

But that question took him aback.

'What do you mean?' he said.

'It's a standard question,' Black replied. 'Some of them embarrass me too.'

'Do you think it was started deliberately?' Heather's tone was sharp.

'We can't rule out anything until we've established what did happen.' Black looked questioningly at Alex and Heather again. 'Might anyone have wanted to upset you?'

'I don't know anyone who would want to do anything like this to us,' Heather said.

'Nor me,' Alex said.

'We do get strangers calling sometimes,' Heather said, 'Jehovah's Witnesses, jobbing gardeners, that sort of thing.'

'Has there been anyone recently?' Black asked.

'There was somebody who wanted to clean the gutters,' Alex said. 'But I do that myself.'

'Do you know who?' Black asked.

'He said he would be in the area for only a short period of time. He had an Irish accent.'

'Interesting. What did he look like?' Black asked.

'Let me think,' Alex replied. 'About medium height. Stocky. In his thirties. Brown hair. A sort of sallow complexion. An outdoor look to him.'

'I don't suppose he gave a name?'

'He left a card.'

'Do you still have it?'

Alex gave a sardonic laugh. 'I put it in the drawer in the hall where we keep all the tradesmen's cards, but that will have been destroyed in the fire.'

'We could check. You don't remember what it said on it, do you?'

'There was a phone number which I didn't even read. The card didn't have an individual's name. It did have a trading name. Logistical Home Maintenance. Odd title. But it must have made sense to him.'

'Striking enough. And he might have left that card somewhere else. We can ask around about that.'

'True,' Alex said.

'And I have to continue with my standard questions, I'm afraid,' the inspector said.

'Do you?' Alex said, thinking that sounded ominous.

'I need an account of your movements last night, Mr Ross, and yours, Mrs Ross.'

'In case we fancied making ourselves homeless.' Alex was embarrassed at how cutting his reply was.

'You'd be surprised what happens,' Black replied. 'But no,' he said. 'I'm just trying to build up a general picture.'

'I was in Elgin,' Alex said, 'at a conference to do with work. I was in company all evening, first at a lecture, then in the bar, which is where I was when the phone rang, and I was given the bad news.'

'Thank you. And your movements, Mrs Ross?' Black asked. 'Your husband said he expected you to be asleep at home?'

'Thank God I wasn't. It must have been a worry to him though,' she said, shooting a sympathetic look at Alex.

Then an odd look appeared on Heather's face. 'And whoever set fire to the building probably thought I was inside at the time?'

'It would be possible,' Black said.

'Surely not?' Alex said.

Heather did not say anything, just stared, then said. 'You mean I might have been lucky?'

'We don't know yet if the fire was started deliberately.'

Alex wondered how truthful Black was being; they were being interviewed by a police inspector; they must have suspicions.

'But you'll get that worked out?' Alex said.

'Oh, yes,' Black replied. 'And where did you say you were?' he asked Heather.

'I had a phone call from a friend.'

'Yes?'

'Margaret Affleck. It's not long since her mother died, and she needed to talk.'

'You were at her house?'

'That's right.'

'From about what time?'

'I must have gone out – I don't know – about nine.'

'And the first you knew about the fire was when you came back, which was about one?'

'That's right.'

'That sounds clear enough.'

The look on Black's face was satisfied. 'And it's a relief you were elsewhere,' he said. 'The incident would have been much worse if you hadn't been.'

'And then some,' Alex said.

'It doesn't bear thinking about,' Heather said.

'I won't bother you any more at the moment,' Black said. 'You're under enough pressure as it is. Can I ask if you two could find time – at some point in the next few days – to come into the local station to give statements?'

'Surely that can't be necessary?' Alex said.

Black gave him a benign but firm look.

'It's routine. If you want us to sign off on this so you can make a claim to your insurance company, we have to dot our i's and cross our t's.' Black's smile was indulgent.

'I suppose,' Alex said.

'It's no trouble,' Heather said. 'Is it, Alex?'

Alex gave her a wearisome look.

After Black and his sergeant had taken their leave, Heather turned to Alex. 'That was easier than I thought it would be.'

'I suppose,' Alex said.

'Were you trying to annoy him?'

'Definitely not,' Alex said.

He knew better than to anger Heather. At least they had come across to the inspector as a couple who got on with each other – he hoped. He gave her what was meant to be a reasonable approximation of a smile.

Heather's look at him became more patient. 'We've been through a lot.'

'Yes,' Alex said.

'Thank God for a tolerant inspector.'

Alex didn't reply. He played safe and tried a vague smile as he stood up.

'Shall we get coffee?' he said.

'I'm not sure I could manage anymore.'

Alex sat down again feeling awkward. He thought he'd behaved reasonably to Inspector Black. It was Heather's mood that was uncertain. One thing that did please him was how convincing Heather had been when telling the police inspector her alibi, but then, when he thought about it, she always was.

SIX

Alex had been putting off phoning his mother but had decided he could do so no longer. He was listening to the phone ring at the other end of the line. It was ringing and ringing. What was keeping her? Was she all right? Then an elderly female voice was speaking in his ear. 'Hello,' it said. His mother always used to answer with her phone number, but he had managed to train her not to do that. He'd told her some people dialled random phone numbers so it paid not to tell them which one they had reached. She didn't understand why anyone would do that, as, he had to confess, he didn't, but he knew it happened. He also told her not to give her name which she had usually insisted on. So it was music to his ears to hear the simple hello. Was he as fussy about his own safety? Possibly not, going by the present situation he was in.

'It's Alex,' he said.

'I thought I was the one who owed you a phone call. Is something wrong?'

She was as sharp as ever.

'A problem came up,' he said.

'You've smashed up your car.'

He had done that before, not long after qualifying to drive; he'd been driving fast for the first time. Though it was a long time ago, Mother still didn't let him forget.

'The car's all right,' he said.

'Do you need to borrow money?'

Mother always treated him as so much younger than he was, which, though irritating, was also refreshing. He did not feel middle-aged when talking to his mother.

'When have I ever needed to do that?' he asked.

'You were always running out when you were at university.'

And how long ago was that?

'I was poor then,' he said. 'Everybody is when they're students.'

He wondered if other people's mothers were the same after their children had grown up. At least she didn't treat him as if he were ten anymore. He had been embarrassed by that as a student. It had been too amusing for his friends.

'Though this is worse,' he said.

'Is it?' Alarm shot through his mother's voice.

'You're not going to believe it. I don't think I do.'

'That sounds bad. Out with it then. What's happened?'

The pause at his end embarrassed him, but he did not know how to phrase this.

'The house has burned down,' he said.

There was silence for what seemed a long time, then her sharp voice said, 'You're joking aren't you? Is this April the first?'

'Hardly. It's November.'

'How did it happen?' she said, and words started tumbling out from her. 'Is anyone injured? Heather's all right, is she? And Anna?'

'There was nobody in the building at the time. It's just the house that's been damaged. Which is bad enough.'

'How did it start?'

'They don't know yet. They think it might have been a firework. There were kids larking around in the area. Or it could have been an electrical fault. They're investigating.'

'This is awful. Can anything be rescued?'

'They're assessing it. But I expect it'll need a complete rebuild.'

'Oh no. I am sorry this has happened to you, Alex.'

'Thanks. So am I.'

'Not that it was a nice house in the first place.'

'You always said that.' She had too, as Alex remembered well.

'I was disappointed you bought that one. Such a poor sitting room. I thought that one you looked at in Auldearn was better.'

'And more expensive,' Alex said. 'We got this one at a good price. Our solicitor couldn't believe it.'

'I could.'

And it had been Alex's pride and joy. And Heather's. Neither of them had ever seen what mother disliked about the place.

'Yes, mother.'

'What are you going to do now?'

'We're still working that out. We're staying in a hotel for now.'

'Will the insurance pay for that?'

Would it? He had no idea.

'Because you can come and stay with me in the meantime. You know that?'

Alex did. He also knew how Heather would react to it. His mother would treat them like kids. Heather could put up with her in small doses only. Perhaps if his father had lived, he would have tempered mother. Well, Alex had done his duty. He had kept her up to date. And, no doubt, worried her silly.

'Are you still keeping up with Betty?' he said.

'She's a scutter these days.'

'You are getting company?'

Alex knew his mother needed to talk everything over with somebody. Who was she friendly with now?

'I was going over to Eileen's this afternoon,' she said. 'I could depress her with your news. How could you let such a thing happen, Alex?'

'You might well ask,' Alex said.

'Do you have clean underpants and shirts and so on?'

'All up in smoke but plastic is a wonderful thing these days.'

'Plastic?'

'Plastic cards. Useful for buying things in shops.'

'I had a picture of you walking around in a plastic bag.'

'We're not that desperate.'

'If you need anything from me–'

'We only have to ask. I know. And I'm grateful.'

'Come round for a meal tonight.'

'Thanks, but we need to get on with things.'

'How's Heather coping? She was always such an anxious thing.'

'Heather?' He thought about how to reply to that.

'She hides it beneath all that bossiness,' his mother said. 'But she'll need a lot of help from you to get through this. I can't think how I'd cope if it happened to me.'

'We're working through things together. Don't worry.'

And he hoped they would.

'And Anna? How's she taking it.'

'She doesn't know yet.'

'You haven't told her? Why ever not?'

'It takes time to tell people. We've just told you.'

'Don't take forever over it. You don't want her finding out from a newspaper or friends.'

That was true. The problem was how Anna would react. It had been difficult breaking the news to his mother – and she was mature.

'How are you taking it – really?'

'I'm coping, I suppose. We're in a hotel. I think I told you that.'

'You did. Which hotel is it?'

'It's a Premier Inn in Inverness.'

'Do they change the sheets regularly?'

'At the price hotels charge I would hope so.'

'You'd be surprised how slack some of them can be.'

There was a pause. Alex had run out of things to confess to.

'But what a thing to happen,' his mother said. 'I'm concerned about you.'

'Nothing to be done but get on with it.'

'That's a sensible attitude. Are they giving you time off work to do what you need to?'

Work? His mother did ask the right questions. She always had. And he would have to tell all of this to his boss as well. And ask for time off. How would that work out with everything that was going on?

'I'm sure they will,' he said.

'You haven't told them yet?'

'Give me time.' He was beginning to feel exasperated.

'You've always been slow in getting around to things. You have to think about a problem ten times over before doing something about it. You have to be pushed into doing anything.'

'We'll get through this.'

'This phone call has been a shock. I'm going to do nothing but worry about all of this. And you're going to have so much to do after a thing like that. And you can't stay in a hotel forever.'

'The house is fully insured,' Alex said. 'And we'll get everything done we need to. It'll work out.' And he hoped he sounded more confident than he felt.

'I hope so. You usually pull through in the end. Even when I don't expect you to.'

'We'll keep in touch.'

'I don't understand why anyone would want to do this to you.'

'What are you talking about? I didn't say the fire was set on purpose.'

'It could have been. You haven't been sleeping with someone else's wife, have you?'

'Of course not.' Now he was beginning to get annoyed – which he tried to curb. But what a question to ask. Had his mother noticed something about him lately? What?

After the phone call had ended, Alex felt drained. It had felt as if he had been consoling his mother after her house had burned down. But his mother was simply his mother. And she had never been the same since she'd been left on her own. The part of her that had died with his father had been the stronger part. But some of the questions she'd asked were good. How were they going to cope with this fire, and would they? At the moment, collapsing in a heap was the most constructive thing he could think of to do, which was at least better than following his mother's train of thought and trying to work out who might have done such a thing to them.

SEVEN

Alex acknowledged his suspicions about Heather were just that – suspicions. There was nothing solid to support them, except the distance he knew had grown between them, and perhaps that was normal after so many years of marriage. Then again, it was usual for a lot of marriages to break up. Was that what was happening to his? He dismissed the thought. Or tried to. He started thinking about the ways he'd noticed Heather had changed lately. Then told himself not to do that. People don't stay the same and he hadn't either. Concentrate on the present. Surely they had enough things to deal with already?

Alex parked the car across the street from where their house had stood. It was now a dismal scene of charred remains and ash surrounded by a police tape with its brightly coloured keep-off message. Alex groaned. He glanced across at Heather as she pulled herself out of the car and walked over the road. She looked as depressed as he felt, which did not surprise him. He locked the car behind him and stepped after her. She had already manoeuvred her way over the tape. This was their house. What was wrong with them looking around to work out what was left of it? He followed her. They started picking their way through the ash.

The singed smell was almost overwhelming. He looked at blackened remnants and tried to work out what they were the remains of. This was unrecognisable as the house he had lived in. Alex stood where the living room had been and tried to picture it. His enormous TV screen, much mocked by Heather, had stood there, dominating their evenings with an Ultra HD vision of a more fascinating world. It was bent and charred and useless now. That other sorry mess had been the Swedish-designed Stressless leather couch, which looked anything but stressless. The picture over the fireplace, painted by a friend of Heather's, must be somewhere in the pile of ashes. It had been a view of somewhere he and Heather had spent a holiday, though the place had been better known to the friend who had painted it. It had been a pleasing aspect of loch, hills, and sky, which had spoken to Alex of a yearning for something though he had never defined what that might be. Every thoughtful dab of paint on that canvas was now gone. As was their whole posh living room. Derided by Alex's mother it might have been, yet they had filled it with expensive items that displayed their feelings about their status, such as it was.

It had been odd that Heather had shown less motivation about housekeeping in the last year. She had only tidied up when someone was coming round – and why had Heather become like that? Alex had become fixated on the fear she'd become interested in someone else. Alex wandered through to the kitchen where Heather was picking up something indefinable from the floor.

'We shouldn't have come in,' Heather said. 'It's still cooling off.'

'If we don't look through it, someone else will be in to see what they can get,' Alex said.

Heather held out an oddly shaped object to him.

'It used to be a serving spoon. Do you think there are other good finds around here?'

Alex stared at it.

'It's difficult to believe everything has gone up in smoke.'

Alex continued to survey the rubble that had been home. He grunted but was not sure himself what emotion that expressed.

'The wall safe in the study,' Alex said. 'We need to look at that.'

'And whatever was in that?'

'Lots of useful things,' Alex said. 'Insurance policies, everything financial.'

Heather gave him a questioning look. 'You never let me look in there.'

Alex gave thought to that. 'You never asked to,' he said. He wondered what she had intended by the remark. What did she think might be in there? Porn? Didn't she know him anymore?

Heather turned and picked her way past more remains. She picked up this and discarded that. The look of agony on her face was such that Alex was surprised she wasn't shrieking, and it was how he felt too.

He worked his way into the study. This had been his private space. It had also been a statement of himself, an understatement had been his joke. The things he'd decorated it with, the African carvings, and the unusual bookends he'd found in junk shops, were destroyed along with everything else. This room had looked out onto one of the best aspects in the house, over the golf course and to the sea behind. The view was underwhelming today with that burned mess in the foreground.

He walked over to what had been a wall cupboard and hauled at what was left of the door. The wall safe was still there, blackened and looking sorry for itself, but intact. The numbers on the lock mechanism were indecipherable but he could remember the layout. He pushed in the code, and, to his relief, the door eased open. What was inside had survived.

'They weren't lying in their advertising,' he said.

'They weren't?' Heather said. She was peering over his shoulders into the safe.

'They said documents would survive any conflagration in there. And they have.'

He pulled out files and placed them in a bag he had brought with him.

'Let me see,' Heather said.

'We can look at them back at the hotel,' Alex said, 'but everything's there: the insurance policies, the car document, the mortgage agreement. Our life's intact even if the building isn't. Though if you disagree, you have a good argument.'

Alex gave the remains of his house a rueful stare. It summed up unspoken fears. He dreaded his marriage ending like this. Why was he so anxious about Heather?

EIGHT

They had just driven into the hotel car park again when Alex noticed Elsa standing at the side of it.

'I was just going when I saw your car drive up,' Elsa said. 'I called at your room to try to find you.'

'It's good to see you,' Alex said. Which it was. Elsa had been a real comfort on the night of the fire.

'Is everything OK?' Heather said, as if reacting to something in the way Elsa was behaving.

'You're the ones in trouble,' Elsa said. 'Are things all right with you?'

'I suppose,' Heather said.

Alex studied Elsa. Her face held a kindly expression, but there was anxiety there too.

'I thought I'd check up on you,' Elsa said.

'We've no cleaning for you to do,' Heather said.

'There would hardly be any of that,' Elsa said.

Alex gave Heather a surprised look. What was she being rude about?

'Come on in,' Alex said, and they walked into the hotel together.

'The room's cramped,' Alex said. 'Join us for coffee in the lounge.'

He chose a different corner from the one they had shared with the inspector, which didn't stop the memory of that interview returning. Alex put his jacket on a seat and walked over to the counter to order coffees. Elsa had asked for a latte which was simple enough, and he was quickly back with a tray of drinks he passed around. Then, there he was, seated, with another espresso in front of him he didn't want to drink. He looked across at Heather and took in her tired expression. Heather was looking at her Americano as if it might bite her. They had been doing too much sitting around drinking coffee.

Alex took a sip. 'I've tasted worse,' he said, 'but I can't remember when.'

Elsa tried hers. 'It's nice,' she said. 'Thanks.' But she still looked on edge. 'I wanted to ask,' she said, 'how is the hotel?'

Alex looked around. 'As you can see,' he said. 'It's a hotel. It's clean. The bed's almost comfortable. The chairs in the room aren't. The TV doesn't have BT Sport. It's hardly home – but it's OK.'

'I feel for you.' And the anxious look was still there. 'I was going to say – it must be awful to be stranded like this. Like being washed up on a beach after a shipwreck.'

'A colourful thought,' Alex said, 'but accurate.'

'But I could help.' Both Alex and Heather looked at her with interest.

'You won't know this, but I have a granny flat I could lend you.'

'You do?' Heather said.

'That would be good of you,' Alex said.

'We would pay rent, of course,' Heather said.

That had been what Elsa's anxiety had been about – would they allow her to help them? They must look in need of pity. It was a surprise their cleaner was sitting there with a spare flat she could lend out, but, when he thought about it, how much did he know about her? He had never paid her any attention. She flitted in and out with her cleaning stuff and, beyond noticing what she'd done, and paying her, he hadn't given her any more thought, which, when he thought about it, was arrogant. Elsa was a person as well as a cleaner.

'What's the flat like?' Heather asked.

'Two bedrooms,' Elsa said. 'And there's a sitting room, and a bathroom – and a kitchen, of course. It has its own entrance. It's private.'

'That sounds good. Is it furnished?' Alex said. 'What we had went up in smoke.'

'Oh, yes.'

'It sounds great,' Heather said.

'And I wouldn't expect you to pay rent.'

'Oh, but we should,' Heather said.

'We'd definitely insist,' Alex said.

'I regard you as friends not just clients.'

Alex noted the word she used instead of customer. She always did try to give her service an upmarket gloss, he supposed, difficult though that might be for a cleaner.

'We would insist on paying rent to anyone – even if you were a close relative,' Alex said.

'Definitely,' Heather agreed.

'Come round and look at it before you make up your minds to accept or not,' Elsa said.

'We should shower and change first,' Heather said. 'We've been grubbing round the remains of our house.'

'That sounds an awful thing to have to do.'

'It was,' Alex said. 'And you must smell it on us. The place is all ash and cinders now.'

'You should see what my lovely kitchen looks like,' Heather said.

'God,' Elsa said. 'You only put that in a year ago. It doesn't bear thinking about.'

'A bit less than that,' Alex said. 'It's not past its warranty, not that we could claim.'

'Do you live by yourself?' Heather asked.

Alex tried to remember what he had heard about Elsa. She was a young widow, wasn't she? Or had she never married? He wondered if she led a lonely life. He did know the street she lived on from the monthly bills for the housework Elsa did. There were a lot of older stone buildings there, some of them almost mansions in size. He'd assumed Elsa lived in a rented flat but, if she had a place she could lend them, that sounded unlikely. Was Elsa well off? Her cleaning business was well spoken of, but it couldn't pay that well.

As if reading Alex's thoughts, Elsa said, 'I'd an inheritance from my parents. I live next door to the flat, but we're well separated. It's private. And, yes,' she said, looking at Heather, 'I live by myself. No children running in and out to disturb you.'

'I didn't mean–' Heather said.

'This is a godsend,' Alex said. 'We can't thank you enough.'

'No, we can't,' Heather said, and Alex noted the gushing. Heather had been worried about finding somewhere to stay, which was hardly surprising. 'It's so good of you to offer.'

'It's the least I can do,' Elsa said.

Her concern for them was genuine, which Alex found touching. He thought back to the neighbours he'd come across at the scene of the fire, how anxious and caring they had seemed – and Alex had hardly spoken to some of them in years. Perhaps he was discovering the kindness of others.

He sipped his coffee, which was another one that had been forgotten about and lost its heat. What did that mean? Perhaps he was too caught up in his anxieties to focus on what he ought to. He looked at Elsa and tried to take her in.

NINE

'What do you mean the house has burned down?'

Alex had managed to reach Anna on the phone at last. Heather had received no reply when she tried. Alex expected Anna was in another strop with her mother and he could only guess what it was about this time. Anna was prone to sulks, and he had given up assuming this was a stage. It was the person she was growing into. Anna sounded upset on the end of the phone right now, but he had to admit a house going up in flames was a big event. Alex responded with directness.

'It caught fire and cremated itself.'

'What?'

'And yes, I'm being serious. There's nothing left but cinders.'

'But how did that happen?'

'I was away at a conference when it happened. I had to drive straight back when they told me. So I don't know – and they haven't worked it out yet.'

'They?'

'The fire brigade was round – no surprise there – and the police. It was a big thing. There were crowds out watching it.'

'How horrible.'

'Very.'

'But how are you coping? Where are you staying?'

'We're in a hotel, but we think we may be able to rent a flat.'

'Rent? Welcome to the joys of my generation, Dad.'

'I look forward to them.'

'And you really don't know how it happened? Nobody did anything stupid, did they, like leaving clothes to dry over an electric fire? You've warned me about that often enough.'

'You should know us better than that.'

'I thought I did, but the house still managed to get torched. Well, it had nothing to do with me. I was in Aberdeen. It couldn't have been my fault.'

'Nobody suggested it was. How are things with you?'

'You're the one who ought to be asked that. So, when did it happen?'

'Friday night.'

'And you're just getting around to phoning me?'

'We've been busy – as you ought to be able to imagine.'

'You're quick in getting word of a flat. How did you manage to get something as fast as that?'

'Elsa says she has one she's going to lend us. Did you know Elsa owns property?'

'Of course. She has a pile up Seabank Road. Everybody knows that.'

'It's a pile? And she's our cleaner?'

'You should get a different job, Dad. Get down on your hands and knees and scrub some floors. It obviously pays better.'

'It does? I didn't know that. So, how are your studies? Or are you planning to clean floors too?'

'They're going great.'

'And why are you avoiding your mother's phone calls? She wasn't able to get through to you about the fire.'

'Nothing to do with university. It's Zac. She needs to shut up about him. Zac's all right.'

Alex thought of Zac. He was a young man with a tattoo of some Celtic pattern across his forehead in black ink, and he was in the process of deciding on what to have done to his cheeks. He was Anna's boyfriend of the moment. Though she'd only known him for a couple of months. Alex was not surprised Heather was nagging Anna about him.

'Has anything survived the fire at all, Dad?'

'Only what was in the safe.'

'Do we have a safe?'

'A small one. For occasions such as these. To protect documents from fire.'

'Did you rescue anything else?'

'We were left with what we stood up in.'

'Look on the bright side, Dad. It's a chance to buy yourself a new wardrobe. You've no idea how out of date your togs had become, have you?'

'Are you paying for them?'

'I'm lucky if I can afford lunch at the cafeteria. Hey. Wait a minute. My stuff must have gone up in that fire too.'

'I'm afraid so.'

'Damn. And oh no. My diary's gone up in smoke as well.'

'You keep a diary?'

'And my books must be gone. Dad, how could you be so stupid as to let the house burn down?'

'I didn't give it permission.'

'And don't be flippant, Dad. It's a horror story.'

'Definitely. And I am upset about it. Obviously.'

'Right.'

'And it's worrying your mother sick.'

'Of course.'

'And she's been anxious about you. You never answer her messages.'

'Is she there?'

'Not just now. I was taking the chance to phone you in private.'

'I'll phone her. In fact, I'll come over.'

'Are you planning to stay?'

Anna fell silent as she thought about that. 'Does it matter? Couldn't I stay at Elsa's flat with you?'

'If we do move in there maybe. There are two bedrooms. Not that we've even seen it yet. We're going round to look at it tonight.'

'I need to come over and talk to you.'

'I know.'

'I can manage from Aberdeen and back in one day. There's an early bus I can get.'

'Let me know what time you're arriving and I'll meet you.'

'Do you mind if I bring Zac?'

'Zac?' Alex said.

Why did Anna want to bring him at a time like this? Maybe they were developing into a genuine item. But there were enough emotions going around about this fire without the complication of Zac.

'Do you have to bring him?' Alex said.

'Of course I do, Dad. This is a big thing. I'll need Zac there as well.'

Alex finished the call shortly after that. It felt rude but that was the effect Zac had on him too. Like Heather, he didn't much like Zac and he had unpleasant memories of their last meeting.

TEN

When they walked into the flat Elsa was offering them, the first thing they noticed was there were open windows everywhere. Alex supposed the flat had been shut up for a while and had needed to be aired. He was also struck by the size of it. His eye was drawn to the old-fashioned cornices in the high ceiling of the living room and the large bay window with sash windows, from which hung long, brown, velvet curtains. The expansive couch and armchairs were worn but looked comfortable. There was a grandeur to the place but it was faded.

A large open fireplace with cast iron grate gave a centre to the room. Alex forced himself not to frown. It was years since they'd made use of an open fire. Fortunately, Alex could see from a radiator there was central heating too. Above the fireplace hung photographs of Highland views. There were pictures of mountain landscapes on other walls too.

'I let it out,' Elsa was saying, 'but my last tenant left a month ago and there hasn't been anyone suitable.'

'I hope we are,' Alex said.

'Definitely,' Elsa replied.

Heather stood saying nothing as her eyes swept the room then roamed round it again. There was a tightness to her lips that was noticeable.

'Let me show you the rest,' Elsa said.

She led them through to the main bedroom, which also had high ceilings with ostentatious mouldings, and tall windows. There was a fireplace here too, in addition to the radiator. Alex's eyes were drawn to the cast iron bed.

'The bed's only two years old,' Elsa said. 'My tenant said it was comfortable. The design fits the flat – or so I thought.'

'It'll be fine,' Heather said. She smiled but her eyes still looked preoccupied.

'The bathroom's opposite,' Elsa said as she strode out of the door and waved her hand at it.

Heather wandered into it, as Alex looked past her. There was a modern suite in bright blue, which stood out against the white tiles. He didn't like it but would definitely not say so.

'We've landed on our feet,' Alex said. 'We're grateful to you.'

But he glanced anxiously at Heather as he tried to read her.

'Yes,' Heather said, and the open smile did express gratitude. 'I don't know what we would have done without you.'

Alex was relieved. He knew Heather did not like to have to feel in debt for anything.

'The other bedroom,' Elsa said as she turned and pointed, 'is there. If you want to put Anna up any time, feel free.'

'I was wondering about that,' Heather said.

'She does honour us with a visit from time to time,' Alex said. 'It's good of you.'

Heather walked into the room and cast her eye around. It was narrow, with space for the single bed it held, but not much more.

'The kitchen,' Elsa said. 'I haven't shown you that yet.'

She strode down the hall. Heather and Alex followed her to a sizeable room with pine-fronted units and a deal table with four matching chairs round it. It was a well-lit space with wide windows.

'The washing machine's here,' Elsa said as she opened a door. 'There's even a dishwasher.' She indicated another unit door.

Alex was pleased to see the polite expression still in play on Heather's face.

'The electrical stuff works,' Elsa said. 'I've just had it PAT tested again. But if there are problems, say. I've been told it's a good oven. Makes great cakes.'

'We'll take the place,' Heather said.

'Not that there was any doubt about that,' Alex added. 'I'll get the bags from the hotel today.'

'Do you want me to leave you here?' Elsa said. 'There's tea in one of the tins, this one.' She picked up a bright yellow tin labelled TEA. 'Obvious enough. I've put milk in the fridge. If there's anything else, just say. I'll be out this afternoon. I have to go now. But I'll be back in a couple of hours.'

'Thanks,' Alex and Heather said, almost together.

After Elsa left, they found themselves looking at each other with uncertain expressions on their faces.

'So, this is what we've come to,' Heather said, which Alex thought a bit unfair on the flat Elsa was offering them.

'It could be a lot worse,' he said. 'We're lucky.'

Heather made a grimace.

'Where are my brand new Bosch appliances?'

'Up in smoke.'

'You said it.'

'This is temporary,' Alex reminded her.

But that did not take the frown from Heather's face. She went around the kitchen opening doors; she explored the fridge, the freezer, and the oven. She groaned.

'Look at the size of that fridge. We won't get much in there.'

'It's all very clean.'

'I'll allow Elsa that.'

'It's generous of her. And it's OK. Enough for our needs.'

Heather looked around for a moment or two longer, then reached a decision. 'It'll do,' she said. After a moment's pause, she added, 'For now.'

She flashed a look at him that might either have been a command or a warning. She was going through a lot, and, he had to admit, compared to their modern house, this was a come down, even if they were lucky to be offered it.

'Anna will hate that room,' Heather added.

'She lives in a uni halls of residence, and this isn't slumming it.'

'She'll complain,' Heather said, 'and complain again. And I won't be able to disagree with her.'

'We'll get through this.'

Heather frowned as if doubting that.

'I'm glad you were able to talk to Anna,' Heather said. 'I haven't managed to get through to her.'

'What are you two arguing about?' Alex asked.

'What do you mean? We haven't been quarrelling.' Heather closed her mouth with a prim expression. She glanced away then looked back at him decisively. 'The horror boyfriend. What else are we going to do but disagree about him?'

'She thinks the world of him,' Alex said.

'He's arrogant.'

'That's what teenage boys are like. They cover up a lot. He's young.'

'If he's concealing serious self-doubt, he's doing it well.'

'Didn't you have boyfriends?'

'Nobody like him.'

'There was me. I'm hardly perfect.'

Heather gave him a questioning look.

'My father did warn me about you. Over and over.'

'Did he?'

'He said you wouldn't settle down to marriage. You'd had too many girlfriends.'

'That wasn't fair,' Alex said.

'And he was right. Don't think I've forgotten.'

'That,' Alex said.

'Yes, that.'

'It was a long time ago. Why do you insist on bringing it up?'

Because it kept him on his toes so well. Heather didn't miss the opportunity to do that.

ELEVEN

There was a tap on Alex's shoulder as he was watching a queue of travellers disembark from the bus Anna had said she would be travelling on. When he turned round, he found himself face to face with her.

'Anna,' shrieked Heather. 'Trust you to give us a surprise. You didn't get here by bus.'

The reason was obvious enough. It stood beside her with a Celtic tattoo on its forehead. Zac looked his inauspicious self with his battered leather jacket, and the torn jeans over skinny legs, revealing sickly pale skin.

'Hi,' he said. His wide grin showed teeth that ought to be looked after better, but there was something gauche and genuine about the smile that went some way to excusing them. Alex shot a warning look at Heather who was making no attempt to hide her dismay at the appearance of Zac in Nairn.

'Zac drove me,' Anna said. She had a smug, proprietorial look on her face as she said this.

Heather was battling a grimace which she managed to turn into an attempt at something approaching a smile.

Alex was pleased to see Anna. Like Zac, she wore a leather jacket but hers made no attempt at the bohemian, worn look and was a neat, shiny black. Alex had difficulty in understanding how girls like Anna ended up with boys like Zac. Anna's auburn neatly cut bob shone, as did her eyes, and her carefully applied lipstick had a sheen to it that caught the light. Her skin was as well made up as ever though there was a spot she'd not been able to completely hide. It was a pity about the regular sulks that overtook her face but at the moment her smile was entrancing. Alex was pleased Anna had not copied Zac in having her face tattooed, though he knew she did have one butterfly on her right wrist. Heather had shrieked at her about that, but there you are, Alex had thought, they will be themselves. Thank God for that. Who would want children who were carbon copies of their parents?

'Pleased to see you again, Zac,' Alex said. He held out his hand and they shook.

'I was surprised the snail made it.'

'Snail?' Alex said.

'Just what I call it. It's a Citroen 2CV. It's the basic model, the one French farmers used to drive round their fields.'

'I didn't know there were any of those left.'

'It's a bit like the last of the Mohicans,' Zac said. 'The only one remaining of its tribe.'

Did Zac really say that? They wandered over to the car park where Alex was able to view an ancient green Citroen with surprisingly little rust but a bash on its rear fender that might indicate someone had taken a dislike to it.

'Stylish,' Alex said.

Zac ignored the sarcasm in Alex's voice.

'It's cool,' Alex said, trying for politeness this time but sure he still managed to sound sardonic.

'A compliment,' Zac said. 'And I agree. If a car's not cool, what's the point?'

'The best type is the kind that goes – and this one doesn't always.' Anna flashed a smile at Zac.

'You have to send up prayers to the Citroen god,' Zac said.

Alex did his best to stop himself wincing at that.

'Can we go straight to the house?' Anna said. 'I need to see it.'

'After that drive you've had? I was going to take you somewhere for a coffee and maybe a bite to eat first,' Heather said.

'I want to see the house,' Anna said. 'Don't mollycoddle me.'

'I'm not. You've had a long journey. Don't you need to unwind?'

'I want to see how bad the disaster is,' Anna said.

'I suppose,' Heather said. 'Though why you always have to have your own way, I don't know.'

'I take after you, Mum.'

'And that's uncalled for.'

'But true.'

'To the house,' Alex said, before an argument began. 'Follow us.'

He led Heather to the car and opened the door for her, possibly just in time. Anna looked as if there were a few more things she would have liked to say to her mother, but all she had the chance to say was, 'I do know where it is.'

'But of course you do,' Alex replied.

Then he opened the door on the driver's side and climbed in as Anna and Zac walked over to Zac's car.

'She's no better,' Heather said to Alex.

'She's Anna,' Alex replied. 'And she's all ours.'

'I doubt if Zac thinks so. And he looks as much a sight as he always did.'

'Maybe he'll tattoo the rest of his face and you won't be able to see that either.'

'Don't suggest it to him.'

'I think he is planning to have something done on his cheeks, isn't he?'

Heather pulled a face.

'I wish she'd get rid of him.'

'He was trying to be pleasant.'

'And all he managed was slimy and repulsive.'

Alex started the car and eased it away. He looked in his mirror at the green Citroen behind him as it lurched into motion.

TWELVE

That blackened outline was the bay window of their front room. That jagged stump had been an apple tree. Alex was sitting in his car looking at the scene. He and Heather had just arrived, and Alex could hear the Citroen pulling up behind them. Alex forced himself to leave the Audi and confront the scene in front of him. Heather followed after with as much displeasure. Anna was quickly out of the Citroen and looked more white-faced than Alex had ever seen her as she peered at the remains of the house she had grown up in.

'Horrible, isn't it?' Alex said to her.

'How could you let this happen?' Anna said. 'How could you be so careless?'

'It didn't take any effort,' Alex said.

'Did you say how could we let this happen?' Heather looked at Anna in disbelief. 'Have you any idea what we've been going through?'

'Look at it,' Anna said.

'We're both just pleased to be alive,' Heather said. 'Aren't you glad about that?'

'You're adults,' Anna said. 'You're always on about taking more responsibility. Couldn't you have taken more than that?'

'Poor Anna,' Zac said, putting his arm around her.

Anna tried to repress a sob but failed. She put her head on Zac's shoulder.

'Zac, could you tell her this isn't our fault?' Alex said.

Anna looked in despair at her father; he gave a mystified stare in return.

'I thought you said they didn't know how the fire started?' Zac said.

'You don't seriously consider it had anything to do with us?' Heather said.

Zac shrugged his shoulders. 'They've still to decide that,' he said.

Alex tried to work out which was worse, the rudeness or the stupidity. 'That's no way to speak to us,' he said.

'This is dreadful for Anna,' Zac said.

'And us,' Alex said.

'Leave it, Zac, if they don't get it, they don't,' Anna said.

'I'll look after you,' Zac said.

'I doubt if you can look after yourself,' Heather said.

Heather's voice was soft, and Alex wasn't sure whether that was meant to carry or not, but it did.

'That's no way to talk to Zac,' Anna said.

Heather decided she'd had enough.

'But you don't know how to look after yourself, Zac. Do you know what you smell like?'

'Zac showers every day,' Anna said.

'Is that what he tells you?' Heather said.

Zac's arm was still round Anna.

'Don't worry about your mother,' he said. 'She can't touch us.'

Heather gave Zac a withering look.

'Zac is my boyfriend. You need to treat him with more respect than that.'

Alex had no idea how they had arrived at this moment. They'd been looking at the scene of the fire that had destroyed the house, and now there was this argument about Zac.

'He should treat himself with more respect,' Heather said, 'instead of destroying his face with tattoos.'

'You live in the past,' was Anna's reply to that. 'You don't understand young people.'

'I do,' Heather said. 'And he's not worth bothering with. You've no comprehension of the feelings of a mother. I worked hard to bring you up and you bring that home?'

'Don't call him "that". Don't dehumanise him.'

'He's supposed to be human?'

'Heather, you're getting a bit strong,' Alex said to her.

'And where were you when this fire started?' Anna said to her mother. 'How come it was able to get so bad it burned the house down?'

Alex cringed. What level of argument was this developing into?

Anna continued. 'Dad was away working but you weren't. You weren't with a boyfriend, were you?'

Which was the sort of thing Alex had definitely never heard Anna say to her mother before.

'Anna!' Heather said. 'I was at Margaret Affleck's.'

But Anna was in full flow.

'Margaret Affleck? You don't even like her anymore. You said so. Are you trying to make us all believe you went round to see her?'

'Be reasonable, Anna. She's a friend. And she's in trouble. Her mother has died of cancer.'

Anna did pause at that, then continued.

'It's sudden the way you've changed your mind about her.'

'You don't know what other people are feeling, do you? It's about time you tried to work that out. You're not a child anymore, Anna.'

'I don't know what other people's feelings are? Have you any idea what Zac's are? He lost his job only a few weeks ago.'

'He's lost his job, has he?' Heather said. 'Isn't it time you wised up to him?'

Alex looked across at Zac who at least had the sense to stay out of this. The look on Zac's face was now of horror.

'It was a good job in a garage. He was unlucky with the boss he had. That was all.'

'How did he manage to lose it?'

Alex looked at Zac again. Zac was looking elsewhere.

'He was being picked on.'

'Is that what he told you?' Heather said. 'I suppose he would. If a boss picks on someone he has a reason. In Zac's case, he was probably slacking.'

'You haven't bothered getting to know him, have you? Zac tried very hard. That man he worked for was a bully.'

'You don't see through him, do you?' Heather said. 'One day you will. I hope it's not too late.'

'Zac's driven all the way over here to try to help me. You have to give him credit for that, and this is no way to treat him in return for it.'

Alex was impressed with how well Anna was holding up her end in this argument. And he wasn't sure why Heather was going on like this.

Zac pulled himself up to his full height, which at five foot eight wasn't impressive, but, taking in the self-righteousness on Zac's face, Alex did wonder what was coming.

'I've heard enough,' Zac said. And there was authority in his voice. 'Whatever you think of me, you should be treating Anna better than this. Anna, it's time we left.'

'But–' Anna said. And the expression on her face made Alex wonder again what else she might want to say to her mother.

'We can't help them, Anna,' Zac said. 'They won't let us.'

'Help?' Heather said. She let loose a peal of laughter.

'I'm not hanging around for any more of this treatment,' Zac said.

In different circumstances, Alex might have liked to have had a pleasant chat with Zac and get to know him better, talk with him about his job and how he was coping with losing it – but that wasn't going to happen.

A weary look appeared on Anna's face. 'You're right, Zac.' She turned to Heather and Alex again. 'We'll go now. We need to get back to Aberdeen. I've classes in the morning.'

They turned and left. Alex looked across at Heather. There always was a wall of anxiety in her, that could turn into anger so quickly. And now it had led to Anna storming off again to get away from her.

THIRTEEN

There was something ominous in the opening to this interview with Inspector Black. The way he addressed them was business-like; there was also something very attentive in the way his sergeant held his notebook and pencil, and the sergeant had seated himself this time, as if this meeting might take some time.

They were in the front room of the flat Elsa had lent them. Heather was looking with irritation at a cup ring on the oak coffee table in front of them, though Alex gauged that was because she couldn't look at the eyes of Inspector Black. He had refused coffee though it had been offered. This was not a personal visit.

'We know now how the fire started,' Black was saying.

Alex stared at him with apprehension. Heather opened her mouth to speak then closed it again.

'And it wasn't an accident.'

Alex swore, which he regretted, but at least he had said the word quietly. Black gave him a surprised look.

'Petrol was poured over inflammables which were then lit,' Black said.

'What?' Alex said.

'That was how the fire was set.'

'It does sound very deliberate,' Alex said.

'But who would do that?' Heather asked.

'That's what we would like to know,' Black said. 'Which is why this is now a police investigation.'

'It wasn't already?' Alex asked.

'Cause of fire is established by a fire investigation officer,' Black replied. 'If it's wilful fire-raising, that's when we take over.' He paused and looked the two of them over. 'And you haven't been down to the station to give your statements yet.'

'Give us time,' Alex said. Damn. They had meant to do that. There had just been so much going on.

'You've had time,' the inspector replied.

The absence of Black's usual friendliness struck Alex. He had not met Black in this mood before.

'We're sorry,' Heather said. Alex glanced across at her and took in the nervousness on her face.

'It's us you're investigating?' Alex said.

'Your insurance company would require us to – if you want payment from them.'

'I see,' Heather said. 'We need to get down there and make statements, Alex. Unless you can take them now?' she said to the inspector.

'Just find time to go down to the station.'

Firm, Alex thought. And they had better do that.

'First, finance,' Black said. 'How is that?'

Alex and Heather stared. It was Alex who spoke first.

'We both work,' he said. 'We have a steady income.'

'And outgoings?'

'We have them,' Heather said.

Alex gave her an irritated look. 'Particularly you,' he said.

He wished he wouldn't let himself be annoyed so easily. His mood had been so variable since the fire – just like Heather's.

'That's an argument between you two, is it?' Black asked.

Heather gave Alex a glare. 'If someone hadn't made a mess of the investments that would have helped.'

'Investments?' Black asked.

'The company Alex put money into went bust.'

'It was a good prospect,' Alex said. 'It wasn't my fault the management was taking too much money out.'

'You and your dodgy friends,' Heather said. 'We should have gone to a personal finance adviser. I said that at the time.'

'It sounds unfortunate,' Black said.

'It was my money from my grandfather that was lost, as well as our savings, so Alex can't complain about my spending.' She pulled a face at Alex.

'To cut a long story short,' Alex said. 'We owe a lot on our cards.'

He glanced across to the sergeant who was writing with speed.

'Which doesn't mean we set fire to our place for the insurance,' Alex said.

'I didn't suggest that,' Black replied.

Heather was giving Alex one of her despairing looks. He wasn't sure what the expression on Black's face meant. He sighed.

'But you daren't lose your jobs,' Black said.

'Which is true for most people,' Heather said.

Alex bit a nail. Heather glowered.

'How is work, Alex?' Black asked.

'It'll come out,' Heather said to Alex.

Alex wished she hadn't said that. Why did she have to bring it up now? It made him sound in desperate trouble at work, and he wasn't, was he?

'There is talk of restructuring in the company he works for,' Heather said.

'And your reaction to that, sir?' Black asked.

'Nobody's brought up anything with me. If I could read minds, I could tell you,' Alex said.

'Are your bosses pleased with your work?' Black said.

'He tells me they are,' Heather said.

Alex wished she would leave him to answer for himself.

'I'm good at my job,' Alex said. He was competent at most things. He knew that. When things went wrong it was caused by the unexpected, though that didn't mean he always escaped the blame.

'What is your job, sir?'

'I'm the marketing director with Norplace.'

'The electronics firm.'

'That's it.'

'Are they in trouble?'

'I wouldn't have said so, but firms never stop doing reviews. They're always trying to maximise profits even if they're already good. The rationalisation Heather talks about is only a rumour and you know how much faith you can put in them. I could answer your questions better if I were telepathic. Even if they do want to make cuts – or restructure – nobody has any idea what areas they might be looking to make changes in.'

If forbidding, Black had been relaxed since this interview began and Alex noted his unruffled air had not altered.

'So you tell me, sir.'

And comments like that made him even more irritating.

'I can only tell you what I know.'

'Precisely, sir.'

Black's eyes swivelled towards Heather.

'And your work?' he asked.

Heather was slipping one of her rings up and down her finger, a habit that never failed to annoy Alex. He looked across at the inspector, who was sitting with the same patience on his face as he waited for his answer.

'I work for the NHS,' Heather replied. 'I've been employed at Nairn Health Centre for twenty years. No one has problems with my work. And there's no shortage of work for nurses.'

'Thank you,' Black said. 'We will check up with both of your employers,' he said.

'Do you have to do that?' Alex said.

'Yes. Do you?' Heather said. 'How's that going to sound at work?'

'We'll phrase it diplomatically,' Black said.

'I'll bet,' Alex said.

'We will.'

'Do we look suspicious?' Alex asked. He was aware of his temper rising and did nothing to prevent it.

'I'm looking for background information,' Black said. 'And there's nothing illegal about owing a lot on your cards – or about having problems at work – if you are. But I still need to ask questions.'

Alex did not like that look in Black's eyes. But why should he worry about this? He hadn't done anything wrong.

'Though I've noticed there's tension between you two,' Black said.

'That's hardly illegal either,' Alex said.

'Quite, sir.'

'Our house has burned down. Anyone would be upset and tense at a time like that.'

'But there's something else, isn't there?'

'What do you mean?' Alex thought Heather was going to do damage to her finger the way she was working at that ring.

'How well would you say you two got on?'

'That's rude,' Heather said.

'And it's none of your business,' Alex said.

Alex thought of the underlying acrimony there had been lately, which was about more than the fire. How could he explain that to a police inspector? Was it middle age and too many long hours at work causing the strain between him and Heather? The edge that failed investment had brought into their relationship didn't help. Alex cursed Tom. He was reckoned to be such a financial whizz-kid at work and look at what his advice had led to.

'We get on great,' Alex said, shooting a comforting look across at Heather.

Perhaps they got on as well – or as badly – as any other long-married couple. Wasn't that enough? Then he thought of his feelings when his mind turned to Jasmine. Something had been awoken in him there. Best to bury that. He looked across at Heather and wondered why she was making no reply.

'We don't have problems,' Heather said.

But there was nothing convincing in the way she said that – which wasn't in his imagination, was it? Heather flashed a brilliant smile, which was more reassuring.

'We're still very much in love with each other.' And the way she spoke made him want to believe that.

'I'm glad to hear it,' Black said. Alex was beginning to wish the expression on Black's face would change now and again. Then he realised that Black was indifferent to whether they were the ones guilty of setting fire to their house, or whether it was someone else. But if they had done anything, he would find out. As the next question proved.

'But we do need to check up on both your alibis now,' Black said.

'Mine's easy enough,' Alex said. 'You have my work details. And my secretary will be able to corroborate all my arrangements for that weekend.' Then he duly gave the number to call.

'Thank you,' Black said, then turned to Heather.

'And can you give me Margaret Affleck's details?' Black asked her.

He hadn't forgotten her name, Alex noticed.

Heather told Black Margaret's address, and even found her telephone number quickly enough when she scrolled through her phone. Though Alex had to wonder at the nervousness as she did so and wondered if Black had noticed that as well.

But Black's only reaction was an affable smile.

'And we've finished ticking those boxes you'll be glad to hear.'

'Very,' Alex said.

Heather had put her phone away and was now fiddling with her ring again.

'You'll be interested to hear there's an MO to this fire.'

'What does that mean?' Alex asked.

Heather was staring at Black.

'The use of accelerant. The fact the fire started in an outhouse. There have been others like that in the last few months. And in this area. One on the other side of Nairn. One in Auldearn and one in Ardersier.'

'Then why are you putting us through it?' Heather asked.

Because Inspector Black enjoys doing that to people was the thought in Alex's mind.

'It's the forms we have to fill in,' Black said. 'You'd be surprised how many of those there are.'

'Forms?' Alex said. 'This is confidential, isn't it?'

'Of course,' Black replied.

'Apart from what you share with the insurance company.'

Black gave him a questioning look. 'You haven't told us anything that would invalidate an insurance claim.'

'Thank God for that,' Heather said.

'And when a crime fits into a wider pattern, that's the significant factor.'

'Do you have a suspect?' Heather asked.

'We know the profile of the kind of person who often commits crimes like this.'

'Which is?' Alex asked.

'I don't see the harm in telling you that,' Black said. 'You might have come across someone like that.'

'Who does that sort of thing?' Heather asked.

'Quite often it's a teenager with emotional problems, usually male.'

'Oh, one of those?' Heather said.

'One of those?' Black asked.

'She means what you read in the newspapers,' Alex said.

Black shot Alex a questioning look. He continued.

'Someone with problems at school, with parents, later with work probably. With a chip on his shoulder he needs to give expression to.'

Black looked at Alex and Heather.

'Do you know anyone like that?'

Alex thought of Zac. But they already had enough problems with Anna and Zac without mentioning him to the police.

'We don't mix with many teenage boys,' he said.

'I don't suppose so,' Black said, 'but if you do think of anybody, let us know.'

Heather had gone very quiet. Alex glanced across at her. When she did speak, what she said was sharp.

'Someone's been burning down houses around here and you haven't any idea who it might be?'

'This is the first house that's been burned down,' Black said. 'The other fires didn't spread so far.'

'It's an escalation?' Alex said.

'Yes.'

'And what exactly does the same MO mean?' Heather asked.

'The fires are started in the same way every time – as I described it to you – and he's starting to make bigger piles of kindling and use more petrol.'

'So these fires could get even worse?' Alex said.

'Yes.'

'And someone might be killed next time.'

'That's what we want to avoid. Which is why we have to catch him. If you can think of anyone we ought to be questioning, we would be grateful if you would let us know. Has there been anyone one hanging around your house?'

'There was that man who wanted to clean our gutters,' Alex said. 'I told you about him.'

'We questioned him,' Black said.

So they hadn't been doing nothing. Then his mind turned to Zac again and that tension he had always noticed in him. But, thinking of the look in the inspector's eyes, for all his talk about MOs, Alex thought Black liked Heather and him for this fire.

FOURTEEN

Heather

Heather was in her little white Peugeot, driving to visit Margaret Affleck. There were various reasons for her not doing that before, none of them good it seemed to her now. In the first place, the sympathetic Inspector Black hadn't even asked for Margaret's address. Now that he had, and in such an official way, Heather wondered whether she could ask Margaret to lie. But she didn't want Alex finding out where she'd really been.

Achareidh was an area in Nairn where Heather didn't like driving. The roads were narrow and there were too many cars parked outside these bungalows and semis. How were vehicles supposed to negotiate a way past each other? Heather braked as she allowed a van to drive past.

Achareidh was a pleasant enough area with its seventies-designed low houses with their well-trimmed hedges arranged in rows beside each other; and it was an area Heather knew Margaret liked; it was quiet, and she knew people there. But Heather was glad not to own one of these bungalows; they were so close together.

Heather noticed she was biting her lip, something she hadn't done in years, and it annoyed her. When had she started doing that again? She pulled up in front of Margaret Affleck's house.

This was a particularly neat bungalow with a freshly painted fence and well-mown lawn. Margaret took pride in it, perhaps too much so; it was something she was always spending money on; that double glazing was new, and it gleamed.

Margaret was someone Heather knew from the Health Centre, where Margaret also worked as a nurse. Their socialising had not extended beyond work, but Heather had seen her a few times lately. Heather pulled herself out of the car and walked up to the door.

Margaret welcomed her. It pleased Heather that Margaret was glad to see her. Heather found herself seated in an elegantly furnished if small front room with a view to the street outside. There was a trace of a previous generation in it. Heather's glance took in the ballooning and varicoloured dresses of Royal Doulton ladies shining in china – which Heather knew had belonged to one of Margaret's aunts. And an oil painting of a country scene showed to effect in an ornate, gilt frame which Heather thought was the best thing about it.

'So, how are things?' Heather asked.

'I might ask you that. I heard what happened to you.'

'It was awful,' Heather replied, and she was embarrassed at her tone of horror.

'I dread to think what it must be like for you.'

Heather didn't reply. What could she say?

'I was so grateful for that long chat about my problems the other day,' Margaret said.

Heather was pleased at her saying that as she didn't want to talk about the fire. That was too upsetting. 'Losing your mother must be dreadful.'

'And talking about it helped – so much.'

Heather's reply was a smile.

'So tell me about your problems,' Margaret said.

But that was direct.

'Those,' Heather said. 'I want to forget about them.'

Margaret's smile was patient, but Heather could see she wanted her to continue. Heather looked away and bit her lip.

'When do they expect you back at work?'

'Not till Monday, which may be too soon for me, though it'll be a relief to go in when I have to. It'll give me other things to think about.'

'You're staying at Elsa's, aren't you?'

So Margaret had heard about that? Heather supposed she and her family were the main topic of local gossip at the moment.

'Is it a pleasant flat?'

Heather considered her reply to that. It did not do to show ingratitude.

'It'll do. It's nice enough.'

'I can tell you don't like it.'

You can? Heather thought. Damn. 'It's good of Elsa but I don't think I would like anywhere just now. I must admit it's comfortable.' What else could she say? 'It meets our needs.' It wasn't a place she'd have chosen to stay in if she'd any choice.

'That house you and Alex had was lovely. So modern but spacious, and with such a large garden.'

Yes, Heather thought. Hadn't it been nice?

'It was too expensive for us when we moved in,' she said.

'I can imagine.'

'But we managed. And the mortgage stayed the same. And salaries went up over the years.'

'The time you've been in that place you must have about paid it up.'

'Only a few years away from that.'

Heather felt her emotions threatening to overpower her again. Talking about things didn't always help, though it was what she criticised Alex for not doing.

'Elsa's been cleaning for you for a while now, hasn't she?' Margaret said.

'A friend of Alex recommended her. She's good. Reliable. Always there when she says she will be. And she does a good job. She's been cleaning for us for a couple of years.'

'She's divorced, of course, which is why she provides for herself.'

'I know.'

'The husband I know nothing about. I gather she's been on her own for some years now. She keeps herself to herself, but is supposed to be good-natured for all that. She's probably a good person to rent a flat from.'

'She's always seemed OK,' Heather said. 'And the flat's fine. It's just not my house.' She wondered if she could turn the conversation in Margaret's direction. 'So are you getting through your mother's stuff?' she said.

'That,' Margaret replied. 'I've made a start. All her clothes now sit in carrier bags waiting to be ferried to the Cancer Research charity shop.'

'You're doing well,' Heather said. 'It must be a horrible thought getting rid of her things, but it will help.'

Then Heather paused.

'It would be nice to have any things to sort through,' Heather said.

She became aware of the knife edge in her feelings. Tears were close.

'Poor you,' Margaret said. 'Is Alex helping?'

'He's being the strong man but if you gave him a slight push he'd fall over.'

'You must be glad of each other.'

'Yes,' Heather said. But her thoughts wandered.

'You're not?' Margaret said.

'We're both in the same boat. Which means we're both tense and ready to snap at any moment. I'm not sure we help each other much.'

'You'll pull through.'

'I suppose.'

But Heather was starting to wonder. Alex had become so distant.

'If there's one thing about Alex, he's a good worker. I expect he'll lose himself in his job,' Heather said.

Margaret said nothing as if working out how to reply.

'Of course, there is that rumour his firm is downsizing,' Heather said.

'Is there?'

'I suppose he feels he has to make himself indispensable.'

'He's been with them for a long time, hasn't he?'

'Twenty years.'

'He's not last in. They're the first to go – so they always say.'

'Except Alex isn't young.'

'He's not old.'

'He might be seen as that in his workplace.'

A thought struck Heather.

'I suppose that's why the running.'

And she'd thought he was getting fit for some unknown flame. She felt guilty about that, but she still wondered if she should dismiss the thought altogether.

'The running?'

'Oh, never mind. How about you? Are you getting more used to things?'

'Do you ever?' Margaret said. 'Every time I go over to mother's house, I keep expecting to see her. It's dreadful to think she won't call through from her bedroom anymore, asking for things. Her ghost doesn't linger though. I thought it might.'

'You're taking the right attitude to things.'

'I need to place her house on the market as soon as I can.'

'That'll be a wrench. But it'll be a relief when you've done it.'

'I'm going to have to try to put things into the past, though you find you don't want to do that with your own mother.'

'You were good to her.'

'I tried to be. Now I can't stop thinking of all the things I should have done with her.'

'You've nothing to reproach yourself for.'

'I felt a lot better after that chat with you.' Heather noticed Margaret kept on saying that. She must have been low. 'Thanks for that again. I kept going over the same things in my mind, and you lose perspective when you're doing that.'

'I'm glad.'

Then Heather paused. 'There's just one thing. That chat we had was on Friday afternoon. You wouldn't say it was on Friday night, would you?'

'The night of the fire?'

'Yes.'

Margaret's look was quizzical. She was wondering why the request for a lie. Heather prepared herself for the big persuasion.

FIFTEEN

Heather held out her hand and studied a nail. There was a crack just there – in the perfect pink. That was annoying. There was a crack somewhere else too – in her world, which was exploding inwards. The thought plagued her, no matter how hard she tried to dismiss it.

Heather was seated on a park bench under a beech tree. A blackbird trilled somewhere near, and a breeze played on her skin. A young man cycled past in an orange jacket and cycling helmet, and she was struck by the certainty in his movements. There was an arrogance there and she was jealous of it. She could almost murder him for that self-assurance.

But it was Alex who was really bothering her.

What was annoying her about him? For one thing – those early morning runs. The way he eased himself off the bed in that attempt at quietness, which was a waste of time as the alarm had already wakened her too. Then the creak of floorboard as he crept about. More virtuous attempts at noiselessness, then the slam of the door on the way out. It wouldn't close properly unless he did that. There was that excuse. But if he didn't get up to go for a jog there would be no problem. Why did he suddenly have this compulsion to go out and push his middle-aged body into all that effort?

Men had to be watched when they reached a certain age. Her mother had told her that, and Alex was becoming strange. What was he getting in training for – or who? What Heather did know for certain was that she needed a good night's sleep to do her job properly at the Health Centre.

At least work had never been a problem with Alex. As a person he was capable – and strong – Heather sometimes felt too much so. If he would show weakness, he would be more bearable. But that was not something Alex preferred to display. He might have even had problems with his work for all Heather knew, but he would not talk about them.

That was a problem with him. He never talked anything through. That had appealed to her when she first knew him because it made him seem strong. But if he wouldn't discuss his own problems, that meant they couldn't talk about any difficulties they were going through together. So they mounted up till the next shouting match.

Lately, he had been working longer hours, and it worried her. Was he always at work? Or was he seeing someone? These might be unworthy thoughts. But she didn't know. Now there had been this fire, and that had strung out her nerves big time.

She took out her phone and looked at it. It was time to ring her parents. She'd put that off for too long. That was why she'd come to the park. There wasn't enough space in the flat – and she hated being in it. She pressed on the contact number.

'Hey, Dad.'

'Hello, Heather. How are you?'

'Don't ask.'

'That bad, huh? What's up?'

Heather buried her head in her hands. Which wouldn't help.

'Heather?' Her father's voice boomed down the phone. 'Heather?'

She struggled with her emotions then did manage to say something.

'You won't believe how bad this is,' she said.

'I won't? What's been happening?'

Heather could hear her mother's voice in the background. 'John? Is something wrong? Is that Heather?'

A silence gathered before the words burst out of Heather. 'The house has burned down.'

'What?'

'On Friday night.'

'You're saying your house burned down on Friday night?'

Yes, Dad, Heather thought. I did. You are listening? Then there was her mother in the background again.

'And this is the first of her telling us? Give me the phone.'

There was a noise on the phone which must have been her mother snatching it out of her father's hand. Her voice then sounded clearly down the line.

'Heather? Are you all right? Talk to me.'

'Yes, Mum.'

She became aware that something in her own voice had changed. She sounded girlish. And she realised why. This took her back to her teenage years – the fear of being urged to confess to something stupid she had done – except she hadn't done anything, which had often been the case back then from what she remembered.

Heather's attention was drawn upwards to a white trail of cloud flowing behind a plane, and she became alive to the fact her mind had gained clarity. Perhaps even a conversation as strained as this was helping.

'We're OK, Mum. Really. No one's hurt.'

'Thank God for that. But how did it happen?'

'Someone set fire to it.'

'But how can they know that?'

'Whoever it was used petrol.'

'That's awful. Are you sure no one was hurt?'

'Yes, like I said, no one was. But, Mum–'

'What?'

'I could have been in the house at the time. I should have been. I ought to have been asleep in bed.'

'Thank God you weren't. Where was Alex?'

'He was away at a conference.'

'Another one of those.

Her mother felt Alex left her alone too much, which Heather had to agree with. Heather sighed and pursed her lips. She held out her hand and studied her nails again. The crack was still there.

'But where were you, Heather?'

'At a friend's. Margaret Affleck. You know her. Her mother died not long ago, and she needed to talk.'

'I see.'

There was a pause from her mother as she attempted to absorb this information, and Heather wondered if she believed her.

'And Anna must have been away at university?' she said.

'Yes.'

'Did you manage to rescue anything from the fire?' she asked.

A giggle erupted from Heather. Nerves, she thought, and not a good sign. 'Nothing,' she said.

'Oh God. That's awful. But where are you staying?'

'The police found us a hotel for the first night, and then Elsa, our housekeeper, stepped up and loaned us her granny flat, so we have a roof over our heads.'

'You could have come over here. You know that.'

'Oh, Mum. That would have been impossible.'

'Why do you say that? I'm your mother. I want to be here for you. You could come over now if you want. Wouldn't that be better?'

'There's not the room.'

'We have a spare bedroom.'

'But there's Anna—' Then Heather paused. Anna had definitely left home. And yes. Why hadn't they done that? 'We have somewhere now,' she said. 'And it's fully separate. We have our independence.'

'I'll do anything I can to help. What are you doing for stuff?'

'The flat's furnished, but we're having to buy things, lots of them. We only had what we stood up in. The hotel provides toiletries, but you need more than that.'

'Are you all right for money? If you're not–'

'I don't want to ask for that. I'm an adult.'

'Of course. But anybody can find themselves stuck.'

Then there was the sound of a voice in the background. 'I'm sending her a cheque whether she likes it or not. Get her address.'

Heather knew she could not afford to turn it down. How could they cope with an emergency like this by themselves? They owed too much already – which was Alex's fault. That stupid investment idea of his. Heather sighed. She thought of her father. He'd always managed finances well. Thank God for fathers.

'What's the address you're staying at in case we need to get in touch?' her mother asked.

And thank heavens for tactful mothers. She gave her mother what she'd asked for. 'There's no landline,' she added. 'But you can reach my mobile phone.'

'How's Anna taking it?'

'Not well. We're all struggling to adjust to this.'

'You have to be there for her.'

'I'll try.'

A pause fell.

'There's something else though, isn't there?' How did her mother make that out? She must listen to every inflection.

'She has a loser boyfriend,' Heather said. She noticed the break in her voice and forced herself to control it. 'I don't understand her. She goes away to university where she could meet all sorts of more than eligible young men and she gets mixed up with a mechanic. And he even managed to get sacked from that.'

79

'When it doesn't work out, she'll turn to you. Or she should. If you're judgemental she might not. You don't want to turn Anna away from you.'

Which Heather thought she probably had. Why was everything such a mess? She remembered that difficult post-natal depression after Anna had been born. What was it she said to herself about that? It had been as if there was an enormous black cloud above her head that blotted out all sunlight. She was feeling something like that again.

Heather noticed a woman walking past with four dogs on different leads, all hauling away in indiscriminate fashion. An overambitious dog walker probably. Heather took in the different directions the dogs were attempting to haul the woman in and wondered what it must be like to try to control them. She took in the fractious look on the young woman's face. That reminded her of something. Herself. Life was pulling her every which way – with her not knowing how to manage it.

SIXTEEN

It was a pity about that sulky look to the chin because Anna's face was as well-made up as ever, the eyeliner carefully done, the line of the gloss lipstick clear. Even the hair escaped Heather's criticism; that bob brought out the height of the cheekbones well. Did Anna realise that? Perhaps her artifice was improving. She took after her mother after all. It was a pity about the perennial peevishness. She thought back to how Anna had been as a child and wondered where this sullen teenager had come from. Heather shifted in her seat as she became aware of her own scowl.

Heather was seated in Costa's in Aberdeen where she had arranged to meet up with her daughter. It had been a long drive, but she had needed to see Anna again. Or had she? Perhaps she just wanted to. She wondered when had life become one big café. It seemed to be what happened when people lost their house. The only private space to meet someone was a public one. And it would be like that for a while because that flat would never feel like home, and it wasn't somewhere she wanted to invite anyone to.

Anna gave Heather a wave that looked not so much casual as curt, then turned to queue for her latte. Her stance was slouched. Lassitude apparently overcame her in queues. After collecting her coffee, she stomped over and slumped herself opposite Heather. Surely Heather had taught her to be more elegant than that?

'Anna,' she beamed at her.

She did hope this conversation would go better than the last one, but her hopes were not high. Things had been difficult between them for so long.

'Hello, Mum.' Heather noticed Anna was giving her a concerned look. Perhaps this would not go as badly as Heather had feared. 'You were right,' Anna said. 'We do need to meet up. And here I am.' The openness of the smile she gave surprised Heather, but it was followed by the usual critical look. 'You look dreadful,' she said.

'You make me feel so much better about myself,' Heather said. 'Thank you.'

'Things are getting to you,' Anna said.

'They are?'

'You look haunted.'

Heather reached for the almond biscuit on the table beside her and nibbled. She tried to think of a reply to that.

'How's Zac?'

Deflect, she thought. That usually works. Though turning any conversation onto Zac was risky.

'As he always is,' Anna said. 'Fun.'

Heather wished she'd come up with a better topic than Zac. She tried desperately to think of something appeasing to say about him.

'Losing his job must bother him.'

And was that the best she could come up with? She hoped Anna was here to make some sort of effort.

'Every so often he threatens to blow up the garage he used to work in.'

'He does?' Heather shot a worried look at her daughter.

'Then he laughs about it.'

'Oh good.'

'He's just larking about. Really.'

'You're sure?'

'Yes, Mum.' Anna's tone was wearied.

'Is he looking for something else?' Heather asked.

'He won't get his dole money if he doesn't.'

'Does he have universal credit already?'

'It's a while since he lost his job. They gave him nothing at first, of course. He was asking for help from his mother.'

'I suppose he would.'

'Which did put him in a bad mood at the time.'

'Did it?'

'He has feelings.'

'Perhaps we trampled over them when we met.' Heather thought she had better probe Anna's reactions to that encounter. 'I should have given more thought to what I said.'

'He won't forget some of those comments.'

'He won't?'

'No.'

'Will you?' Heather asked.

'Probably not.'

Anna's stare at Heather was icy. Heather looked away, sipped coffee, nibbled, then looked back. Anna was still gazing at her, but her look had become surprisingly concerned.

'But you're under strain, Mum. Are you coping?'

Heather didn't reply to that. She was thinking about how it must have been for Anna. 'It must have been awful for you having to look at the mess your home has turned into.'

'It was.'

'But it wasn't our fault either. It's not as if we were anywhere near it.'

'And I shouldn't have said it was. OK. I'm sorry.'

Anna looked ready to listen and Heather wasn't used to that from her.

'It was difficult for all of us, of course.'

'And then some,' Anna said.

'But we now have somewhere to put you up between terms – or any other time.'

'Thanks, Mum.'

'And we will get through this. The insurers will come through.'

'Are you totally rebuilding or what?'

'I suppose. We hadn't thought about it yet.'

'It'll take a while. You're back at work now?'

'Monday.'

Heather decided to switch the conversation away from herself again. It was a pity it was still only Anna's boyfriend that came to mind.

'Are you happy with Zac?' she asked.

Anna looked surprised at the question. 'Yes,' she said.

'It's just – How did you meet him?'

'At a uni dance. He was a laugh. He had this ancient uni scarf he'd got from somewhere. It couldn't have been his own. He must have borrowed it.'

'Why would he do that?'

'It was his line. He was a university student. Like us. Of course, everybody saw through it. He was funny though. I went along with it to see what he was like.'

'So he's a con artist?'

'It was for a laugh. He admitted to it. He had to in the end. It was cool, Mum. Really. I admire him for it. It took a bit of nerve. Anyway, he's good-looking and fun. He's got more chutzpah than most of the first-year nerds I was meeting. They're boring. Only there because of daddy's money and the fancy school he paid for.'

'I don't know why you're so picky about them,' Heather said.

'And he's sexy. Don't you think?' Anna looked at her mother. 'Obviously not.'

'Does he treat you OK?'

'What do you think? Of course, I know he has issues, but he'll get through them. He needs someone like me, that's all.'

'You think. You won't change him, Anna.'

'I'm not trying to. Why would I want to do that?'

Heather lowered her voice when she leaned over to speak again. 'When we were talking to the police—'

Anna interrupted that.

'The police? What have the police got to do with Zac? Mum. Really.'

'They told us the kind of person who might have set that fire.'

'What?'

'A teenage boy with authority and anger issues.'

It was predictable, of course, but Heather could tell their conversation was now a lost cause. That look of Anna's was designed to kill.

'You think Zac would do something like that? That's gross. How could you say such a thing? You haven't told the police you think that?'

And Heather was glad to be able to say totally truthfully, 'Of course not.'

'You have, haven't you?'

'No.'

'I wouldn't put it past you. I bet you have.'

Mother and daughter glared at each other, Anna with self-righteous anger, Heather with frustration and not a little guilt. She shouldn't have suggested a boyfriend of Anna's might have started the fire. But had he?

'I'm sorry, Anna.' She was making too many blunders here – again. 'It's been difficult lately.'

'I'll say. But Zac would never do a thing like that. And, if he did, why would he do it to you? I'm his girlfriend.'

Heather had to admit the logic of that.

'All right. Then he wouldn't. You're the one who knows him. I don't.'

And God this was hell. The house reduced to ashes and all this agony afterwards. But the house had to have been set alight for a personal reason. By someone who knew them? So why not Zac? Even if she couldn't think why. Why would anyone do it? Would a person who did this sort of thing reason things out? Who knew. But at least she'd managed to suggest to Anna, awful though the thought was, she had to admit it was possible Zac had done the fire-raising, which, she now realized, was why she'd arranged to meet up with her in the first place. Then Heather's mind bounced around again. It had been doing that lately. And she shouldn't be saying this to her daughter either, but she did.

'Anna, do you think your father could be having an affair?'

Anna's mouth hung open, which almost amused Heather. She hadn't seen quite that expression on Anna's face before.

'You must be joking, Mum. Dad? See someone else? What makes you think he might be doing that?'

'It's just – he's been odd lately.'

'And you haven't been?' What did Anna mean by that? 'The fire's getting to you.'

'You don't think he might do that?' Heather asked.

'No.'

That was clear, as was the hard look Anna was giving her.

'No, Mum,' Anna said. 'Dad's not having an affair. Are you?'

SEVENTEEN

Heather was thinking she had never expected to have to kowtow to her cleaner. Though she had to admit it was a snobbish thought. When had she become like that? Perhaps she always had been that way. She told herself it was defensible to resent having to ingratiate herself with anybody, though she would have to get on with things and do just that in her reduced circumstances.

She knocked on Elsa's front door. Why did Elsa not have a doorbell like everybody else? Was that a form of pretentiousness? The knocker was in the shape of a horse's head which Heather was having to hammer onto a horseshoe. That was bad taste. Heather wondered what she would find inside the house. As Elsa opened the door, Heather had her face fixed into her best attempt at an appeasing smile and hoped it was convincing.

'Hi, Elsa, I don't like to bother you, but we don't seem to have any coffee. I was wondering—'

'Come in,' Elsa said. 'Sorry. I should have checked.'

There was such graciousness in the way Elsa said it, that Heather felt ashamed of her resentments, and the flimsiness of her excuse for coming over. As she entered through the hallway, Heather found herself walking on a pink-and-white Chinese rug over a dark, varnished, parquet floor. There was a faint smell of what might be bread baking. Did Elsa find time to do that? Heather was jealous. They entered the kitchen.

The kitchen was a bright room with units in pale cream, with black marble worktops. The gleaming white Aga looked pristine despite the two loaves cooling on the worktop beside it. Everywhere looked spotless as might be expected from someone of Elsa's profession. On the wall were prints of Iona with beaches as pale and clean in appearance as the kitchen units. Heather had to admit the place was more pleasing than she had expected. Elsa opened a cupboard and brought out coffee.

'I have loads,' Elsa said. 'I've always had this fear of running out of things.'

'Have you?' Heather said as she wondered why. She switched her curious gaze from the kitchen to Elsa.

'Would you like a mug of coffee now?' Elsa said. 'I was going to take a break.'

Heather did not refuse. She could not help noticing the almost fluorescent pink of the kettle as Elsa filled it with water. Now that stood out. Elsa switched it on, took out a filter coffee pot and spooned in grains.

Heather realised what was odd about Elsa's kitchen. There was nothing personal in it. It was a room of anonymous surfaces that gleamed, with no photographs of the people Elsa knew. When Heather thought of her own kitchen, there had been photos of Anna and Alex – and her – stuck all over the fridge. And there was clutter that had been laid down by busy people on their way to somewhere else and not picked up again. Heather wondered if the rest of the house was as tidy as the kitchen.

When the kettle had boiled, Heather found herself seated at the kitchen table opposite Elsa, holding a mug with a view of Loch Ness on it, and a chocolate digestive biscuit she was wishing she had refused.

'Someone was saying you were married once?' Heather said. 'Not that I mean to pry,' she added, though she did.

If she was having to accept the favour of the flat, she might at least find out something about the woman who was lending it to them. She was annoyed with herself for not already knowing more about Elsa. In Heather's mind Elsa had only existed to take care of the practical chores that bored her. Now she had been forced to realise there was more to Elsa than she had realised.

Elsa took a sip and looked back at Heather with an expression on her face that said nothing. Then she frowned.

'For four or five years,' she said. 'Long enough.'

'But that's barely time to get to know him,' Heather said.

'That was the problem. I was getting to.'

'There's been no one else?' Heather said.

'I learned my lesson.'

There was a coldness in her eyes and in her tone, and Heather wondered whether it was a good idea to pursue the topic. But Heather could not resist another attempt to find out more about her.

'What age did you marry at?' Heather asked.

'Nineteen.'

'Young,' Heather said.

'I suppose,' Elsa replied.

'I don't think girls understand much about men at that age. I know I didn't. You tend to take them at face value. And there's always something they're hiding. Don't you think?'

'Or you don't know how boring they're going to be when you start to live with them all the time.'

Heather laughed at that. But Elsa didn't. That had been a serious comment.

'How long have you been married to Alex?' Elsa asked.

'Twenty-two years,' she said.

She tried to catch the tone in her own voice as she said that. Was that surprise or regret?

Elsa smiled. 'Lucky you. You must have one of the good ones.'

'You admit there are some?'

'I suppose,' Elsa said. A smile appeared on her face. 'I go in and out of a few houses in my line of work and there are a lot of husbands I wouldn't want anything to do with, but I do notice when things are going well, and you two are contented with each other.'

Really? Heather thought.

'You get on well. It's obvious.'

Heather was thinking that had not been true for a while.

Then she found herself glancing round the room again. That empty fridge door. Her own was filled up with notes. Reminders about this and that. And there were inane magnets brought back from unmemorable holidays. She wished there was something individual in this room. Then she realised what the overpowering presence in it was: emptiness – as if, at the centre of Elsa lay a vacuum. She looked at Elsa again. Did that sum her up? There was an inner emptiness she filled with an obsession for neatness and cleanliness; and the work she did held a repetitiveness that was also essential for that?

'It's good that you have each other,' Elsa said. 'It'll help you through this. And you will get through it.'

Elsa gave her a blazing smile which Heather thought was manufactured well. Or might Elsa mean it? There was kindness in the expression.

A thought occurred to Heather. Alex hadn't noticed Elsa, had he? He wouldn't be interested in someone like her? Perhaps that vacuum at the centre of Elsa sucking him in. An appalling thought. But she'd had this nagging feeling about Alex for a while.

EIGHTEEN

The bland, the impersonal: Heather's life was filled with coffee rooms, hotel lounges, and borrowed flats. She hauled her top over her head with a flourish and plunged into the personal. She draped her arms around Stuart as she devoured his lips with hers. They might be in an anonymous hotel room, but it was going to be so much more than that. She tugged at Stuart's top. Between lunging at each other and tearing off clothes, they made slow but enjoyable progress towards the bed. When they reached it, they merged into the moment. Afterwards, they lay and looked at the vapid décor of their hotel room with its tasteful greys, as they luxuriated in the slowing of their heartbeats.

Stuart was someone else Heather knew from the Health Centre; he was a physiotherapist. Heather felt more relaxed with him than she had with anyone in years. He was tall, fair, lean, with a winning smile, and so much younger than her, about ten years – perhaps that was why every glance at him pulled at her heart. She did not attempt to justify her affair with him. How could she do that? But falling into bed with Stuart had been the natural thing to do. As if she were falling back into the youth she had left behind.

Though she had also been falling into guilt. She could not look at Alex without feeling that. Perhaps that was why she was watching Alex so carefully. She would feel better about her own affair if Alex was having one too. But she felt no regret. She enjoyed her times with Stuart so much. They did seem to lead to snappiness with Alex, or perhaps that tension had always been there, and she had just become more aware of it. Maybe it was why she was having the affair.

Heather continued to lie on the bed and listen to the shallowing of her breath and Stuart's. This was a moment to savour. Then she supposed she should force herself to broach the subject that needed to be discussed.

'Friday night,' Heather said.

'Hmm,' Stuart said. 'It was wonderful.'

'Of course, and it was also the night of the fire.'

'That,' Stuart said.

'No small thing.'

'It must have been a real shock going home to that.'

'And there was Alex standing watching me as I returned from you.'

'You didn't tell him where you'd been?'

'I should have been asleep in my bed when the house went up.'

'Just as well you weren't.'

'And I had to come up with some sort of excuse.'

'What did you say?'

'I said I was round at Margaret Affleck's.'

'Quick thinking.'

'Which meant I had to ask her to lie for me.'

'Will she?'

'Yes.'

'That's handy.'

'But I had to tell her where I really was.'

'Can you trust her not to say?'

'That was the most difficult conversation I've had in some time.'

'And?'

'She's all right about it. Shocked but not self-righteous. She did have an affair once. Which makes us birds of a feather.'

'I didn't know she was married,' Stuart said.

Heather frowned. 'She's not now.'

'If Alex asks her anything, she'll back you up?'

'Yes. But that's not the problem,' Heather said.

'Isn't it?'

'Alex and I had to make statements to the police about our movements that night. Which we had to sign.' Heather was aware of how anxious her voice was as she spoke.

'That's awkward. But they can't suspect you of burning down your own house – as you didn't do it. The statement's a formality – isn't it?'

'Maybe – but if they check up with Margaret it could be difficult.'

'She's said she won't lie to the police, only Alex?' Stuart said.

'I shouldn't think it's occurred to her she'll have to talk to the police.'

'You don't think she will lie to them?'

'I don't know what she'll do,' Heather said.

'If the police find out about you and me, all that does is give you an alibi.'

'Does it?'

'Don't you think?' Stuart said.

'But then Alex will know.'

'Not necessarily. You could ask them to keep quiet about it. If it came to a court of law, of course, they couldn't, but why should it come to that?'

'I suppose,' Heather said.

They lay in their hotel bedroom for a while afterwards. Heather had always felt happily separated from reality when she was with Stuart. But it was muscling in. Perhaps she ought to acknowledge the place she had reached in her relationship with Alex and make a decision.

NINETEEN

Alex

A photograph of Al Pacino in *The Godfather* film was directly opposite Alex, and he found the menace in the actor's face off-putting, as he did the other references to Italian Mafia Hollywood culture in the décor. It was quite a theme in this tiny Italian restaurant in the centre of Inverness. Was it a hint the restaurant was robbing people with its prices? Alex checked his sense of humour. He had read the menu before entering. The tables were positioned very closely to each other. Apart from offending his need for personal space, there was the chance that he and Jasmine might be overheard.

It was lunchtime and Alex was seated at a table beside her: Jasmine, with that sweep of hair and the quick smile that had its way with him on the night of the fire. What a way to put it, he thought. He had been more than a willing accomplice. They had been together in his hotel room enjoying their unexpected and prolonged encounter when his mobile had rung, and a voice had chattered senselessly about his house being on fire. Jasmine had since insisted on this lunchtime meeting. They needed to talk.

Alex was not long back at work. Everyone had been sympathetic when he returned but there had been so many threads to pull together after only a few days' absence that he felt fraught with the effort and was glad of the chance to relax in a city centre restaurant. At least he hoped this was going to be relaxing. He still had to make up his mind what to do about Jasmine.

Jasmine looked up from her menu and flashed a sympathetic smile at him.

'You're shaken,' she said.

'Watching everything you own going up in smoke would do that to most people.'

'True,' she replied.

'It's – I don't know,' he said.

He put the menu down, unable to concentrate.

'I don't know how anyone begins to replace everything they had,' he said.

'I know.'

'And Heather – I dread to think what it's doing to her. And I shouldn't have been unfaithful to her,' he said.

'That's not complimentary to me,' Jasmine said.

'Heather's all over the place.'

'Is she?'

'How else would she be?'

The waitress appeared at that moment, a dark Italian type with deep brown eyes and a swirling mass of black curly hair. Normally Alex would give her more than a glance, but now he just looked hurriedly at the menu and stabbed a finger at it. The young woman made a note on her pad. There was a sense of ease on Jasmine's face as she gestured at her copy of the menu. This was her choice of restaurant and she was at home here.

'Do they know anything about how the fire started?' she asked Alex.

'Oh, yes,' Alex replied.

'So what happened?'

'The opposite of accidental. Petrol poured over what they call inflammables, then lit.'

'No. But who would do a thing like that?'

'That's what they're trying to find out. As long as they don't decide I set it on fire for the insurance money.'

'Are they likely to do that?'

'Who knows what bizarre conclusions they could come up with?'

'It's lucky neither of you were at home when it happened. You wouldn't be here to talk about it if you had been.'

'We really thought Heather might have been in the fire.'

'Thank God she wasn't.'

'She was at a friend's house.'

Jasmine gave Alex a questioning look.

'A female friend. Whose mother died recently of cancer and she needed to talk. And they chatted into the small hours.'

'Lucky for Heather.'

'Thank God for Margaret. Not that I can remember meeting her. But Heather has talked about her.'

'She does exist then?'

'What do you mean?'

'You're sure Heather was with a female friend?'

Alex looked across at Jasmine.

'You don't know Heather,' he said.

But his reply did not impress.

'You weren't with a male colleague,' Jasmine said.

'That, ah,' Alex said.

'And you don't look as if you regretted it.'

Alex looked across at Jasmine and sighed. He liked her and didn't want to upset her feelings. He could bed her again happily. He was meeting up with her again, wasn't he? What was it with those eyes of hers? Even when they were questioning him as they were now.

'Heather had to put Margaret's name down on the police statement when she explained where she was at the time of the fire. She does exist.'

'The police?'

'Naturally they're involved. And they're suspicious of everybody until they can prove them innocent. It's their job to be like that.'

'You haven't told the police about me?'

'No,' Alex replied. 'I was away at a works conference. That covers it.'

Jasmine's smile was feline, Alex thought – and smug when directed at him. Which was appealing. It was good to feel Jasmine had proprietorial feelings towards him. And that time in his hotel room had been fun. It was a pity it had been interrupted in the way it had been. Jasmine put her hand on his. He squeezed hers in return. Then he took his away with an abruptness that surprised him.

'What Heather's going through is awful,' he said. 'Have you any idea how I feel about that?'

'You still asked to meet up with me again.'

Alex pondered her.

'Yes,' he said.

'We did enjoy ourselves.'

'Yes.'

And if his feelings were easy to understand it would help.

'When something like that fire happens, I don't know,' he said, 'you reconsider everything.'

'You do?'

'I shouldn't be doing this to Heather, and I feel bad about it.'

'Oh.'

Jasmine looked down at the table then away through the window at someone on the street walking past the restaurant.

'Do you really think I should be hurting Heather like this?' he said.

Jasmine looked back at him.

'I don't see what happened between us has anything to do with Heather. It was about us. We needed to do it.'

Alex tried to take that in.

'It was good,' he said. 'It's not that I regret it.'

'I should hope not. I'm a catch, aren't I?'

There was a teasing tone in Jasmine's voice, and it appealed to him.

'It was good,' he said. Then the decision formed itself apparently against his will.

'But we should leave it at one night.'

'That's not fair to me.'

'No. But we should – and I'm sorry,' Alex said.

There was a pause. Now her eyes were accusing him, and he had to look away.

'That fire,' he said. 'It turned everything upside down and it made me look at things. And I don't want to make my life even more chaotic.'

Jasmine's look was growing fiercer.

'You're a disappointment,' she said. 'I thought there was more to you than that.'

'I've let you down,' Alex said. 'I'm sorry.'

He was regretting this. But he'd decided to be sensible; there was nothing else to be done.

'Look, we're adults,' Jasmine said.

Alex braced himself for what she might mean by that.

'If you don't live for the moment, you discover it's gone.'

Alex was puzzled. Was that not what he had said – the moment was over?

'We have to make the most of things while we can,' Jasmine said. 'And that's all we did. I don't feel guilty about that, and I don't think you should.'

'It was good,' Alex said. 'It was very good.'

And he did mean that. They looked at each other.

'If it wasn't for the fire,' he added.

'The fire wasn't my fault. I shouldn't be punished for it.'

'I'm sorry.'

'But if your house hadn't burned down, you'd have been happy to keep on seeing me?'

'You make me feel like a heel.'

'You don't know Heather was with Margaret. She was probably having it away with someone else. You often leave her on her own. What do you think she is? Inhuman?'

There was such seriousness in Jasmine as she said it, Alex was intimidated, but he wasn't going to back down.

'I don't know anything to suggest Heather's having an affair.'

'She would make sure you didn't.'

'Or not,' Alex said.

He thought back to their moments of passion, the scent of Jasmine's skin and the touch of it. He shook his head as if to shake the thought away. He put his hand across and over hers.

'I'm sorry,' he said.

How many times had he said that to her in this conversation?

'But with all that's happened I can't keep this up. I don't think I can handle it. And it's not fair on Heather.'

And that was that. He'd succeeded in sticking to his decision. He pulled his hand away.

Their food arrived and the half bottle of wine. His pasta looked good. He had looked forward to it but knew it would be spoiled by the quarrel. He glanced across at Jasmine and tried to work out just how strong the fury was in those eyes.

TWENTY

When Heather's father had warned Heather about Alex's female conquests before he'd met her, he had been telling no lies. Alex came from a family of several sisters with himself the only boy, and they'd spoiled him, which had given him a good understanding of women, and a fondness for them, so he usually did have at least one girlfriend. When Heather was pregnant with Anna and lost interest in sex, Alex soon found himself with another offer, from Mia, Alex's date before Heather, not that he had to say yes, but he did.

Heather was being difficult at the time, and he couldn't cope with it. She was moody, unpredictable and, as far as Alex was concerned, selfish. He'd never known her like that before.

He felt guilty about taking up with Mia but that hadn't stopped him. What Heather didn't know wouldn't harm her. The callowness of youth. And of course she did find out. He didn't like having to give Mia up. The sex had been good – and he'd been getting none from Heather.

After Anna was born, Heather's time was taken up with Anna, and she'd gone through all those mood swings. It was after that her doctor was consulted, and Heather had been given that diagnosis of post-natal depression which made Alex feel like a heel. It was his fault. He'd been interested in his own needs and had neglected her.

Later on, he came to realise one of the best things he had done in his life was give up Mia. He did love Heather and was so glad when she cheered up and became her normal self again; and it had eased his guilt to help her through her illness. He also enjoyed his fatherhood with Anna.

That had been twenty years before but Heather had never let him forget the betrayal, which he really did come to regret because it seemed to give Heather such power over him. She had the last word in every argument. But he had come to realise how much he valued Heather. So he blamed himself. It was because of his bad behaviour – with Mia.

And now, despite their troubles, things were good with Heather; she was fussing over him in a way she hadn't in years; she made his favourite meals and turned up with items of clothing she was sure he must have forgotten to buy. He didn't think he had ever had so many pairs of socks. The shock of the fire had brought them together. It didn't occur to him there might be guilt on Heather's part.

They were relaxing over a glass of Pinot Noir after a dinner of venison casserole – when was the last time Heather had cooked that? – when the doorbell rang and Alex found himself face to face with Inspector Black and Sergeant McPherson again.

'Good evening, sir,' Black said with a disarming smile that worried Alex. 'We have developments to discuss with you. May we come in?'

'You do?' Alex replied. 'By all means.'

He ushered them into the lounge and waved them into seats. Soon they were seated opposite Alex and Heather. There was something ominous in Black's manner that reminded Alex of his headmaster – never more dangerous than when at his most benign.

'Have you caught him?' Heather asked.

'Yes and no,' Black replied.

Alex wondered what that could mean.

'I did say the fire fitted an MO.'

'Yes,' Alex said.

'Outhouses in different places in this general area have been set alight destroying the outbuilding but doing no other damage and causing no risk to life – though the fires have been getting bigger, so that yours could have been set by the same person. It was started in exactly the same way.'

'But you've changed your mind?' Alex said.

'We caught him.'

'What's the problem?'

'He's the type of person we expected to arrest: an eighteen-year-old lad of limited intelligence who did badly at school, and in the workplace, and who has recently been sacked from his job.'

Oh no, Alex thought. It's Zac.

'As an apprentice car mechanic?' Heather said.

'No,' Black said, looking at her. 'What makes you say that?'

'Just a thought,' Heather said. 'I don't know really.'

'A precise thought,' Black said. 'He's a young man called Stephen Brodie. He lives in Nairn – in Tradespark. Do you know him?'

'I don't think so,' Heather said, and there was a note of relief in her voice.

'No,' Alex said, and he was definite about that.

'Did you think it was someone else?' Black asked.

'It's a bit of a shock,' Heather said, 'finally knowing.'

'You're sure it's him?' Alex said.

'He's made a confession,' Black said.

'Great,' Alex said.

'To an extent,' Black added. 'He's admitted setting fire to the others. When we asked him why, he said it made him feel good. It warmed the heart. Not that he'll think it funny for long. The only thing is, he says he didn't set fire to your place. He says he didn't intend real harm in the fires he started. He liked shocking stuck-up people who thought they were better than him. A bit twisted but what can you expect? And he already knew the people whose buildings he set on fire. Which is why we'd like to ask you to come down and have a look at him. See if you recognise him.'

'Of course,' Alex said.

'Definitely,' Heather said.

'We did tell him the extent of the damage this fire caused. And told him it could have been worse, that Heather might have been caught up in it, even killed. Which could be why he's denying doing yours. Can you come down this afternoon?'

'How did you catch him?' Alex asked.

'He was boasting to a pal. He's not bright. He didn't think anybody would rat on him, which, of course, they did, after hearing what happened to your house.'

'I'm trying to think if I've come across him at the Health Centre,' Heather said. 'But I don't think I have.'

'We haven't finished checking every camera in the area,' Black said. 'If he showed up on anything near your house that would help us. He has shown up at another of the sites – on a neighbour's security camera. Not that it was incriminating by itself.'

'Does he express regret?' Alex asked.

'He's feeling sorry for himself because he was caught, which isn't the same thing. He has an alibi for your fire which we've yet to check out. If it holds up, it would rule him out but you never know with alibis. People often lie. Don't feel we expect you to recognise him. If you do, good, but if not, don't worry about it. There's always the chance he didn't do yours.'

'I see,' Alex said.

'We wouldn't want an innocent person convicted,' Heather said.

'No,' Black agreed.

TWENTY-ONE

With its navy-blue-painted concrete walls, its grey metal-framed windows, its smell of cleaning fluids, its alarmist posters of robbery and rape, and its funereal black-tiled floor, the corridor was a depressing place. Alex and Heather were seated in their local police station at Inspector Black's request. Black had said Stephen Brodie would be led past them to an interview room, and this accidental meeting would give them the opportunity to see if they recognised him.

A door was opened further up the corridor and there was the sound of two sets of feet. One sounded firm and confident, the other not so. Alex looked up. He found himself staring at a police constable and a young man. Brodie was an unprepossessing teenager. He had pale skin, a long, beaked nose, and hair that spiked out in untidy directions. The expression on his face was downcast and the look in his eyes sullen. Alex pondered him. Had he seen that unsightly individual before? He was distinctive and there was something familiar about him, which might not mean anything. Nairn was a small town, and it would have been easy enough to have noticed him in the street. Stephen saw Alex stare at him and glared. Alex looked away. There was something disturbing in that look. He thought he would have noticed Stephen if he had been hanging around their house but did not remember him.

Stephen Brodie and the policeman walked past. Alex glanced at Heather, who was looking after Stephen. She shrugged her shoulders as if to indicate Stephen did not ring any bells with her. Alex thought that Black would call them into his office to discuss Brodie, but he didn't. They sat listening to the wall clock opposite tick out its official time, which felt longer than that elsewhere. Alex listened for the sound of Black's door and of Black's feet but there was only silence and the sound of a car passing by outside.

'Have you ever seen him before?' Alex asked Heather.

'No.'

'This is a waste of time,' Alex said.

'Yes.'

'You don't think they want another look at us?' Alex asked.

'I can't think why. Brodie must have set fire to our house. He did the others.'

'It makes sense to me. The police try to be too clever for themselves sometimes.'

'If the insurance company suspects us, they won't pay out.'

'Maybe that Stephen Brodie is the one trying to be smart,' Alex said.

'That makes sense to me,' Heather said.

The sound of another pair of feet was eventually heard. Alex looked up and found himself looking into the eyes of Black. They were particularly authoritative. Alex forced a compliant expression onto his face as he smiled up at him.

'Has he talked?' Alex asked.

Black's smile was non-committal.

'If you'd like to come into my office,' Black said.

When they followed him, they found themselves in a room designed for function. Shelves containing files stretched from floor to ceiling. A glass and steel desk dominated the centre of the floor, allowing Black ease of access to the chair behind it, and room for interviewees in front of it. The centre of the desk held a large computer, and there were several piles of papers stacked around it. Black's hand gestured to two plastic chairs. Alex tried to convince himself of his self-confidence. Black gave an expansive but intimidating look.

'Our friend, Stephen Brodie, did you have a good look at him?'

'Yes,' Alex said and looked across at Heather who nodded.

'And?'

'He's not unfamiliar,' Alex said.

'Which means?'

'That's a good question. I might have seen him around Nairn at some time or other. It's a small place. But, if I did, he can't have registered.'

'Accuracy is what we're looking for. If you don't know him, say so.'

'I might have seen him hanging around the house,' Heather said. 'The day before the fire.'

Alex gave her a surprised look.

'You might have done?' Black said.

'Or, if it wasn't him, it was someone very like him. I looked out of the kitchen window and noticed someone staring at the house. I'm sure it was Stephen Brodie. When he saw me looking at him, he looked away. I thought no more about it, but, when I think back now, it was a bit strange.'

'You're definite it was him?'

Heather considered for a moment, then said, 'Yes.'

Alex thought that odd considering Heather's reaction when Stephen had walked past.

'Anyway, he must have confessed by now?' Heather said. 'Has he? He must have done it. It stands to reason if he set the other fires.'

'That would be convenient,' Black said. 'But, as I've told you, he denies doing yours. We've tried to press him on it.'

'He must be lying,' Heather said. 'The charge for our fire is more serious, isn't it?'

'He boasted about the others. But not yours,' Black said.

'He was showing off?' Alex said.

'Oh yes, he's proud of them. Thinks he did something clever. "That'll show them," he says. Whoever "they" is supposed to be. He's an angry person. And confused. They'll have a psychiatrist at him to try to work him out. But, when we asked him about your house, he was more surprised than anything.'

'I don't believe him,' Alex said.

'And I don't,' Heather said.

'Then you don't,' Black said, 'but it doesn't prove anything.'

TWENTY-TWO

What windows remained were gaping holes giving views onto the blackened remnants of walls, and floors. Ash was strewn everywhere. Alex was at the scene of the fire again, pondering the debris of the home he had shared with Heather, who stood beside him now. Alex's desk had stood over there. On that wall had hung a photograph of them on their wedding day. Alex groaned. Their time in this house had crackled and burned; a whole life had been obliterated in one night.

Beside them was the insurance company investigator. He had introduced himself to them as John Matheson. Alex had expected a man in a suit who looked a bit like an accountant, but, in overalls and flat cap, Matheson looked like a builder, and said he was. He had shown them his identification, and the photograph matched. Alex supposed the man would have to work out how to reconstruct what lay in front of them.

He wandered about, pointing a camera, and writing down things on a paper pinned to a board. He probed and tutted. Left to their own devices, Alex and Heather felt aimless, so they walked about, and looked around too. When Matheson returned to them, there was a questioning look on his face.

'I've seen the reports,' he said.

'Yes?' Alex replied.

'This fire started in an outhouse. Could you point it out?'

Alex did, and the man strode over. He poked and peered; he turned over charred pieces of wood; he probed through ash; he wrote more notes; he took more photographs; he pushed bricks about; he frowned; he looked around more and wrote even more down. Alex assumed that, as well as being conversant with the building problems in front of him, Matheson was well trained in the causes of fires. A decisive look appeared on Matheson's face as he straightened himself up, then walked over to them. He had seen what he needed to see.

'Starting again from scratch,' he said.

'What?' Alex said.

'The rebuild. An obvious enough conclusion to reach. You only have to glance around. Your insurance company will cover it. The good news is the only thing the policy does specify is the sum involved. The design's flexible. People often build something different. If you're rebuilding anyway, why not?'

That perked Heather up. 'When can we look at different designs?'

'You can only use trusted builders. They specify Tulloch or Mackay. Which of them is up to you.'

'So the insurance company will meet the claim?' Alex asked.

'Your payments are up to date,' the man replied. Then he paused.

'So there's no problem?' Alex said.

'This is wilful fire-raising,' Matheson said. 'That's in the fire investigator's reports – and I can verify that from what I've seen. That can slow things down.'

'I knew there would be a snag,' Heather said.

'But we're not the ones who set the fire,' Alex said.

'And I didn't say you were. But it takes longer to settle the claim.'

'Why?' Heather asked.

The man put on his most professional look.

'Due process,' he said. 'The police need to eliminate possibilities. Then the company will meet the claim.'

'In other words, they think we might have done it?' Heather said.

'What lovely bureaucratic minds,' Alex said.

'Well,' Matheson replied, 'they have processes to go through. It's a difficult thing to assess.'

'Is it?' Alex said.

He could not read the look that Matheson gave him in reply.

'We've nowhere to live,' Alex said.

'And building a house takes time,' Heather said. 'At least a year, isn't it?'

'It varies but often not as long as that.'

'But they need to get started as soon as possible,' Heather said.

'Will the company give us money to help with temporary accommodation?' Alex asked.

'That's not in your policy. You receive the cost of the rebuild.'

'If they meet the claim,' Alex said.

'This is inhuman,' Heather said.

Matheson did not reply.

'How long do you think it'll take to resolve this?' Alex said.

'I don't know,' Matheson said. 'It depends on the police.'

Then he added, 'But, with any luck, not long.'

As Matheson left, Alex noted the expression on his face. Despite his polite reactions, Matheson was untouched by their conversation. This was a job of work to him. But, in Alex's opinion, Matheson did think it a serious possibility they had started the fire themselves to claim the insurance money.

TWENTY-THREE

'I hate that carpet.'

They were in the living room of their flat. The room was not as intrinsically annoying as one might have thought from Heather's reaction to it. It was not to her taste; something pale and Scandinavian would be more in tune with Heather's modernistic sensitivities – but there was more than that trying her patience. She simply expressed this by complaining about the carpet, the fussy cornice and the over-elegant velvet curtains, or anything else in the flat that caught her eye when her feelings were getting the better of her – and the same thing that was worrying her was upsetting Alex.

'What if they don't pay up?' he said.

He took in the look of horror on Heather's face.

'That would sink us,' Heather said.

'What do we do?' he said.

'Pray?'

'Be serious.' He gave her his most withering look.

'Nothing then,' she said. 'There's nothing we can do, unless you know anybody who could be useful?'

'With influence at an insurance company?'

'Your boss is always going on about his contacts, isn't he?'

'Not in insurance, no.'

'But these CEOs – a lot of them know each other, don't they?'

'It's a dream, Heather.'

'We've got to try something.'

Alex sighed. He stared out of the window. There was a wind outside. It wafted the conifer opposite. There was rain too, slanting down at its odd angle, savaging the pond in Elsa's garden. Odd how the weather was echoing his mood.

'People who know people,' Alex said. 'That's what ordinary folk think makes the world go round.'

'Isn't it?'

Alex turned his head towards her.

'I don't even know that I'm that well in with my boss right now.'

'That streamlining,' Heather said. 'Has he said he's getting rid of you?'

'I'm in the wrong age group. Once you're over forty, you have to work twice as hard to justify yourself.'

Heather gave him a piercing look.

'They probably think I might drop dead at any moment.'

Heather's gaze did not alter. Perhaps she thought that too.

'That's why I go to all these conferences you object to,' he said.

'You should have set up something of your own ten years ago. I did try to persuade you to do that.'

'You need capital for that.'

'If you hadn't lost all grandfather's money in that stupid investment.'

'That was bad. I admit it. I've always regretted that.'

'And it was my inheritance.'

'I've said I'm sorry.'

'Which doesn't help. And if we don't get the insurance pay-out for the house, we've nowhere to live. Don't get sacked on top of that.'

Alex averted his gaze and looked at the rain. Then he summoned the nerve to look at her again.

'Heather,' he said.

'What?'

'Come here so I can give you a hug.'

Heather gave him a disbelieving stare.

'Have you any idea how annoyed I am by you sometimes?' she said.

'Yes,' he said, then walked over and hugged her.

She was stiff at first but then returned the embrace. He kissed her but she pulled away from that. He looked at her. This was Heather, the person who meant most to him in the world – and the mother of his child. How had things become so strained between them?

'It's the kind of situation that can bring people closer,' he said, 'when you're working through problems together.'

'Great theory,' Heather said, but her look didn't agree. 'I don't know, Alex. How did we get into this situation?'

'A mixed-up teenage boy with a grudge against the world took it out on us.'

'And he denies it.'

'And we don't even know him. Did you see him near the house like you told the Inspector?'

'What?' A confused look came over Heather's face. 'Oh, that. I don't know.'

'That's what you said.'

'It must have been him. Who else could it have been?'

Alex stared at her.

'I saw somebody. And there can't be that many fire-raisers around. It had to be him.'

Alex was disappointed in her, but words failed him.

'It was set in the same way as the others,' Heather said. 'The same MO the police said.'

'Perhaps it's the most obvious way to set a fire.'

'Don't look at me like that,' Heather said.

'All right. All right.' Alex sighed. 'Is there anybody we know who might have wanted to do this to us?'

'The police asked that.'

'And we said there wasn't. But is there?'

'They'd have to be crazy.'

'Crazy people go to Health Centres,' Alex said. 'Where else would they get treatment? And you work in one.'

'True.'

'Have there been any incidents there?'

Heather's brow furrowed.

'There was one old man. We had to give him a prostate examination and he didn't half object afterwards. You'd have thought he'd been molested.'

'And?'

'That's it,' Heather said. 'But the doctor dealt with that. She talked to him.'

'You can't talk round someone who's crazy. Was he?'

'It was a while ago. And hardly a major incident. He wouldn't do this.'

'It wouldn't make sense. But setting fires doesn't make sense, does it?'

'All the same, I couldn't mention him to the police.'

Alex supposed not. Heather didn't betray confidentiality anyway.

'Have you given someone a bad deal?' she asked.

'I do that all the time,' Alex said.

'So lots of names spring to mind?'

'If there's a real reason to complain they'll sue.'

'Your company gets sued a lot then?'

Alex laughed. 'Oddly enough, no.'

Then a thought struck Alex. Something had come to mind. Derek could still owe him a grudge for being sacked. But Derek had been lucky to get away with just being dismissed. Derek had his hand in the till and Alex had been the one to rat on him. Alex's own boss thought the police should have been involved but Alex had persuaded him not to get in touch with them. Derek had been best man at Alex's wedding and that shouldn't have any influence on Alex, but it had. What had happened to Derek anyway? He hadn't seen him in years, but he couldn't see Derek doing something like this.

'It's someone who has it in for us.'

'Maybe it was something random.'

'That would make it difficult to work out who it was.'

'You're right there.'

Heather was now the one to gaze out of the window. Alex wondered what was going through her mind.

'Could it have been one of Anna's friends?' she asked.

A picture of Zac came into Alex's head, the tattoo blazing from Zac's forehead.

'Zac's crazy enough,' Heather said.

'Maybe. Or maybe not,' Alex said, 'but he's fallen head over heels for Anna.'

'You think so?'

'Don't you?'

A puzzled look appeared on Heather's face.

'Who knows what goes on in the mind of someone like him.'

'He looks odd, I know,' Alex said.

'He looks as strange as he can manage. He likes getting up other people's noses.'

'If you suggest Zac's name to the police, Anna will never forgive you.'

'If the police keep on asking us questions, his name will crop up.'

'Are we looking for a fall guy?' Alex asked.

Heather fixed a look on him and Alex wondered what was going on behind those innocent hazel eyes.

'It would be good to find out who did it,' she said.

'To persuade the company to meet the claim.'

'They know the fire was started deliberately. If they're not looking at someone else, why would they stop suspecting us?'

Alex didn't know what to say in answer to that. The two of them stared at each other until Alex had to stop. Eventually, he did look back.

'If they can't prove we did it, that'll count for something – and they'll be obliged to meet the claim.'

'You mean we could be getting more pressure from the police over this?'

Another silence fell. Alex studied Heather. Was she going to come up with schemes to get them off the hook? But what she asked him was a surprise.

'Did you do it for the insurance money?' she asked.

'Of course I didn't,' he said. The words had rushed out. 'I'm neither that crazy nor that stupid.' Alex realised how angry Heather had made him feel. 'You should know me better than that. We've been married for long enough.'

'We must be high on the police list of suspects,' Heather said.

'I can't think why,' Alex said.

'We have financial problems. The insurance payment would help.'

'We'd have no more mortgage payments to make – but that wouldn't solve everything. And they don't pay out if you set the fire yourself. I know that.'

'When people are under strain–'

Alex did not allow her to complete the sentence.

'Really?' he said.

'And with the downsizing at work.'

'That's quite a case you're building there.'

'Have they told you they're letting you go?'

Alex could not believe it. Heather did think he might have done this.

'Do you think so little of me?'

Heather shook her head.

'Of course I don't,' she said. 'Of course not.' Why did she need to repeat that? 'You're Alex. You're the guy I've known all these years. You wouldn't do that.'

Then she paused before a quizzical look hardened on her face.

'But you didn't, did you?'

There was indecision in her eyes and Alex tried to take it in. Heather wasn't sure, and it hurt. How had his marriage come to this? How had his life reached this point? He stood there searching for words, as he and Heather continued glaring at each other. Her distrust shook him to the core. Even if she hadn't said it, he knew what she was thinking. If Heather had died in the fire, that would have solved any financial worries, because of the tidy sum her life was insured for. Heather was trying to work out whether he had tried to murder her.

TWENTY-FOUR

In contrast to the glass, steel, and Formica-surfaced office that Alex inhabited, his CEO's office was imposing. The man seated in front of him was behind a sweeping mahogany desk with a green leather top. He had a padded leather mahogany 'captain's' swivel chair that he had turned towards Alex. Mark Bright had been studying something on his Mac before Alex's entry. To his rear was a view through a window of the river sweeping out, and the mountains behind. Everything must look set fair to him from where he was seated, was the thought in Alex's mind. Alex himself found being called into the boss's office ominous.

When it happened, it was because sales figures were down, there were problems with the employees, or with the programme. Alex's mind was working on what the difficulty could be this time.

The man looking back at Alex was a large man. Mark had put on at least a stone since he'd become CEO, as if growing into the weight of office, Alex thought wryly. Mark's skin shone and sweated. He was a man of only medium height so that the acquired bulk did not suit him, and it gave a ponderousness to his movements that showed now as he stood up and gestured Alex to a seat. It belied what Alex knew to be the quickness of Mark's brain.

Mark had come to the company on the back of impressive results in his previous firm, and he had overseen a quick expansion of this company and rising profits. Alex knew him to be hard-working. He also knew him to be punctilious.

'Good of you to drop in,' Mark was saying. 'Please take a seat.'

Alex nodded and seated himself.

'So how are things with you, Alex?'

It was a simple question but not one Alex wanted to answer.

'Fine,' he lied. 'No problems.' Now why had he said that?

'Glad to hear it.' There was a smile on Mark's face but its false avuncularity threatened. 'I've been looking at your spreadsheet reports.' Mark now paused and flashed his smile again. 'Excellent figures – as always. Your results are consistently high.'

'I do my best,' Alex said.

'And you do well.'

There was another pause in Mark's delivery, and Alex pondered the direction of the next remark.

'Now regarding the rumours going around–'

'Rumours?' Alex asked.

'About the company.'

'Yes?' Alex said.

'I'm sure you've heard them.'

'There's always gossip,' Alex said, 'about this – and that.'

'But these particular stories–'

Then Mark's voice stopped again. He was dragging this out, wasn't he? Alex could feel his impatience rising, which might be what Mark intended.

'Regarding downsizing.'

'Even more talk about that?' Alex said. He made an attempt at a light laugh. 'The ladies in the typing pool make them up for a lark.'

Mark gave a laugh in reply, but it was not light.

'On this occasion, the gossip is not all fictitious.'

Alex wished Mark would stop taking these pauses. It made it so obvious there was some sharp comment at the back of his mind.

'Drive and energy,' Mark said. 'That's what's got this company where it is,' then added, after another pause, 'and youth.'

And that was it. The word 'youth'. Age discrimination of course. Which he might have expected his CEO not to bring up. But then, this was Mark speaking to him.

'Hard work got us here,' Alex said.

'Quite. But trading conditions are changing, and there are even more competitors out there. Results are still good. But we have to keep them that way – and project ahead.'

Ah yes, Alex thought. Radco. The new kid on the block. He was wondering what response the company would make to them.

'Energy. Drive.' Then the same pause. 'Youth.'

Did Mark have to repeat that? Alex took in Mark's quizzical look.

'What's your response to that?'

'You're telling me I'm past it.'

Mark laughed with a surprising heartiness. He slapped his hand on the desk in front of him, then leaned back in his padded chair with an indulgent look on his face.

'You're anything but that, Alex. You're at your peak. But I do have to find ways of keeping you there. And yes, though I look to youth to drive us forward, I do know we need older and wiser heads. The young need leadership. I need to know you're going to continue to supply it.'

'You need be in no doubt about that.'

Then Mark switched tack. Perhaps to the one he had intended to pursue. 'How are things at home?'

'Absolutely awful,' Alex said. He had allowed himself to be irritated by the question. He didn't like things being dragged out of him, which he could tell was going to happen. 'I've kept you up to date on it. My house was burned down, and we're trying to cope with that.'

'I tried to make sure you were allowed ample time off for it.'

Alex noted the genial tone but wondered at the genuineness of it.

'It was good of you,' he said. 'It was needed.'

'And how are things progressing?'

'We have somewhere to live,' Alex said. 'Things are settling down to a sort of even keel. There's been a police investigation, and they think they know who did it – a teenage fire-raiser who's known for this sort of thing.'

The teenager had been the suspect. Alex had not quite worked out why he felt the need to suggest that was still the case. But he didn't want to share his fears with Mark that the police might have decided he and Heather had started the fire themselves.

'And the insurance company?'

'Will pay out at some point.' Alex said that with as much confidence as he could muster. 'Once the police have finished with their reports.'

'Will those cause a problem?'

'No,' Alex said. 'But these things aren't instant.'

'I suppose not,' Mark said.

And Alex wished that look of sympathy looked more sincere – or was he just on edge himself?

'Because, as employers, we do care about the welfare of employees. After all, how can they produce their best work when there are problems at home?'

'Indeed,' Alex said. 'And, to use the vocabulary of insurers, this was an act of God. Unexpected and out of my control.'

'Quite.'

'But I can handle how I react to it. And I am doing that.'

'I hope so,' Mark said.

Alex looked at the well-fed face in front of him. He knew the expression that now lay on it. This was Mark weighing up things so that he could reach a decision. He also knew Mark would wield the sack without hesitation if he thought that the best solution.

'Because you are someone the company values, Alex. You're the experienced head amongst the young ones. The calm one. The person to be leaned on in an emergency.'

'It's good to know you think of me in that way,' Alex said. 'I do try to live up to it.'

'I'm glad to hear it, Alex.' He gave Alex a beatific smile, though it did not last. His mind had moved on. 'Oh, the rumours. There will be restructuring, though nothing drastic, just as a means of maintaining our competitive edge. Not that any decisions have been taken.'

'Thank you for letting me know,' Alex said.

And, with a wave of the hand, Alex was dismissed.

After he left, Alex thought about the interview and, for some reason, an image of a snake came into his mind. Well, Mark would continue to slither away in his office. And he would have to continue working out how to cope with a police inspector with a similar look in his eye, the good Inspector Black.

TWENTY-FIVE

Heather

There was a stubbornness about Heather as she pushed with her legs and pulled with her arms. She swam steadily and strongly but, though it was her favourite stroke, the slowness of her breaststroke had always annoyed her. Too many other swimmers rocketed past. She glided past the shine of the tiles in the local authority pool easily enough, just slowly. She exhaled as if trying to expel her irritation.

To Heather's left was Anna, and her stroke was not only more elegant, but Anna had to slow down when she was swimming with her mother. Heather envied her daughter's competence in the water. Then Anna extended her stroke towards the end of their length, and Heather had to watch the white-capped head surge past. Anna couldn't resist showing off.

Heather was not tired unduly by her swim, but they were reaching the end of the first twenty lengths and that was always when she and Anna had their break. After Heather's hand touched the tiles at the end of her length, she stood beside Anna for a moment before they hauled themselves out and tramped over to the steam room, where they draped their bodies on the tile benches as they relaxed in the luxury of heat.

They did not usually exercise together but Heather had needed to talk to Anna yet again, and insisted she come over. Did seeing Anna make Heather worry less about her own problems? She had convinced herself she needed to see Anna for Anna's sake. And there were things that needed to be said, especially the way that last conversation ended.

It was Anna who began the conversation. 'Have the police finished their investigations or what?' she asked.

At least she wasn't interrogating Heather about the possibility she was having an affair. Had denying it worked? The very idea Heather had said. Though she was.

She supposed the reason Anna had agreed to swim with her was because she wanted to know about developments in the police investigation. And Anna was as blunt as ever, Heather noticed; though sometimes painful, it was not difficult to discuss things with Anna.

'They haven't told us that,' she replied.

'But they know who did it, don't they?'

'Stephen Brodie?'

'Yes.'

'He was their suspect, but they can't get a confession out of him.'

'Do they need one?'

'Apparently. He has admitted to other fires, but not ours.'

'But it must have been him.'

'I think so,' Heather said. 'But ours was the only fire that did real damage. It's obvious why he's not admitting to that one.'

Her tone was peevish; that had annoyed her.

'If they don't think it was him, who do they think did it?' Anna asked.

'They will look at us.'

'You're joking.'

'For the insurance money.'

Heather and Anna sat in silence, breathing in the steam. Then Anna said, 'Did you?'

'Get real,' Heather said. And there was anguish in her voice, which she hated.

'I don't believe Dad would do something like that.'

'Nor me. He must have thought I was in the house. He would hardly try to kill me.'

'Yeah. Right. As if.'

'And you can't think I would burn down our house?'

Anna did not reply straight away, and Heather realised Anna was considering the possibility.

'I definitely didn't.'

She glared at Anna before looking away. Sweat was trickling down her from the steam. This ought to be relaxing.

'I don't suppose–' Heather said, then stopped herself.

'What?'

'Alex has never said anything like "I wish your mother was dead", has he?'

Anna's response to that was to laugh, which was a relief.

'Don't be ridiculous, Mum.'

'I'm glad you think I am.'

'If Dad did try to do anything like that, he'd probably set himself on fire.'

'Hmm,' Heather said, but she was not sure that was true.

'So stop being so hard on him.'

'What do you mean?'

'You're always on at Dad. I don't know how he can relax at all sometimes.'

'And that's not true.'

'He always has to account for what he's been doing, especially when he's working away.'

'If there's nothing to hide, there's nothing to hide,' Heather said.

'That's one of the reasons I'm glad to be away from home now.'

'What do you mean?'

'You nag all the time, Mum.'

'I get worried about you,' Heather said.

'As if there's anything to worry about.'

'What do you know about it at your age?'

Anna did not reply to that. Heather continued.

'There's no way I'd want to push you away from me. You can't think that, can you, Anna?'

'No. That's not what I'm saying. Why would you think so?'

Heather studied Anna's face but did not know what to make of the expression on it.

'If the police dismiss Stephen Brodie as a suspect – and neither I nor your father did it, who else does that leave for them to suspect?' she said.

'You definitely can't mean me, Mum. I was miles away.'

'Zac does fit the profile the police describe.'

'You're on about him again? I've told you. Zac's in love with me. There's no way he would do that to you.'

'He's a dysfunctional teenager.'

'What?'

'And there's all that anger in him, some rage at the world. Which he has no way of letting out.'

'There isn't any anger in Zac. Mum, you haven't really told the police this rubbish, have you?'

'Of course not,' Heather said. 'I would hardly do a thing like that without discussing it with you first.'

'You mean you are going to?'

'He ought to be questioned.'

Anna's face took on a serious look, which Heather found uncomfortable. 'If you point the police at Zac, I'm finished with you. You know that, don't you?'

'Anna, be reasonable.'

Anna stood up and pointed her finger at Heather. Oh no, Heather thought. This was going to be Anna in full flow. She would be shouting and waving her arms about next. But she didn't. She started to say something, then stopped herself before flouncing towards the pool.

God, she's really annoyed. What have I done? Heather thought. And I won't be able to undo it, will I? Heather pulled herself up and walked after Anna. She needed to talk more with her. At least Anna was still at the pool. She had dived in again without looking towards her mother. Perhaps a chance to discuss things more with her would come at the end of her swim. Anna might have calmed down by then.

Meanwhile Heather continued with her swim, not that she would be able to keep up with Anna in this mood. Anna would leave her floundering far in her wake.

TWENTY-SIX

After a few more difficult words with her mother at the end of the swim, all in defence of Zac, Anna disappeared leaving Heather on her own by her car outside the pool. She was unlocking the car door when Black came up behind her.

'Mrs Ross?'

Heather whirled round at the sound of the voice. And she was not reassured at the sight of Black. What could he want, and could she cope with him? She was already feeling drained.

Black was contriving a reassuring smile.

'I didn't mean to alarm you,' he said.

So you say, thought Heather.

'You didn't,' she said, though he had.

'I was passing and just noticed you there,' Black said. 'Have you had a good swim?'

A good guess, thought Heather. She could have been working out in the gym, but there was only a fifty per cent chance of being wrong.

'So-so,' she said. 'I ought to go more often.'

'I don't have the time to work out as much as I'd like,' Black said.

Heather supposed he hadn't stopped her to discuss exercise. What did he want?

'There are some questions I want to ask you.'

Here it comes, Heather thought, and braced herself.

'You seemed determined to think it was Stephen Brodie who set fire to your house?'

'You said you thought it was him at one stage,' Heather replied. There was that note of irritation in her voice again.

'It was a field of inquiry.'

'You've dismissed him?' Heather asked and she wished she didn't sound disappointed.

'At this stage in the investigation, it seems less likely it was him.'

'Seems? That's considered good enough?'

'It's logical.'

'Oh.'

'Inquiries can only be evidence-led.'

'I suppose,' Heather conceded.

'Do you actually know Stephen Brodie?'

'I've already told you that. No.'

Black considered this.

'Looking at the circumstances of the fire, it was intended to spread to the house and cause considerable damage. That doesn't seem to fit with what we know of Brodie. There's something ineffectual about him. We don't think he's got as much malice as that. He would think it great fun to burn down someone's garden shed but it wouldn't occur to him to go any further than that.'

'I see,' Heather said.

'So is there any reason why you might want to implicate him?'

Heather noticed the menace in Black's voice. That had her even more on the defensive.

'I don't mean to point a finger at anybody,' she said. 'All I know is my house was burned down. I don't suppose you have any idea what it's like to go through that.'

'I do have sympathies for you, Mrs Ross.'

'You tell me Stephen Brodie has been starting fires all over the place around here. I would have thought any of the rest of them could have led to serious consequences too. He was lucky they didn't. That's what I think. I don't understand why you're dismissing him from suspicion of burning down my house.'

'I see,' Black said.

But to Heather's annoyance all he did now was put on another patient smile. And there was nothing more Heather could say.

'There was something you said earlier that aroused my curiosity,' Black said.

'Yes?' Heather said. Why couldn't the man get on with it?

'You said you thought the fire-raiser might be an apprentice car mechanic?'

'Is that not what you said Stephen was?'

But, even as she said it, Heather knew bluster would not work with Black.

'I didn't say what Stephen was employed as.'

'I–' But Heather couldn't think of a reply.

'Who's the apprentice car mechanic?'

'I didn't mean – what makes you think I know one of those?'

But she knew Black would continue trying to winkle out what lay behind her remark.

'Who were you thinking of?'

'It was nothing,' Heather said. 'A silly comment. Please forget I said it.'

'Why?' Black said.

And Heather knew where this was heading, where Anna had told her she must not go. She was going to tell Black about Zac.

'Let me decide if the person you were referring to was important or not,' he said.

Heather was at a loss. She didn't see how she could keep on lying. In any case, she did think Zac might have done it.

'I'm not sure I can share this with you,' she said. 'My daughter has warned me not to. She says it's complete rubbish.'

'Try me,' Black said.

And Heather told him.

'It was Anna's boyfriend I was talking about,' she said, and once it was out, she discovered she was pleased.

'Your daughter has a boyfriend who has been dismissed from a job as an apprentice mechanic?'

Black was going to have every bit of it out of her. Wasn't it lovely?

'But he would never do anything like this,' Heather said.

'Possibly not,' Black said. 'All the same. What's his name?'

And she proceeded to tell him.

'It's Zac. Zac Main.'

'And?'

'He lives in Aberdeen.'

'Do you know his address?'

'No.'

'But your daughter will?'

'Yes.'

'Is there friction between you and Zac?'

'We don't row or anything. I make my daughter's boyfriend welcome. What kind of mother do you think I am? Even someone like Zac. Honestly.'

Black's look was quizzical. Heather didn't think he believed a word.

'He has a tattoo on his face,' she said, by way of explanation for what she was not sure. 'He was a loser at school. I know that much. Look,' Heather said, 'when

Anna went away from home to go to Aberdeen University, that's not the kind of boyfriend I expected her to come back with. And she thinks the world of him.'

Heather stopped talking. She didn't want to burst into tears, which she felt might be a possibility when she thought of Zac.

'I would like to talk to him,' Black said.

'You would?' Heather said, and, though a large part of her was delighted, the other part dreaded what Anna would say.

'So we will need his address from Anna.'

To which Heather could only reply yes.

TWENTY-SEVEN

Back in the flat, Heather found herself in a state of panic. When she'd phoned Anna to find out Zac's address for Inspector Black, the conversation had been painful. Anna had yelled at her down the phone and Heather had only managed to defuse the situation by saying that Black was standing beside her. The gist of Anna's complaint was she had told her mother not to mention Zac to the police – and that was what she'd done. Though it was expressed more forcefully than that. Heather explained that Black had given her no choice, but this explanation did not impress Anna, who said Zac had enough problems on his plate. He did not need interrogations from the police. Heather tried to explain that the police were bound to want to talk to anyone connected with the family, so how was it possible not to mention Zac? They had to question Anna and when they did, she would have to tell them about her boyfriend herself. Anna calmed down slightly. She gave Zac's address and phone number, if with bad grace.

But that did not cheer Heather. Anna had threatened to finish with her if she pointed the police in the direction of Zac. Suddenly it felt as if the floor was collapsing underneath her and she had to sit down.

Heather noticed her breathing had become difficult and her pulse was racing so she tried breathing more deeply, to see if that would slow her heart rate down. Eventually her body started to behave and she began to feel more normal, but Heather still could not concentrate her mind. And all there was around her was an impersonal rented room she hated.

Eventually, she was able to walk over to the window, and found herself looking at a view of Elsa's high hedge, which she didn't like either. She stared at the nails on her right hand. One had been done serious damage at some point. She would have to trim that right down.

She gave her hair a flick. It felt brittle after her swim. Another shower with lots of herbal shampoo was in order. Had she remembered to put on moisturiser? Some more wouldn't do any harm. She walked over to a mirror and looked at herself. Her reflection was like her inner state – distressed. And she'd already wondered if she was losing Alex. How could she hope to keep a husband if she let herself go? She sighed.

Alex had been taking more care over his appearance lately; she'd noticed he'd started using Grecian, and she hated a man using colouring on his hair. He wasn't doing that to please her. If he was doing it for someone else, who might it be? Someone at work probably, maybe somebody she had never even met. Heather hated suffering doubts like these. What to do about this? Do some digging about so she could dismiss the idea? She would feel less guilty about her own behaviour if Alex was being unfaithful as well, though she hated the thought and dreaded having her suspicions confirmed. At least she would know what she was dealing with. But how to go about it?

She could look through Alex's things – what was left of them. She could do that now as he was out of the flat. She marched into the bedroom, buoyed up with what false courage she could muster, too embarrassed to admit to herself that what motivated this was paranoia. Where should she look first?

She started off with the wardrobe and searched through the work suit hanging there. It was the one Alex had been wearing at the conference. The pockets were empty which was only to be expected as, now she thought of it, he'd sent the suit to the dry cleaners. Was he having his things cleaned more often? He might be. Did that mean something? She felt her pulse starting to race again. She went over to the bed and sat down, forcing herself to concentrate on slow, deep breaths.

But her thoughts wouldn't stop racing. Could there be proof of anything in Alex's Audi? She could give that a search, except Alex was using it. She supposed the opportunity would occur.

She stood up again and looked frantically around the room before walking over to the dresser where she feverishly rummaged through the drawers containing Alex's present collection of clothes. At least there were only two and the drawers weren't even full, not surprising in the circumstances. Might she find something in the clothes he'd put aside for the wash? Wrinkling her nose, she rummaged through them.

She stopped searching. What was she looking for? What evidence could there be? A packet of condoms? That would give the game away – if she found one.

Or was it proof her husband had something to do with the fire that she was looking for? She reminded herself that he had been away at the conference. How could he have started it? Could he have slipped back? It was an hour's drive to Elgin and back – at least. Was there a gap in his alibi that would allow him time for that? And did she really think Alex wanted to kill her? Where was she going with this? Alex wasn't that kind of person – was he?

She sat down on the bed again and tried to stop the whirling of her brain but to no avail. She thought of Alex's moments of thoughtfulness through the years, the surprise bunches of flowers, the spontaneous presents of jewellery. If Alex had decided to kill her, he must have undergone a personality change. Unless the gifts had meant there was somebody else at the time. Perhaps she had never really known him. Which wouldn't be possible – would it?

She turned to the wardrobe again and looked through the drawers there. Alex didn't even have anything in these. Hardly surprising after the fire. She supposed there hadn't been much chance of finding anything. But had she missed something?

She caught sight of herself in the mirror again. What kind of anxiety basket case was she? She decided she would have that shower.

TWENTY-EIGHT

Anna

Zac was leaning under the bonnet of his beloved green Citroen in his parents' garage, doing something mysterious. His mum and dad didn't live far away from Anna's student halls of residence in Aberdeen, and, as Zac still lived with them, Anna found that useful.

Zac appeared to be succeeding only in covering his hands with oil and improving the fluency of his cursing.

He could have been replying to something Anna had said to him, though Anna would have been surprised if anything had registered.

'Do you know what she thinks?' Anna said.

'Of course,' he said.

'What's that then?'

'Eh?'

'What's my mother thinking?'

Zac stopped what he was doing and straightened himself.

'How can you expect me to know what's going on in someone else's head? What do you think I am? Telepathic? If you let me get on with this, I think I've nearly got it.'

He bent under the bonnet again.

'She thinks you set fire to their house.'

Then Anna gave Zac a kick on one of his calves. Zac raised himself erect again and glared at her. She had to admit he could be intimidating with that scowl on his face. But Anna persisted with her questions.

'Did you hear what I said? She thinks you set fire to their house and burned it to the ground.'

Zac's stare was now mystified.

'She thinks you drove over to Nairn, broke into the outhouse, put a bundle of sticks and rags together, doused it in petrol, and set light to it.'

Zac did not say anything. Then anger took over his face.

'She's stark staring mad. You don't think I did that, do you?'

'Of course I don't,' Anna replied.

'So why are you bothering to tell me about it?'

'She's my mother.'

'Poor you.'

'And it matters what she thinks about you.'

Zac scowled again. It made him look butch which Anna found a turn on.

'And it's also why the police are here.'

Zac looked around in alarm.

'Just joking,' Anna said. 'And it serves you right. You've been pottering around in that engine for an hour. You're far more interested in that car than me. Why don't you kiss it instead?'

'Now there's an idea,' Zac said.

He bent under the hood before emerging with an oil stain round his mouth.

'That was OK,' he said. 'You've got competition.'

Anna giggled, then giggled again, then found she couldn't stop. Zac could be funny. It was what she liked best about him. Then she saw Zac was looking past her with a serious expression on his face.

'But it's a pity you weren't wrong about the police,' Zac said. 'At least that's what they look like.'

Anna whirled round to find herself face to face with Inspector Black and his sergeant.

'Where did you come from?' she said.

'You're Anna Ross?' Black said.

'Yes,' Anna said, thinking there must be a scowl on her face now.

'And you must be Zac Main?'

'I must?'

Anna noticed the other man's eyes roaming all over the garage before resting on a petrol can. Black reached into his jacket and pulled out a holder to show his identity.

'Detective Inspector Black,' he said.

The sergeant pulled out his identity card as well.

'Detective Sergeant McPherson,' he said.

'It's you we want to talk to,' Black said, looking at Zac.

'It is?' Zac replied. The expression on his face was angry, but, with an effort, he dismissed it. When he did speak, his voice was neutral.

'What do you want to talk about?' he said.

'You know about the fire at Anna's parents' house?' Black said.

'Of course,' Zac replied. 'And a dreadful thing that was.' Anna noticed how hurriedly that was added.

Black considered Zac.

'So you'll understand why we have to ask questions.'

'I dare say. But why me?' And Anna could see he was getting annoyed again, which she did not think a good idea.

'We're asking questions of anyone with a connection with the family.'

'So you thought of me?'

'Yes.'

The inspector looked across at Anna.

'We'll want to talk to you as well,' he said.

'Oh.'

'But first, Zac. Where were you that night?'

Zac's lips had tightened.

'The fire had nothing to do with me,' he said. 'You don't think it had, do you?'

'You haven't answered the question,' Black said.

'You want to know where I was?' Zac said.

'That's what I asked.'

The words had been spluttering out of Zac and Anna dreaded an explosion from him.

'What kind of question is that?' Zac said. 'I wasn't anywhere near Anna's parents' house.' For the first time Anna noticed there was fear there as well as the anger.

Now the sergeant spoke. And his voice was sharp.

'Is that what you said when you were convicted of shoplifting? "I wasn't anywhere near there, honest."'

'Your lot always bring that up.'

That surprised Anna as she hadn't known anything about shoplifting.

'Have you been behaving yourself?' the sergeant said.

'Of course I have. I learned my lesson. All right?'

'That's what they all say,' the sergeant continued. 'Usually just before they do it again.'

'You still haven't said where you were on the night of the fire,' Black said.

'At home, watching *Line of Duty* on the box.'

'*Line of Duty*?'

'It's amazing what the police get up to.'

Black ignored the jibe.

'You have a witness who can swear to that?' Black said.

Anna opened her mouth to speak then closed it again. She hadn't been with Zac that night, so she could hardly say she had, even if she wanted to. Though she knew for certain it couldn't have been Zac who set the fire. She did, didn't she? She looked at him.

'My parents were in,' Zac said.

'We'll ask them about that,' Black said.

Then he switched tack.

'You've met Anna's parents?' he said.

Anna frowned at the thought but said nothing.

'Yes,' Zac replied.

'How do you get on with them?'

Anna thought Zac wasn't going to reply, but after a pause, he said, 'I get on fine with them.'

Which led Anna to think of some of the more difficult exchanges between Zac and her mum and dad. Zac scratched his nose as his eyes took on a thoughtful look. He shot an apologetic look in Anna's direction before saying, 'I don't think Anna's mother likes me.'

'Did she say why?' Black asked.

'I've got a tattoo stuck all over my forehead.'

'And you must want to shock people with that.'

At that Zac couldn't suppress a grin.

'I wouldn't expect to get on with Anna's parents,' he said. 'I'm from the wrong side of the tracks.'

'As they say in the movies,' Black said.

'And I do,' Zac said. 'I'll never be at university for one thing. Anna is.'

Anna grimaced but Zac contrived not to notice that.

'I couldn't hope people like them would have any time for someone like me. Apart from that, they were all right.'

Black paused. Now he glanced at Anna carefully, but he continued anyway.

'You didn't get on with them or you just didn't like them?'

'They didn't have time for Anna either as far as I could see.'

Anna thought of forceful replies she wanted to make to Zac but perhaps she ought to save those for later.

'What makes you say that?' Black said.

'Anna had gone round to see what the fire had done to their house, and they behaved as if they were the only ones who had been hurt by it. Anna was brought up there. They didn't see what it was doing to her.'

'It's an upsetting time for them,' Black said. 'You need to show patience.'

'They haven't any,' Zac said. And he was getting too worked up now to care what effect his words had on anyone. 'They're an over-entitled pair who only think of themselves. What can you expect from the middle classes? Which is what they are.'

'No they're not and they don't,' Anna said.

These were her parents. How could he talk about them like that in front of her? But she did admire the way Zac was standing up to this inspector.

'What do you do with your time since you lost your job?' Black asked.

'And I can guess who told you about that,' Zac said. 'As you can see for yourself, I spend a lot of time tinkering with my car. While I wait for the dole cheque to arrive.'

'So you could have driven over to their house?'

'Maybe but I didn't.'

'What happened to your job in the garage?' Black said.

'And I might have known you would ask about that, not that it's any of your business.'

'How did you lose it?' the sergeant said.

Zac shrugged his shoulders in an exaggerated way.

'Timekeeping,' he said.

'You can't get up in the mornings?'

Zac's glower at the sergeant was his reply.

'You must have resented losing it?' Black said.

'That garage owner is an arrogant git,' Zac said.

'How did your father feel about it?'

'He hasn't stopped shouting at me, not that it'll get me my job back. So what's the point? It wasn't even a good one. Being an apprentice mechanic sucks. The hours are too long and the pay's rubbish. I don't know why I stuck it as long as I did.'

'You'd just lost another job when you did your stint of shoplifting. Social services said you were feeling "unsettled". Is that how you're feeling now?' the sergeant asked.

Zac said nothing to that.

'It would be a good idea to behave yourself, Zac,' he continued.

'That's what I do.'

'He's straight,' Anna said. 'Really. I would know if he wasn't.'

'Then keep him that way,' Black said. 'What kind of job are you looking for now, Zac?'

Oh no, Anna thought. Zac certainly hadn't been looking for jobs, for all he lied about it at the Jobcentre. That had been driving her mad.

'Anything. Something to do with driving maybe. I like doing that. I have a licence.'

And I wish you would, Anna thought.

'That sounds all right,' Black said. 'You stick to that.'

Black seemed to have found out what he wanted from Zac. He looked at Anna. 'As regards yourself, you don't have a record. You could be good for Zac. Make sure he isn't a bad influence on you.'

'I try to be good for him,' Anna said. 'And he's good for me.'

'And I'm bound to ask you. Where were you on the night of the fire?'

Anna had to admit later she lost it at that point. 'I wasn't at my parents' house fucking burning it down, right?'

Black gave her a surprised look.

'Temper,' he said.

Anna felt her cheeks reddening.

'So where were you?' Black asked.

'She wouldn't fucking do that,' Zac said, swearing in solidarity.

Zac's face was white. Black's showed no expression.

'Where were you?' he said to Anna again.

'I was being a good girl,' Anna said. 'I was studying in the university library. I was working on an essay I had to hand in the next day.'

'Which can be verified?' Black said.

'Yes.'

'And we will.' He studied Anna. 'Keep on being good for Zac,' he said. 'Don't let this conversation "unsettle" anyone.'

This was Anna's first experience of being questioned by the police and she had not enjoyed it. She hadn't known how to handle it, but she supposed getting angry and swearing had not been a good idea.

The sergeant, who had continued to allow his eyes to wander round the garage, walked over the petrol can and lifted it up.

'You don't have a search warrant,' Zac said. 'Put that down.'

But the sergeant was already unscrewing the cap. He sniffed at it, then peered.

'It has held petrol,' he said to Black. 'But it's empty now.'

'It's petrol for the lawnmower,' Zac said.

'It's not much use if it's empty,' Black said.

'Sometimes I borrow from it for my car,' Zac said. 'I'm not supposed to but I'm broke half the time.'

'As long as that's all you're "borrowing",' the sergeant said.

'I didn't go anywhere near Anna's parents' house.'

'We'll see what your parents say about where you were that night,' Black said. 'Are they in?'

Zac nodded his head, but his expression was livid.

After Black and his sergeant had left, Zac strode over to the can and kicked it against the wall. As he did, he shouted, 'Fuck. Fuck. Fuck.'

'They'll hear that,' Anna said.

'So what?'

He had now whirled round to face her.

'Was that really because of your bloody mother?'

Anna could only stare back at him. She'd never seen him this angry and was not contemplating how sexily butch he looked. She took a step back. As Zac strode forward she made sure she was well out of his way. He marched past her, head erect, limbs stiff.

'Where are you going?' Anna asked him.

'I'm going to see your mother,' he said.

'Don't do that. The police might have more to say to you.'

'Try and stop me.'

'Zac,' Anna called after him. 'Don't.'

But after quickly, and surprisingly roughly, flinging precious tools into a toolbox, Zac had the car door open and was in the front seat of the Citroen, switching the ignition on. The engine responded. Zac must have fixed it after all.

TWENTY-NINE

Anna was on the train to Nairn this time, as it was quicker if more expensive. She was in a seat to herself with her legs pulled up as she hugged them close to her. She supposed that was an unnatural position in a public carriage and put her feet to the floor but that didn't feel any more comfortable. She watched the north-east fields blur past. They were monotonous but might have been restful if she'd been in a different mood.

Thoughts about Zac were bothering her. She took out her iPhone to look at her messages. Nothing from him. She decided to text him: 'Zac. Where are you?' Then she stared at the screen for a minute. It didn't do anything, so she rammed her finger down on the keyboard again as she hammered out: 'Zac. Calm down. And go easy on my mother.' She stared at the screen and willed a reply to appear. Nothing happened. She pressed in another message: 'Talk to me, Zac!!!!!' The screen remained blank. And glaring at it made no difference. She put the iPhone in her back pocket.

Why did the train not go any faster? She glared murderously at a copse of trees, then at a field of equally inoffensive sheep. But she did reach Nairn in the end, and Anna heaved herself out of her seat and tramped out of the train. She trudged along the platform onto the concourse as she started on the mile-long walk to the other side of Nairn where her mother and father were staying. When she eventually reached the flat annexe, she rang the doorbell and waited for what felt an extraordinary length of time.

Heather answered the door to her. The expression on her face was urbane and relaxed, which surprised Anna. Had Zac not arrived? And was she not surprised to see her daughter arriving unannounced?

'Anna,' Heather said. The look of pleasure on her face was not feigned, though perhaps it ought to have been. How often could her mother be expecting her to turn up when she was safely ensconced on a university course in Aberdeen? 'So glad to see you. Zac's here. Did you know?'

She knew now. Why was her mother not frantic and upset?

Then Heather ushered her into the flat and, to her surprise, found herself in the middle of a peaceful tableau in which her father and Zac were seated opposite each other with what looked like glasses of gin and tonic beside them. When they turned their heads towards her, she could see they were beaming.

'Anna,' Zac said and his manner towards her was easy.

As she had a good look at him, she tried to take him in. At least he had managed to discard the overalls he had been wearing, but there were still signs of oil on his face from where he had kissed that car engine. Did he really do that? And was her mother actually putting up with hands in that state? And, perhaps even more surprisingly, was this calm Zac the same person who had stormed out, raising his fist in a threatening attitude to the world? Anna took a seat opposite and tried to hide her disbelief. Her mother seated herself too.

'Zac's been telling us about that awful visit from the police,' Heather said.

'Oh that,' Anna said, and tried to look nonchalant.

'We were saying to Zac they treated us in the same way.'

'Did they?' Anna said, who doubted it. Her father and mother did not have a record for shoplifting – as far as she knew.

'The police just have a lot of questions they need to ask,' Heather said.

'I suppose,' Anna said.

'They're investigating a crime,' her father said. His voice held an unctuous tone that Anna was not used to hearing from him. Was this her father? Not the one who had lectured her about money before she set off for university. 'They have a set of routine questions that they go through. They explore the possibilities in a situation. It's not personal.'

Wasn't it? Was her father that naïve? To an extent he was right, she supposed. The police threw out what to them were probably standard questions to see what response they raised. But it had been more than routine with Zac. Now Heather was speaking in soothing tones.

'Zac was ever so upset when he arrived,' she said.

I bet, Anna thought.

'The police ought to learn more diplomatic methods,' her father said, 'particularly with young men. I remember, when I was young, I was pulled up by them and questioned about drugs. I suppose I fitted the profile. Student. Young man. Out and about on the town with friends. I objected like mad. Me? As if I'd use drugs. It felt like a police state.'

As if, Anna thought. If everyone else was doing drugs, she was sure her father would too. Not that he would admit it to her. He felt he had to set the example.

'And Zac wouldn't set fire to anything,' Heather said. 'It's written all over him.'

Anna wondered what it had been like when Zac arrived. She was sure there hadn't been all this saccharine around then.

'I'm glad to hear you're applying for jobs,' her father said to Zac. 'And you sound to be trying for sensible ones.'

Was Zac pretending to be looking for jobs again? Anna thought. All the time she spent moaning at him to do something about work and he paid no attention. Pull yourself together she'd told him. Don't give up. Zac must have been pacifying her parents, which wasn't like him. And what had happened to the foul mood he left in?

'There are always jobs for van drivers,' her father was saying. 'And if you can get a licence for lorries that leads to better pay.'

Which was strange. Her father was the kind of snob who didn't gush on about jobs for drivers. Perhaps he had more nous than she'd thought. Driving vans would suit Zac and her father was right to encourage him if Zac was interested. But Anna could not help wondering how confrontational the conversation between Zac and her parents had been when he first arrived. And how long it had taken to reach this point.

They had seen him when he was hurt. Perhaps that was what had softened them. At least they looked as if they were getting on with Zac now. But previous difficult conversations between her mother and Zac lingered in Anna's mind.

'It isn't that the police suspect you,' her mother was saying to Zac. 'They have to eliminate people from their inquiries.'

'You were at home with your parents,' Alex said. 'What better alibi could you have?'

And he sounded convincing, Anna thought. How furious had Zac been when he first arrived? That must be why her parents were being this diplomatic. Anna could not forget the vehemence there had been in Zac when he stormed out. She had glimpsed something in him then for the first time. At the centre. A deep-seated wall of anger that frightened her. And it must have frightened her parents too.

THIRTY

Alex

It was when he was leaving work that he saw it, the deep jagged score along the side of his car. When did that get there? His Audi had been standing in the car park as always, in the open outside the offices where anyone had access, so Alex supposed it would have been easy to do. There weren't even any security cameras there. Alex looked around but the only person he could see was a middle-aged woman on the pavement opposite, walking a terrier – an unlikely suspect. He looked back at the damage. Who would have done that? His mind was blank.

He swore quietly – then loudly to make himself feel better.

Then a thought occurred. The fury Zac had been in when he arrived – it couldn't have been him, could it? They had to put a lot of effort into pacifying him when he arrived. But he didn't suppose so. If Zac had done that he would have pronounced it proudly. Anyway, he'd gone back to Aberdeen.

Alex would have to drive the car to a garage to have it fixed. Was there time now? And could he manage without the car while it was there? Then there was the thought of the expense. Just when there had been so many outgoings. And insurance wouldn't cover it. Damn. It hurt to think that someone had decided to do this to him.

Perhaps it wasn't personal? Some unknown angst-filled person could have taken his ire out on the nearest available object and there had been the Audi, innocent but defenceless and they had felt in their pocket for a key.

Alex inspected the score again. It could have been done in that way. Simple enough to do if time-consuming to repair. But why?

Alex thought back to a similar scar on a different car, a sleek red Lamborghini; it had been years ago, and Alex had forgotten about it till now. Alex hadn't seen many of those cars around before – and hadn't since – and he'd thought it dreadful to see such a beautiful vehicle suffering damage like that.

It had happened one night when he and some friends had been on a pub crawl. He had been an undergraduate at Edinburgh University at the time. God that was some time ago. They had spent the night railing about the Conservative party; they had all been ardent socialists. Was anyone that anymore? And the Lamborghini had been a red rag to a bull. Not to Alex. He'd just envied it. But he'd joined in when they'd all surrounded it and mocked it. Alex even aimed a harmless kick at a tyre before they turned to go. Then one of them had turned back, taken out a key and run it along the car in savage abandon.

'That's for the mass unemployed,' he'd said.

Despite the genuineness of their proletariat sympathies, the rest of them had launched into him with venom.

'You shouldn't have done that,' someone said.

'Vandal,' someone else added.

'What were you thinking of?' said another.

'We'd better get out of here,' had been Alex's contribution.

And they had started running as fast as they could with all that beer inside them. It had been a relief to turn the corner and pretend to have nothing to do with all of that; they'd slowed down and attempted to walk as normally and as innocently as they could.

Alex had felt so sorry for the owner – and the car. Fortunately, the finger of blame had not been pointed at any of them. After they'd stumbled home, and gone to bed, Alex had forgotten all about it – until tonight, when he'd seen what someone had done to his Audi. Now he understood better what that Lamborghini owner must have gone through. Not that he compared his Audi with that sleek sports model. Though it was also precious to him.

He remembered clearly who had taken their ire out on that vehicle. It had been Derek. Not that Derek was in the habit of doing things like that. It had been the drink. Still, he had gone down seriously in Alex's estimation at the time.

His mind returned to Derek now. If he had been capable of doing that to a car then, he could have done it again. Alex looked up and down the street; he swept his eyes around again, pausing to study every shadow but there really was no one there.

He had done Derek that ill turn when he'd got him sacked. Alex tried to think. Had he noticed anyone around who looked in any way like him? He couldn't say he had. On the other hand, he had not been looking for him.

He hadn't mentioned Derek to the police as a suspect for the fire-raising because the sacking had happened so long ago. Why would Derek turn up and take his revenge now? But now Alex's car had been scratched in this way he wondered if he should have told them about Derek. Though he had nothing approaching proof of anything at all.

But he didn't see why they shouldn't investigate him. The fire could have been caused by anyone with a grudge against him or Heather, and Derek did fit the category.

Alex turned and looked at his damaged car. His house. Now this. His wounds were running deeper.

THIRTY-ONE

Alex was in the flat now, busy with more work for the office. His mood hadn't improved and he was having difficulty concentrating. When he'd discussed what had happened to his Audi, Heather had shown sympathy but no real interest. Apparently there was a limit to the number of disasters she could become strongly emotionally involved with at the same time. And Alex had somehow or other to get on top of some figures for work tonight. He swore.

When they'd been living in their own house, working at home had been easy; in this makeshift flat there was no privacy. He was seated on the couch with his laptop propped on the coffee table while Heather busied herself with things to do in the kitchen, though he didn't like to hazard a guess how long these would last her.

The doorbell rang and Heather called out, 'I'll answer it.'

Alex grunted as he continued to ponder the screen in front him. He became aware of a heavy tread of feet. When he looked up and saw it was Inspector Black, he snapped down the laptop lid.

'Hello,' he said. His voice was tentative and weak. Why was that?

'Sorry to bother you,' Black said.

At least Black was being polite. But why was there that chill in his glance?

'That's all right,' Alex said, though he thought the opposite.

He noticed the rudeness in the stare of the sergeant who accompanied Black. What was that about?

Alex gestured to the chair opposite. 'Have a seat.'

'Thank you,' Black said, as he complied. The sergeant remained standing.

'I'm glad you came,' Alex said, recovering his poise.

'You are?'

Black now looked puzzled.

'My car was vandalised.'

'Oh yes?'

'A scratch right down the side of it. I know it sounds petty compared to the rest of what's happened to us – though it's upsetting enough in itself. The thing is–' Alex tried to work out how to phrase it. 'It brought Derek to mind.'

'Derek?'

'Derek Forbes. He used to work at Norplace before I had him dismissed for embezzling. He deserved the sack – but what was awkward was I'd known him for years. We used to go round together at university. And when I saw what had been done to my car, I remembered I'd seen him damage a car in exactly that way once before – when he'd been drinking.'

'And you suspect him of vandalising your car now?'

'It's not just that,' Alex said. 'Don't you see?'

But the expression on Black's face was questioning. And Alex had thought inspectors were supposed to be smart.

'He could have been the one to set our house on fire – for revenge.'

'So you're suggesting him as a suspect?'

'Yes.'

Black said nothing just looked thoughtful. Then he spoke.

'He could be worth checking out,' he said. 'I'll need contact details.'

'I haven't kept up with him – for obvious reasons. He was ever so annoyed with me. But I can tell you where he used to live.'

'We could start with that,' Black said. But he sounded oddly unenthusiastic.

Alex gave him Derek's full name, and the address he had for him.

'Why haven't you mentioned him before?' Black said.

For which Alex didn't have a good reason. He supposed he hadn't believed Derek would do such a thing to him.

'The scratched car,' Black said, 'you know that won't have anything to do with the fire, don't you? Have you any idea how many times vandalised cars are reported to us?'

'That common, is it?'

'Sadly, yes. Meanwhile, I've an update to give you.'

'There's news?' Heather said.

'Some. We've been talking to our fire-raiser again. He gives full co-operation.'

'And?' Alex said.

'He still admits to the other fires in the area, but not yours,' Black said. 'And now we have proof he couldn't have done it.'

'You do?' Alex and Heather said almost at the same time and with a similar note of disappointment.

'CCTV – and his mobile – put him in the area of both the fires he's confessed to. Not that we have footage of him setting them, but he's made the admission. He's not that tough a boy. He's a teenager who's a bit mixed up. He didn't even realise the seriousness of what he was doing. He does now.'

'So what's the proof he didn't do ours?' Alex asked.

'A CCTV camera in Inverness no less shows him going into a Co-op to buy alcohol at about the time of your fire. He didn't do it.'

'But you said it was the same MO,' Heather said.

'It is,' Black said, 'which makes it a bit of a conundrum. The answer to which might be someone was doing a copycat, which might not have been difficult. Newspaper reports weren't precise about how the first two fires were set – we'd told them not to be – but they might have given enough details. We were trying to find witnesses.'

'It sounds hard to believe,' Alex said.

'It's what we have to go with.'

'He gave someone else the idea?' Heather said.

'You tell me,' Black replied.

'Someone expected him to take the blame for the third fire as well?' Alex said.

'That's the interesting thought,' Black said. 'If it was the plan it might have worked – if it hadn't been for the CCTV camera footage. Faced with the other two, he might have confessed to the third. That has happened in similar cases.'

Black stopped talking and Alex tried to take in what they had been told.

'You've seen the way we work,' Black said.

'What do you mean?' Alex said.

'We talk to people. We investigate them.'

Oh no, Alex thought. He thought of the reassuring things he had been saying to Zac about the way the police went about their job and wondered how innocent he'd been. Black wasn't about to interrogate him and Heather again, was he?

'We've asked at your place of work. They are planning that restructuring.'

'They are?' Alex said.

'And there are questions about you.'

Are there? he thought. Alex hadn't thought his competence was seriously in question. His boss had a habit of keeping his cards close to his chest, but he might have opened up to the police.

'And as well as an insurance policy on your house, you have one for your wife – a large one.'

Alex pondered the gravity of the insinuation. The nerve of this policeman.

'There's an equally sizeable insurance policy on me,' he said. 'We're prudent people, which isn't a crime. Neither is it suspicious.'

'And when we checked up on your alibi–'

'What?'

'What do you think we found out?'

'That I was in Elgin?'

'That there was a period of between an hour, and an hour and a half, when you disappeared from view.'

Heather was staring at Alex, and the look chilled him. He hoped this wouldn't lead to her becoming convinced he was attempting to murder her. That didn't bear thinking about. He glared at Black as he considered his reply. He opened his mouth to speak but closed it again instead.

'We would like an explanation for the missing time,' Black said.

And now Alex realised why the lack of interest in Derek; Black had decided he had done it.

Alex racked his brain for a convincing explanation.

THIRTY-TWO

The look on Heather's face was even more questioning than the one on Black's had been. Alex and Heather were still seated in their living room, where Alex was feeling more disorientated than ever, and Black had gone, leaving them with the consequences of his questioning.

'You went for a walk? Really?' Heather's voice was disbelieving.

'I wanted to clear my head,' Alex said, wishing that didn't sound so feeble.

'Do you think that inspector believed you?'

'Why shouldn't he?'

Heather's brow remained furrowed. Alex looked away and stared out of the window. The silence that fell seemed to last for a long time.

Then Alex said, 'The real problem is the insurance payment – as we both know. If they think we did it, they won't pay out.'

'They can hardly prove it was us.' Heather's glare at Alex became even harder. 'Unless it was you.'

'Of course it wasn't.'

'Going out for a walk to clear your head does sound suspicious.'

Alex glowered back. He considered his reply, but then Heather said, 'Who is she?'

'What?' Alex said.

'If you didn't drive over here to set fire to our house, and I hope to God that's not true, you were with someone.'

'You know I don't play around,' Alex said.

'You have before.'

'A long time ago.'

'And my father tells me to be suspicious of all this time you spend away at "conferences".'

'Does he?'

'He's told me what men get up to when they're away. He's had to work away from home himself and he's seen how some men behave. He wouldn't join in with them, but he has a lot of stories to tell about what some of the others did to while away the time.'

So that was what was going on in Heather's head when he worked away?

'Some men do that. I don't,' Alex said.

'So where did you go on your walk to "clear your head"?'

'Round and about. I went for a walk down by the river.'

'At that time of night?'

Alex knew how weak his explanation was, but he would have to stick to it. He had never been a good liar, and it was a pity he hadn't come up with something better. And if Heather was as little convinced, then the police must think the same. And if they thought that, they must think he had been trying to murder his wife.

Alex took to staring out of the window again. It was better to look anywhere but at Heather. It was evening and the streetlights were on, giving their glimmer of light against the gloom. He noticed how clear the sky was tonight. The stars shone their myriad patterns and he wondered about the pattern in his life. How had he ended up in the place he was, and could he find a way out of it? Perhaps all he could do was tell the truth. He had been with Jasmine. That would give him an alibi. It would wreck his marriage, but, if there was no alternative, he would have to own up to where he really was.

He turned to look at Heather. She was sitting with her back straight and her head pointed at him. He'd often thought she looked like a predator approaching its prey when she was in that mood. She was the wife. She had her rights. That was what was going on in Heather's mind. He was the husband letting her down. He wondered why life had to be so difficult. But he had made this problem for himself by falling for Jasmine. That time with her in the hotel that night had been good, and he had felt no guilt about it then, but he should have done.

He wasn't the man he tried to be. He was still the weak youth he'd been when he had been unfaithful to Heather before. The miracle was she hadn't brought that up more often than she had.

Middle age hadn't improved him. It simmered inside him like a never-ending and unsettling mood. What mood? Dissatisfaction? Frustration? Life hadn't turned out as he'd hoped? As if it could. What did he expect? And that feeling had led to what? A tumble with Jasmine. So little but it had seemed enough at the time. A pity it didn't feel worth it now.

'And what about you?' he said. 'A friend you haven't had anything to do with in ages gets in touch with you out of the blue, so you stay out till one o'clock in the morning talking to her – when I happen to be away from home? How believable do you think that sounds?'

Heather looked at first as if she might spit at him, but she didn't – quite.

'How dare you?' she hissed. 'Now I know for certain you're lying about where you were. Who is she? I want to know. Unless you did sneak back and try to murder me.'

'The police might think that, but you can't. Surely not?'

There was such doubt in Heather's eyes as she looked at him. Despite his resentment of Heather's anger, he felt for her. This was his wife, and she shouldn't have to be on that knife-edge of suspicion.

'You need to tell me who she is,' Heather repeated. 'Then I won't be afraid you might make another attempt to kill me.'

She meant that. Alex thought back to how it had been with Heather when they had first been together. None of the girlfriends he'd had before Heather had lasted for a long time – for different reasons. When Heather had come into his life it had been different. Something had grown between them that had never been in his life before. And something new had seemed to grow in himself. It was as if he had caught a glimpse of a different person in him. As if, with Heather, he could grow into something better – even become the person he had always wanted to be. When he'd walked into a room where she was, her whole face had lit up. She was so pleased to be with him that any doubts he'd ever had about himself had evaporated. She had given him himself. Or so it seemed. And he had destroyed that.

When she'd become pregnant, she had pulled away from him. It was as if she had gone somewhere else, and he could not follow her. He knew he should have acted in a more mature way.

And that affair had damaged him. He'd never stopped living with the guilt of it, which, he told himself, would have been the case even if Heather hadn't kept on reminding him. It gave her the last word in so many arguments and she relished it. Though, despite that, their relationship had recovered. Heather must have found some forgiveness in her somewhere. But now he was destroying everything again and the uncertainty in Heather's eyes was like a cut deep inside him. The guilt of the long-ago affair surged back and added itself to the guilt of this one.

'Heather,' he said, and hoped his voice was as gentle as he intended it to be.

Then Heather's eyes softened, and he held out his arms to her and hugged her. Her body was stiff, but he clung on in the hope it would relax. Then it did as she returned the hug. He kissed her gently at first then with passion. Then she pulled away and looked at him.

'Where did that come from?' she said.

'The usual place,' he replied.

Then it occurred to him they ought to go to bed and he pulled her towards him again.

But what Heather said was, 'Enough.'

When she pushed him away, she seemed to be leaving him with a vacancy inside himself. Then she turned and pulled him towards her and kissed him. They stumbled and fumbled towards the bedroom as they tugged at each other's clothes.

They gave vent to their passion; and the savage uncertainty they had been experiencing gave more power to it. Eventually they pulled away from each other and lay there letting their breathing return to normal. Alex started to relax.

'We needed to do that,' he said.

Heather had turned her head away from him and he wondered why; she seemed to be considering something very carefully. Eventually she said, 'No. You're not trying to murder me,' she said.

'No.'

'But who is she?'

'There's no one,' he said, wishing it so.

He knew he would stick to the lie. He had experience of what it was like when she knew for certain. He gave a moment's thought to whether it might give them the chance to talk everything through and move on but common sense said no. That was naïve. Admit to nothing. The safest course.

Heather had a gash inside her, a bank of anxiety that never left her, and she had to express that through controlling everything, including him, which was why he'd needed the safety valve of working away from home in the first place.

He turned and kissed her on the shoulder. That made her smile and touch his hand with hers. They did have tenderness between them too. And he was enjoying this moment of peace that had somehow occurred. Perhaps they had needed that row. And the passion afterwards. It had been agony since the fire.

But, as they lay there, his mind continued to wander. Had Heather been at Margaret Affleck's? That had been strange. He continued to give thought to this. Had there been anything different about Heather lately? Had there been some extra spring in her step and where had it come from? What were the signs a husband was supposed to look out for? Mysterious phone calls? That were stopped when he came into the room? There hadn't been any he could remember. Should he check her phone? He shuddered at the thought. He didn't want to turn into some personal form of police state. Had there been unlikely excuses for time spent by herself? He supposed he gave her enough opportunity to see someone without need for any of that – if that was what she wanted to do. Had she been spending extra money on clothes or underwear? She spoiled herself with that anyway.

No. The fact she had turned out to be with Margaret Affleck when she was supposed to be at home was the first sign of anything at all, and it had saved her life, so he ought to be glad of that, and bury these suspicions. He had strayed. But was Heather better than him? She had an iron will she tried to use over him too often. Did that mean she had such rigid control over herself? Or the opposite?

He continued to revel in holding her close as they lay there; but were they really so near or were they miles apart in their minds? Who was the person he was lying beside? If she had been unfaithful that night, had that been the first time? Did he know what Heather wanted and needed? And she must be lying there thinking the same about him. He bent his head forwards and kissed her shoulder.

'We need to go away,' he said.

'Why do you say that?'

'With everything that's been going on, we need time to ourselves.'

'How could we manage that?' she said. 'I don't even know if I can get time off work just now. Could you? Would it be wise, with things being as they are in your job?'

'If we wanted to, we could manage it,' he said.

'If we wanted to throw everything else to the wind.'

'Perhaps it would be a good idea to do that,' he said. 'We need time for each other.'

Heather looked at him with what looked like curiosity in her eyes.

'The fire destroyed everything else. We need to find each other,' he said.

Now that look in Heather's eye became tender. 'All right,' she said. And they should have gone away together, but it didn't happen.

THIRTY-THREE

The police turned up at their door again the next day. It was Alex who opened it to them and once again he did not like the alertness in Black's eyes, nor the stern look the sergeant gave him. Alex put on his most appeasing expression.

'Inspector Black,' he said. 'Good to see you again.' And he tried to sound as if he meant it.

There was no answering smile on Black's face; instead, his lips tightened.

'Mr Alex Ross,' he boomed. 'We require you to come down to the station for formal questioning.'

Which Alex did not like the sound of.

'You do?' he said. 'But—'

Several objections were forming in his mind. For a start, why weren't they investigating Derek – instead of arresting him – but Heather interrupted before he could give voice to anything.

'Who is it, Alex?' her voice rang through from inside the flat.

'Inspector Black,' Alex replied.

'Don't keep him on the doorstep,' Heather said. 'Invite him in.'

'Of course,' Alex said, 'but—' He did not know how to complete the sentence.

Then Heather bustled up behind him. She took in Inspector Black's stance in the doorway and the expression on his face.

'Good evening, Mrs Ross,' Black said. 'I've informed your husband he's required to come to the station for formal questioning.'

'Just now?' Heather said.

'It would be convenient,' the inspector replied.

Heather and Alex glanced at each other.

'I'll have to go,' Alex said. 'But are you sure there's any necessity for this?' he said to Black.

'That's for me to decide,' Black replied.

With no obvious alternative, Alex said, 'I'll get my coat.'

'I'll come down as well,' Heather said.

'There's no need for that,' Black said.

'You're taking my husband in for questioning,' Heather said. 'Of course I'll want to be there. I take it this is about the fire?'

'It is,' Black replied.

Fortunately, Black allowed them to drive themselves down. It would have been embarrassing if he had insisted Alex and Heather travel in the police car. They had lived in Nairn for years. Alex's ears burned at the thought of the gossip that would have been provided by being seen in a police car on the way to the station.

After they had parked, they followed the policemen inside. It was intimidating to enter the concrete, steel, and glass of Nairn police station.

But here he was, treading the same path that had led to Hugh Randall's appearances in Inverness Sheriff Court – Hugh Randall of the over-ready fists, definitely to be avoided on a Friday night after he had been in the pub, though gentle enough at any other time. It was the same route Hamish Auchinleck had followed. He was a local teacher who was found with a vast library of child pornography on his computer, one the headmaster had been forced to look through as well in order to check none of the young girls displayed there was a pupil at Nairn

High School. Auchinleck had spent time inside and been put on the Sex Offenders Registry.

At least Alex was innocent. It was something to reassure himself with.

He found himself seated at a table with a far less desirable view than those they had seen on their trip. It was of bare concrete scarcely improved by being painted blue. Heather had been left by herself in the corridor despite her protestations.

Black sat opposite Alex, with his sergeant beside him. To his right was a tape recorder. Black inserted a tape and started the machine. As Black dictated the date, time, and details of those present, for the record Alex supposed, Alex had to wonder what he was doing there. There was a huge sense of unreality to all of this.

'Your name is Mr Alexander Ross?' Black said.

As Black knew well. Alex supposed that was also for the recording so bit back the rejoinder.

'That's correct,' he said.

Black continued to confirm known facts, for the precious recorder, then asked about the exact value of the house insurance.

'We're insured with Direct Line,' Alex said, 'for £300,000, the full value of the house.'

'And contents on top of that?'

'Yes.'

Alex wondered if Black was trying to lull him into a sense of false security with so many obvious questions.

'You also have an insurance policy on the life of your wife, Heather?'

And that was hardly unexpected.

'To the tune of £500,000, taken out six months ago?' Black added.

'There's also one taken out on my life for the same amount – with the same company,' Alex said.

Which didn't appease Black this time either.

'Which may have been how you persuaded Heather to have her life insured for such a large sum.'

Black's gaze at Alex was steady. Black wasn't going to miss anything in his reaction, and Alex wished he had prepared good replies.

'A bit of an assumption, Inspector,' he said, but his tongue stumbled over the words and Alex didn't sound convincing to himself.

'We've had full access to your bank statements now,' Black said.

Oh no, was Alex's reaction to that, but he did not say so.

'Which do confirm you're under financial strain.'

'Most people are these days,' Alex replied. 'I'm sure we're no worse off than most couples.'

'You think?' Black said. 'Between you and your wife you have a total of four credit cards, all close to the limit, which means the amount you have to pay off each month is considerable. Do you think you'll ever be in the position to pay off what you owe?'

Alex stared back at him, and his voice became defiant.

'Why not?' he said. 'In time. It's not as bad as you say.'

'And there are those problems you have at work.'

'I'm on top of my job,' Alex replied. 'Results are good.'

'We talked to your boss and the rumours of downsizing are true.'

'He hasn't threatened me with redundancy.'

Alex supposed the expression on his face was anxious. Though he feigned indignation, he was worried sick – if his boss thought he was under investigation by the police, he could lose his job. Alex forced his right foot to stop tapping its frustration.

'They need experienced men,' he said. 'And leaders. It's not me he'll lay off.'

'You're not calm and collected, Mr Ross.'

'What's that supposed to mean?' Alex snapped, and noticed the satisfaction on Black's face.

'And if you lose your job, you're in serious financial trouble,' Black said.

'Isn't everybody?' Alex said. 'And if it happens, which I doubt, I'll have to deal with it then. You're fishing,' he said. 'An overrated hobby, I think myself.'

Alex supposed the anger made him look more guilty, but there was satisfaction in it.

'And your relationship with your wife is precarious.'

Which wasn't a question but a statement.

'How dare you?' Alex said.

'We've witness accounts of arguments between you and Heather.'

'All couples argue from time to time.'

'And there is the gap in your alibi.'

Black was pressing him, and Alex didn't like it.

'You disappeared from view for about two hours, which is enough time to travel to Nairn, set fire to the house, and travel back,' Black said.

'For all that insurance money, I suppose?' Alex said.

'Yes.'

'You must think I'm desperate.'

To which Black again replied, 'Yes.'

'Which would have meant I was attempting to murder Heather?'

'Quite,' Black said. 'Financial and marital problems solved in one night. Then it wouldn't have mattered if you'd been made redundant.'

'I was only told by my boss about possible re-structuring after the fire happened, which doesn't help that theory.'

'It was mentioned the first time we talked about this.'

'But my boss didn't talk about that with me. It was a rumour.'

Alex really did not like the sardonic tone. His right foot drummed the floor hard. 'And I'd have to be a psychopath to do that,' he said.

'Which you could be,' Black said.

'No, I'm not,' Alex said – and he had to stop himself screaming at the man.

'We like you for this,' Black said.

Then Alex realised what Black was doing. He wanted Alex to break down and confess in response to that comment.

Then he seemed to change his mind.

'At least we think so,' Black said.

A smidgeon of doubt? Alex thought. Surely not?

'I'm nearly convinced – and my sergeant is.'

Alex looked across at him and shuddered at the glare on his face.

Black continued, 'The missing time is awkward.'

Which Alex had to admit. He had been hoping the police wouldn't turn that up; he really didn't want it to come out into the open he'd been with Jasmine, who was as innocent of any of his troubles as she was complicit in the passion they had shared. He swore inwardly. If he told Black of his tryst, it could get back to Heather. In any case, it might suggest motivation and would the alibi it gave him be suspect because of that? Alex did not like this situation. He decided to go for the alibi. It was at least true.

'Can I tell you something in confidence?' he said.

Black's look was curious.

'We're investigating a crime,' he said. 'I can only promise confidentiality up to a point. If things reach court, everything comes out. Of course, if what you say clears you, you won't go in front of a sheriff.'

Alex supposed that was the kind of thing a policeman would say. It was what they said on the cop shows on TV.

'I really don't want Heather knowing about this,' he said.

'Go on,' Black said. 'We'll do our best.'

'I was in one of the hotel bedrooms – with a friend.'

Alex paused at that point. He found it difficult to continue.

'And the name of the other person?' Black asked.

Alex told him.

'It's not something I make a habit of,' Alex said.

'Of course,' Black said.

Which it wasn't, though he didn't suppose Black believed that.

'I don't have affairs. It was just that night.'

Which didn't sound convincing to him either.

'My marriage to Heather does matter to me,' he said. 'I really don't want her knowing about this.'

But if he was looking for empathy from Black, he didn't find any. Black continued probing. Had the affair started that night or had it been going on for some time? And he wanted Jasmine's personal contact details. Alex answered the questions. He noted the thought that she could be in trouble for withholding information from Black didn't seem to concern him. Perhaps he was just rattled.

THIRTY-FOUR

Heather

'They've arrested him.'

Heather's tone was scandalised. She was seated in Stuart's car, which was parked at the Maggot car park in Nairn. The place with such an inauspicious name lay beside the River Nairn. The view from there was not unattractive even on a drizzly, overcast day such as this. An onlooker could see past an iron footbridge to the masts of sailing boats bobbing at their moorings in the harbour, and behind them, in the distance, rolling hills on the opposite side of the firth were just visible. The other direction showed an aspect of vernacular houses along a river front. Not that Heather was paying attention to any of this.

Heather didn't usually meet up with Stuart in Nairn as she considered it risky, so the fact she was doing so held meaning. Stuart, realising Heather was desperate about something, had arranged the opportunity to slip away from his wife and family, but he had told Heather he could not stay long.

'Alex? Arrested? What do you mean?' Stuart said.

'Detained for twelve hours to permit questioning was how it was phrased.'

'Not delicately put.'

'No.'

'But arrested for what? They must have said.'

'Fire-raising.'

'They're saying Alex set fire to your house?'

'Yes.'

'Which means he must have thought you were inside it at the time?'

'Yes.'

'Good God. They think he was trying to murder you?'

Heather could only look back at Stuart, aware of the horror that must be on her face.

'Do you think he's capable of doing that to you?' Stuart asked.

'I'd never have thought so, but, if the police do, maybe he is. Do you think he is?'

'They say you never really know the person you're married to.'

'All the same,' Heather said.

'Quite.'

'But look at us,' Heather said. 'Does May suspect you?'

'What we're doing is a far cry from murder. But no. May doesn't suspect anything – as far as I know. And she would say if she did. Would Alex?'

'It can be hard to tell what he's thinking sometimes.'

'So he could suspect. And have decided to do something about it.'

'The police think so.'

'What happens in this twelve hours they've detained him for?'

'They're doing a search of the flat. Not that we have much in it to look through. I hope they let me back into it tonight, or I'll have to find yet another place to stay.'

'It shouldn't take them long. It's not big, and, as you say, you've just moved in there.'

'They've taken his computer – and his smart phone.'

'And yours?'

'No. Which doesn't mean they won't ask for them. God, Stuart. They'd see all our texts to each other.'

'Have you mentioned me to the police?'

'No.'

'Maybe they won't need to see your phone. Though how would I know? I don't know how the police think.'

'They will. They must.' Heather noticed the panic in her voice. 'And if they ask about you and me, I'll have to tell them, won't I?'

'It would be better if they didn't know about us.'

Stuart's tone was serious; he was terrified of his wife finding out.

'There was a gap in Alex's alibi,' Heather said.

'A gap?'

'Of about two hours when nobody knew what he was doing.'

'So he could have been driving over to Nairn to set fire to your house?'

'But he wouldn't. Not Alex.'

'Did he say what he was doing?' Stuart asked.

'He said he went for a walk to clear his head.'

'Not a great explanation. No policeman is going to believe that. I'm not surprised they arrested him.'

'Do you think he's just seeing someone?'

'It's possible,' Stuart said.

'I had been wondering about him.'

'You had?'

'And it's more believable than Alex pouring petrol over things and setting the house on fire.'

'You'd think his car would show up on CCTV cameras somewhere if he did drive over to Nairn. That's what would happen on cop shows on the telly. I expect that's the kind of thing they're checking up on.'

Stuart's brows were as furrowed as Heather supposed hers were. There was so much to puzzle over.

'Has Alex had an affair before?' Stuart asked.

'Yes. But a long time ago. Which I made him suffer for. And he said he regretted it. I believed him. And as far as I know he's behaved since. But I could believe he's been at it again more easily than I could he's trying to murder me.'

Though Heather was considering that too. How desperate was Alex for money?

'Financially, we could be not that far away from queer street,' she said. 'And there's talk of restructuring at his work. Alex might not be telling me everything he knows about that. And there's the insurance money.'

Heather sighed. Once doubts had begun to arise, it was so difficult to dismiss them.

'It would leave him free to pursue pastures new as well,' Stuart said. 'If that's what he wants.'

'You don't think?

Drizzle was continuing to hit the car windscreen. Heather's hand crept over to Stuart's and squeezed it. Stuart's hand pressed back. Heather looked at his face and tried to work out the expression on it. There was concern there. Was it concern for her or just for the situation Stuart found himself in? Heather had never made up her mind how deep Stuart's feelings for her were.

Stuart leaned forward and took her in a hug. Then he pressed his lips on hers. She understood this and would take comfort in it.

She had met up with Stuart to try to dismiss her suspicions that the police were right in thinking Alex had been trying to murder her. But he'd convinced her Alex had been doing that.

THIRTY-FIVE

After the twelve hours, Alex was allowed to walk free, but that didn't dispel Heather's suspicions. The police kept his computer, which he was told required further examination, though his smart phone was returned to him. Heather found herself with the task of welcoming him back to the flat, which the police had also finished with – and she didn't know how to go about it.

They were seated opposite each other in the living room, Heather on the lumpy settee and Alex on the oddly shaped orange chair. Alex looked relaxed and relieved.

Alex was speaking. 'I never want to go through anything like that again.'

'I bet,' Heather said. 'It must have been dreadful.'

'As far as awfulness goes – on a scale of ten – I would rate it at about three hundred. You'd have thought I was a terrorist the way they treated me. I was expecting waterboarding at any moment.'

'What did they do?' Heather asked.

'They left me on my own in a cell. Which felt bad enough and they certainly kept me locked in long enough for my imagination to run riot with what they might do next. Then they interrogated me. For a couple of hours at a time. Often asking the same questions over and over. They really thought I'd tried to murder you. It was humiliating. And frightening. I thought – what if they assemble a case believable enough to convince a jury?'

'But how could they do that?' Heather asked. 'You didn't do it.' And she was praying he hadn't. Though, after a pause, she added, 'Did you?'

Alex's eyes looked as though they were going to pop out of his head.

'Of course I didn't,' he said. 'You don't think that?'

'So how could you be afraid they might convict you?'

'You don't–' Alex stared at Heather. 'They haven't got you convinced, have they?'

This flustered her. She should be defending him. Shouldn't she?

'Of course not,' she lied. 'But the police are bound to be suspicious about that missing time in your alibi.'

'When I went for a walk?'

'It was a long walk.'

'Though they've accepted now that's exactly what I did.'

How had Alex convinced them of that? Heather wondered.

'They had a sighting of what they thought was my car on CCTV – in Nairn around the time of the fire. But they can blow those up and get better definition on them. When they'd used their bag of tricks it proved it was somebody else's. A similar number plate right enough – the numbers were nearly the same – but that left them feeling foolish. They had to start accepting what I said after that.'

'So that puts you in the clear?'

'It would be great if it did,' Alex said. 'But at least they let me go. Luckily I hadn't already broken down and confessed.'

'You'd be mad to do that.'

'Though I can see why some people might. To get them to stop all that questioning and leave you alone.'

Heather found herself looking at him not without sympathy. If Alex was innocent, he must have gone through hell.

'They went on and on about this clear-cut motive I had. They had to let me go in the end, though I doubt they're convinced that I had nothing to do with the fire. If they turn up anything else at all they'll have me back in there all over again.'

'Why would they turn up anything else?' Heather asked. Or could they? she wondered.

'Oh, they'll be happy with anything that could conceivably be misinterpreted,' Alex said. 'They'll be having a good hard look.'

Did Alex sound innocent? Possibly. So why was she still afraid of him? It was annoying that she often didn't have any idea what was going on in Alex's head; he was so controlled. Or did he just make a point of being like that with her? She'd always admired him for it. She'd thought that was strength, not having to share his feelings the way she did. Though he wasn't all that calm now, was he? And wasn't he talking about things?

To an extent. He could when a situation became serious enough. But he wasn't exactly breaking down in tears and saying how sorry he felt for himself, which she probably would have done. He was just having a dig at the police, wasn't he? That could cover up anything. Which perhaps it did.

She should leave this flat for her own safety. The police might not have enough evidence to charge anyone until there'd been a successful murder attempt on her but then it would be too late. So why was she standing listening to Alex instead of running for her life?

'Alex,' she said, and her voice was quiet.

'What?' he said. His look was sympathetic but it did not touch her.

'Are you trying to kill me?'

'Are you kidding?' Alex said.

His face was angry and that scared her more.

'How could you think anything like that?' he said. 'After all that from the police, I get this from you. It's a bit much.'

'You still haven't explained the missing time,' Heather said.

'I haven't?' he said. 'I thought I had – and if my alibi was better, wouldn't that be more suspicious?'

But was Alex blustering? He was waving his arms about.

'Heather,' Alex said. 'I did not drive over to Nairn and set the house on fire.'

A strong tone in the voice, but was there something evasive in the eyes?

'All those silly questions at the police station and I come home to more?'

And that self-righteousness. Was that put on?

'I'm moving in with my mother,' Heather said.

'You can't mean that,' Alex said.

But she did.

THIRTY-SIX

Heather's mother was glad to see her, as always, which Heather was grateful for. Father was out which Heather was pleased about too as it gave her the chance to explain.

'Your father always said Alex wasn't good enough for you. And he didn't think you should have taken him back after that dreadful behaviour when Anna was born.'

'Maybe he was right.'

'The police arrested him, you said?'

'Yes.'

'But they've let him go now?'

'Yes.'

Heather's emotions were rising up in her and choking any words she might have wanted to say.

'But you think he did it?'

An image of Alex splashing petrol around and reaching in his pocket for matches sprang to Heather's mind.

'I don't know what to think,' she said.

Then she shamed herself by bursting into tears.

Her mother did what mothers do. She brought out tea and sympathy. Heather found herself looking up at a benign smile as she sipped from a china cup.

'Your father's never stopped going on about all those weekend conferences Alex goes to. He doesn't believe there can be so many work meetings and, if any of them are genuine, he doesn't believe Alex wouldn't take advantage of the opportunity to have fun on the side.'

Which didn't make Heather feel any better, even if it did let her know her mother thought right was on her side.

'I thought he just took me for granted.'

'He did that all right.'

'It didn't occur to me he hated me.'

Then another sob burst out of Heather. She was foolish letting her feelings overwhelm her like this. She was being an inadequate teenager again and it was a long time since she'd been that. An image of the night of the fire came to mind and the tears flowed again. Her mother put her arm round her and waited for the sobs to subside.

'Alex is a foolish man. He should value you. And he's self-centred. And unpredictable when things go against him. But I didn't think he had this in him.'

Heather's sobs slowly grew less severe.

'I've thought for a while he might be seeing someone else,' she said eventually.

'Have you?'

'But he always knows the right things to say when you ask him and the right feelings to show. He's difficult to catch out on anything.'

'I don't know what you mean.'

'Doesn't he get my feelings? Doesn't he understand what they are?'

Her mother's stare was puzzled but caring.

'I don't think Alex knows what caring for someone else means. Even with Anna, it doesn't seem to occur to him what someone else is going through,' Heather said.

'Anna?'

'Alex laughed when Anna's boyfriend left her last year. And she was devastated. "It's one of the things teenage girls have to go through," he said. And I looked at him then and wondered how he could be so callous. Maybe that's when I saw him for the first time. He puts on the right face most of the time, but I sometimes think it's just a sham.'

Her mother looked puzzled. 'He can be diplomatic when he wants,' she said. 'Is that what you mean?'

'I don't know. I just don't trust anything he says.'

'You've been through a lot with that fire. You lost everything you owned. That's a shock.'

'And I was supposed to lose my life.'

'We can't be sure of that.'

'Have you not been listening?'

'It's hard to believe. I can see Alex having an affair but not that.'

'When you've stood there watching your house burn down it can change your mind about a lot of things.'

'If he was the one responsible for that he's an evil man – and not the person I thought he was. And you've had a lucky escape. Stay here as long as you want and don't go back. And your father will say the same.'

Heather had something she desperately wanted to say, if she could find the words.

'It was a way out of his problems for Alex. And I can see how little I've always meant to him. Perhaps I've never known him.'

'I don't know what you mean, you know,' her mother told her.

'It's as if I'm seeing him for the first time. For the selfish bastard he is.'

Heather thought of Anna. Was that why Anna had thrown herself on the tattooed misfit – because she was so desperate for genuine male attention? Heather had never thought Alex close enough to Anna, which she'd never understood. How good was the job she and Alex had done in bringing her up? Would Heather have managed better on her own? Lots of women did that these days.

'Mum,' Heather said, trying out the words. 'Alex tried to murder me.'

And saying it made it real. Along with the night of the fire, and everything that had happened since. The need to stay at Elsa's. The police investigation. Alex's arrest. His release. Especially that. Alex had tried to kill her. And he might try again.

THIRTY-SEVEN

Alex

Alex did not like being accused of murder. Who would? He had felt slightly better about it when he'd been released from the police station, but not by much. He wished it had convinced Heather.

Now he'd received that phone call he was even more rattled. It was from Jasmine, and he could tell he had not handled it well. When the police had got in touch to ask her to corroborate his alibi again, she refused to. Which was a pity. The police would have him back in. He'd thought better of Jasmine. Though he wasn't sure he blamed her. He'd dumped her after a one-night stand, enough to pique any woman's pride.

Which was why Alex was doing some frantic investigating of his own. He had hoped the police would have questioned Derek, or made some effort to locate him anyway, but they hadn't mentioned it to him.

Alex was pleased he'd actually tracked Derek down, and he was at his flat now. Derek was obviously in reduced circumstances because this flat block was in a bit of a run-down area. It wasn't like the show-offish Derek he'd known to live somewhere like this.

Alex entered the block and climbed the stairs. The stairwell was in need of a repaint and the carpet was worn. How depressing must it be to live here? Flat 4. That was what he was looking for. He found it and knocked on the door. A woman opened it.

'Angela,' he said.

She stared at him and said nothing at first. Alex had always thought Angela was Derek's better half by a distance. Composed and graceful, she'd smoothed over Derek's indiscretions with competence. And there was always recklessness of some sort with Derek. Now there was a faded look to her and she appeared flustered.

'This is some surprise,' she said.

And it was obvious from the expression on her face it was not a good one.

'What are you doing here?' she said.

'I was in the area and I thought I'd look up Derek,' he said.

She stared at him with what looked like disbelief.

'You're not someone he would have wanted to talk to.'

'He'd been embezzling, Angela. What else could I do?'

'He helped you get a job with that company. He never forgave you for what you did.'

They stared at each other for a few moments.

'You betrayed him. That's how he saw it.'

Though there was a trace of uncertainty in her voice, as if she had mixed feelings herself.

'But what do you mean I'm not someone he *would* have wanted to talk to?' Alex said.

'You haven't heard?'

As Angela stared at him, Alex tried to work out what lay behind the emotions revealing themselves on her face.

'Obviously not. You'd better come in.'

Alex followed her through the hallway and into the sitting room.

'Have a seat,' she said, and he sat himself on a worn-looking settee. But she did not offer him tea or coffee, just sat herself opposite, with a strange look on her face. 'You don't know the story at all?'

'The story?'

'The last couple of years have been difficult. I don't defend Derek for taking the money. And perhaps he shouldn't have blamed you for what you did. He never saw what was wrong with taking it; that was the problem. I explained to him of course. Everyone did. But he never did get it.'

'I don't see – How could he not get that?'

'He had it in his mind he'd only borrowed it and would pay it back, not that he would have managed to pay that much – if he'd ever got round to it.'

Then Angela stopped talking for a moment as emotions built up inside her. Her face screwed up in an attempt to hold back tears, and her hands formed fists as they squeezed at the dress she was wearing. Then she did manage to speak.

'His head just muddled everything up. He stopped making sense of anything and everybody stopped making sense of him.' She had to pause at this point, but when she spoke again, the words rushed out. 'He had a brain tumour.'

'What?' Alex felt his mouth opening wide.

'Not that we knew until long after he had to leave the company. But it must have been in there growing at the time he was taking the money. If he'd been well, I don't think he would ever have done anything like that.'

'Oh,' Alex said. And he did not know how to react to this. 'If we'd realised–' If they had, then what? he wondered. Did the revelation excuse Derek? Maybe. He didn't know. He supposed so. 'Where is he? I'd like to talk to him.'

'He's dead,' Angela said. 'He died a year ago.'

A year ago, Alex thought. Poor Derek. He had let him down. If only he'd known. And there was a thing. From what Angela said, Derek couldn't have caused the fire – or the vandalism to his car.

Guilt shot through him. Suspecting Derek of that on top of everything else.

His mind raced through the things he ought to say to Angela. He couldn't tell her what his suspicions had been. What comforting things could he say instead? He smiled weakly as he tried to frame something kind.

It was a pity it hadn't turned out to be Derek though. It would have solved a few things.

And that was that. He returned to his lonely flat.

THIRTY-EIGHT

Alex was still feeling sorry for himself when Anna turned up. He was pleased to see she was on her own. He could do without the intensity that was Zac. He was in the kitchen washing up dishes after a meal when she marched in.

'Where's Mum?' Anna asked.

Straight to the difficult question, which was typical of Anna, not that he could blame her for asking. In a flat this size it was obvious if someone was missing. And a glance must have told her he was washing up dishes for one. But he had difficulty in answering though the words were simple enough: Heather had left him.

He washed the last two dishes and placed them in the rack, then dried his hands. He took Anna through to the sitting room. He supposed his silence was telling. Anna's compliance with it showed unlikely consideration.

'Is everything OK at university?' he asked. 'We're not used to seeing you this often.'

'Like things are normal here?' Anna said. 'I was wondering how you guys are doing.'

'Shouldn't you be at a lecture today?'

'It's a holiday. You remember them?'

'Just wondering. It would be easy for anyone to be thrown off the rails with everything that's been going on.'

'I'm fine,' Anna said. 'And you?'

Alex had difficulty meeting her gaze – again.

'Great,' he lied.

He sat down on the couch and sighed. Anna slouched opposite. Her eyes seemed to be boring into him.

'Weren't you arrested?'

'You heard about that?'

'Mum texted me. By the way, you look terrible.'

Alex supposed he did. Then it blurted out. All by itself.

'Your mother's left me.'

A frown appeared on Anna's brow. And he noticed her hands clench into fists, then unclench again. She wasn't taking this well.

'That was sudden. What happened?'

Then his words dried up again.

'Come on, Dad. Out with it.'

'I might have convinced the police but your mother's decided I'm guilty.'

'Really?'

'She thinks I drove back to Nairn and set fire to the house.'

'Does she? Are you joking? You didn't, did you?'

'Of course I didn't. Do you need to ask? And she thinks I was trying to murder her.'

'I don't blame her for leaving. But silly Mum. You'd never do that.'

'No I wouldn't.'

Anna looked at him hard.

'Of course not,' he said.

'OK, Dad. You didn't. So what happened when the police arrested you?'

'They put me in a cell and questioned me.'

'I expect they would. Why did they suspect you in the first place?'

'They had CCTV footage that was supposed to show my car in the area – but, when they looked at it more carefully, they discovered it wasn't.'

'Couldn't they have done that before arresting you?'

'You'd think so – but at least they got around to it in the end. They didn't believe my alibi. That was the problem.'

'You said you were at a conference in Elgin. Other people must have seen you.'

'There's a hole in the alibi.'

'What do you mean?'

'An hour and a half when I went out for a walk by myself. The police don't like that sort of thing.'

'Time enough to drive over to Nairn, do the dirty deed, and motor back?'

'Exactly.'

Anna looked at her father carefully. 'What is it you're not telling me, Dad?'

Alex's eyes shifted away from hers. With everything that had been going on, he was beginning to lose his nerve, and Anna was like her mother. She had an instinct for ferreting out lies, which left him in a quandary. His unconvincing alibi had lost him Heather and he didn't want to lose Anna as well. Should he tell her the truth? Was she old enough to cope with that? And would it help him? Things couldn't be any worse than they were. And it would be good to talk. He didn't think this would throw her. And it might help him. Anna could be good at listening to people despite what her mother said. She had enough patience with Zac anyway. Not that he wanted to tell Anna this problem. It would bring him down in her estimation. The best thing would be if it had never happened. Then his tongue took over.

'I wasn't by myself,' he said. 'Which isn't something I've been able to tell your mother, though I'll have to if I want her back. So I'll have to get used to owning up to the truth.'

'What do you mean?' Anna said.

Alex couldn't hold someone's gaze when he told a lie. Now he noticed it could be the same when he told the truth.

'You're going to have to be awfully grown up when I tell you this.'

'What?'

'I was with a woman. Now I know what you're thinking. It's not something I make a habit of. It was a one-off.'

'And that's what you're going to have to tell Mum? Good luck with that one. It might have been a smarter idea to murder her.'

'You think?'

'She's going to murder you. Not literally – I hope – but she's going to put you through it for that.'

'And I'll deserve it. I know. It was bad. And I'm sorry. The opportunity was there and I was tempted.'

'You're not in love with this woman, then?'

'No. And I did finish with her after the night of the fire.'

'You did?'

'I should never have started anything with her. It just happened.'

'Oh yes? Really?'

'Really. Anyway, she had her revenge for my dumping her. When I gave her as an alibi to the police, she denied it. I expect the police round any moment to put me back in that cell.'

'Surely not? Oh God, Dad, you can't half pick them. Who is she? Do I know her?'

'She's someone from work. You've never met her.'

Then a thoughtful look appeared on Anna's face. 'But you maybe don't need to worry, Dad. The police are sharp. They could have just seen through her.'

'You think?'

'Maybe.' Then Anna said. 'But never mind her, how could you do a thing like that?'

And Alex could not find any words to reply with. Guilt was tying his tongue in knots. He felt helpless, frustrated and ashamed.

'And it was on the night of the fire? It's a weird sort of coincidence. You're sure this hasn't "sort of happened" before?'

'It hasn't.'

'You've always resisted temptation?'

'Something like that.'

'I'm not surprised Mum's left you,' Anna said. 'And it's going to make no difference when she finds out what you were really up to. You know that?'

'You're probably right,' Alex said, and his voice was weary. 'And I deserve that. But I regret it. I do still love your mother.'

'So why do it?'

'I thought you might get it. You're an adult. Things can get – complicated.'

'I'll say. And have you any idea what it must be like for Mum thinking you've been trying to murder her?'

'I know.'

'And this is your excuse. Well, for the record, it's Mum I feel sorry for over all of this. You could try crawling to her.'

Alex was finding the courage to look at Anna again. She looked shocked, no, more than that, devastated. It was awful. He had shattered any illusions she might ever have had about him.

'Dad?'

'What?'

'You didn't really try to murder Mum, did you?'

THIRTY-NINE

When your wife leaves you, you rediscover time. What do you do with it? At least the police hadn't turned up to arrest him again. Why hadn't they done that yet? Not that he would go round to the station to complain.

It had been years since he had gone to the cinema by himself but that was what he found himself doing now – and it was the early evening performance, which was the one in all of his years with Heather that he'd never gone to with her. Which might not have been his best idea because when he returned to the flat, he seemed to still have so much time to fill. Then Elsa turned up, and invited him round for drinks, which surprised him, but the caring face was welcome, and he found himself seated in one of the comfortable leather armchairs in her parlour as she poured him a healthy gin and mixed in tonic.

'I was concerned,' she said.

'Yes?' Alex said. Concerned sounded good.

'You were arrested by the police?'

'They had to have a go at somebody. They've a crime to solve.'

'But what did they think you might have done?'

'I fit their idea of a fire-raiser. I did my best to convince them otherwise, but I doubt if I managed it.'

'At least they let you go.'

'They were disappointed at not turning up proof. It's a good job they need that. But I expect they'll keep on rooting around.'

'And they won't find any?'

'I don't see how they can. But possibly the only other person who thinks like that is you.'

'What do you mean?'

'Heather's convinced I did it – and I was trying to murder her in the process.'

'No.'

'So she's left and gone to her mother's.'

'Not standing by her man, then?'

'And Anna's stormed out in a strop – off round to give Heather support.'

'But you'd think Heather and Anna would know you better.'

'The idea I'm a fire-raiser and would-be-murderer doesn't seem to be a surprise.'

'They'll come to their senses.'

'They think they have.'

Alex fixed a gloomy stare on his drink. He'd never been less interested in one. Conversation petered out as Alex became lost in thought. Then he came back to the present with an abruptness that startled him.

'You must think us strange,' he said.

'You're going through an odd experience,' Elsa said. 'That doesn't make you peculiar. And I can't imagine what it must be like to have your house burned down. And then to be accused of doing it yourself. It must be dreadful.'

'It is,' Alex said, and told himself to stop feeling so sorry for himself, then thought why not?

'I had hoped that giving you two the space to get through this would help,' Elsa said.

'Oh, the flat's great,' Alex said. 'I'm ever so grateful. We're a powder keg of a family. That's the problem.'

'They're letting you down.'

'I wish they saw it that way.'

'As for the police,' Elsa said. 'I know they're doing their job, but do they have to blunder about like this? They can't have looked at you properly.'

'Oh, they've had a look, and they see possible motive, so they think they see a criminal.'

'But what reason could you have for doing that? It was your house.'

'They think the insurance money's enough.'

'But it leaves you without anywhere to live.'

'And the insurance money on Heather's life.'

'They must think you're really mercenary.'

'I expect a lot of the people they meet are.'

Alex still felt a harassed wreck but the talk was helping; some of the tension was starting to leave him. He sipped some gin. One thing had been happening after the other lately, and he'd been becoming more wound up by the minute. He gave Elsa a weak smile. She was the one shining light around. He hadn't understood why the flat annoyed Heather. It was something to be grateful for. Everything had to be perfect for Heather. He was sure she'd had difficulty putting up with him for years.

He looked across at Elsa and thought what a handsome woman she was. Perhaps he should have noticed that before this. That was an attractive wave in her brunette hair. He liked the way that shone. And the angle of her chin, and the sway of her breasts. He tried to think of something else.

When had he become such a beast? Did he have to react like this towards every woman? Though that was insulting Elsa. She could hardly be lumped in with 'every woman'. She was Elsa. She had her individual smile and the warmth that exuded from her was her own. He ought to appreciate her more.

He couldn't help noticing the firmness of her body. Elsa had the figure of a younger woman. She was slim, yes, and buxom at the same time. In any case, there she was in front of him, with the scent she used hanging in the air between them. He shook his head and forced himself to think of other things.

'I expect Heather'll see things differently later,' he said.

'You think so?'

'It's been a strain for her. If the police suspected me enough to arrest me, it's no wonder she started wondering about me.'

'She's your wife. And she ought to have more faith in you.'

'You don't know Heather.'

'What do you mean?'

'At the centre of Heather' – he tried to think how to phrase this – 'is a tight ball of nervousness. She structures her whole life round calming that.'

'Really?'

'She has an assured manner and elegant ways, but, underneath, she's a complete anxiety basket case. She'll be up the wall now, wondering if I'm going to be coming after her with an axe. And I didn't do a thing.'

Elsa had been watching him carefully, and now she moved towards him and placed a gentle kiss on his forehead. Where had that come from? Elsa's head was still close to his, and he was acutely aware of the smell of her body. And the warmth of it. She was so close. Close enough to reach out and touch. Then he did that. He put his hand on her shoulder as he drew her face towards him and kissed her on the mouth.

And he was at it again. It seemed he was ruled by his passions now. What was going on with him? He supposed his life was on edge and his feelings were raw. And he could not stop himself following where they were leading him. He should show strength. But strength was the problem, the strength of the passion thrumming through him.

He kept on kissing her. Over and over. It was a release from the agony of all the emotions he had been going through. That anxiety – and that anger against Heather – it was seeping from him. Wasn't it? He started to relax into the embrace. Worry about consequences drifted off.

FORTY

Alex was woken by a kiss on the cheek. There was an impression of the softness of lips and the tang of feminine scent. He opened his eyes to see Elsa's face close beside him.

'Good morning, lover,' Elsa said.

The voice was smug and brought back the sensations of the night before. Those had been exhilarating. Then a pang of guilt struck him before disbelief took over, followed by a feeling of self-satisfaction.

'Good morning,' he replied, as shame hit him again.

'Who was a lovely surprise packet then?' Elsa said.

'Oh,' Alex said.

He took Elsa in. She was standing above him, fully dressed in work clothes. She must have woken and dressed while he still slept. A yawn overcame him, and he stretched out on the bed. His head was full of memories of Elsa without clothes on. He reached out an arm, and she leaned down towards him as they kissed properly on the lips.

'I've got to go,' she said, and there was a business-like air about the way she said that.

'What time is it?'

'It's only seven,' she said. 'You can lie there for as long as you like.'

'That's a relief,' he said.

His eyes were full of sleep, but he was taking a good look at Elsa as she stood above him. She bent down and they enjoyed another lingering kiss.

'Goodbye can be sweet,' Elsa said. 'Hello can be better. I'll be back about two in the afternoon.' She straightened herself up. 'I'll be at work. Stay here as long as you like.'

She turned and strode to the door where she stopped again, and blew him a kiss, which he returned. After she had closed the door behind her, he listened to her walk downstairs, open the outside door, and close and lock it behind her. He gazed at the ceiling.

What had he done? But he was pleased with himself. Should he be feeling that? Then his thoughts returned to the embraces of the night before, and he stopped wondering. He lay there for some time as he waited to wake up properly. He came to the conclusion he could stay there in a dreamlike, self-congratulatory state all day. But he supposed he should re-acquaint himself with reality and forced himself out of bed and into the shower. As hot water poured over him a sharpness returned to his mind. Shower over, he dried himself. His shaving stuff was in the flat as were his toiletries. He put on his clothes and found the kitchen.

What did Elsa keep in her fridge? He ought to go back to the flat and eat there but he didn't have the energy to go that far yet. He was enjoying being where he was. Why not? Heather had left him and, as she'd done so, she'd accused him of trying to murder her. There was no reason not to luxuriate in his experience with Elsa. He was entitled to think of himself. Why not? And Elsa was a good catch, a fine-looking woman and an independent one. He was doing well with her. Feel smug, he told himself.

He sat at Elsa's breakfast bar and ate muesli and fruit. He was in a good space here. When had he last felt so relaxed? So much had been going wrong in his life. It made a nice change for something to work out. So what if Heather did find out? She had asked for it. Though he supposed that would make no difference. She would still hold him accountable. Which he supposed was right. He had to accept responsibility for his own actions. Though wasn't that what he was doing? With no second thoughts so far.

He discovered Elsa's cafetière and brewed a strong coffee. That would wake him properly. Though he wasn't sure he wanted to be completely awake. Being half asleep and pleased with himself felt good. He poured coffee, turned on Elsa's kitchen TV and seated himself opposite to watch the early morning news.

That was as gloomy as always – financial problems and Brexit – but it at least helped focus his thoughts. He ought to go back to the flat, but he needed to do something about these breakfast things first. Though he did not leave even after washing those and leaving them on the drainer. This was a haven. Why be in a hurry to leave it?

He walked into the living room and looked around. It was bland if relaxing – and in good taste – but he could find nothing of Elsa in it. He noticed the lack of photographs and personal mementoes. Did Elsa live here? Elsa had never projected much of her personality in the time Alex had known her – until last night that is. She was a self-effacing and self-contained person, and that was what this room reflected. The colours did not dominate. There was nothing brash about cream and white. And there was no hint of loudness anywhere. The pictures were of inoffensive nature scenes that blended into a quiet, unnoticeable background. All the furniture was reasonably new, as if any with memories of the past had been dismissed. This was the home of a woman who lived in and for the present, which he supposed was refreshing.

He wandered down the hall and tried a door but discovered it was locked. That surprised him. He continued with his exploration of the floor. There were other rooms upstairs too, but they held nothing of interest. They were kitted out as spare bedrooms but did not look as if they were much used. He went back downstairs and tried the locked door again – which would still not open.

And it was beginning to annoy him. It was the only mysterious thing in the house. And what on earth would Elsa need to keep secure from prying eyes? His curiosity had been woken. More than anything, he wanted to go into that room.

Was that bad? It was probably inexcusable. Elsa had welcomed him as a guest, and he wanted to return that favour by breaking into the only place she kept private? But it was obvious why he wanted to do that. Elsa's house was such a contrast with what his and Heather's had been. It was possible to tell so much about them from the rooms they used and impossible to find out anything about Elsa from the space she inhabited.

Was Elsa such a disciplined person she could sweep anything and everything of her personal life behind her instinctive good taste and professional cleaning habits? The whole place was a showpiece. Was that the word he had been looking for? He decided it was. His eyes raced around but he could find no trace of the woman he had bedded the night before. His mind returned to the locked door.

Was that where she was? And what would he find if he opened it? He knew something now of Elsa's secret personality. The rawness and sensuality that had never shown on the surface before. What else was there to discover? Or was he letting his imagination run riot? He shouldn't be so curious. That could lead to trouble and he was already in enough of that. But he still found himself walking towards that beckoning door and trying to work out the best way to open it.

He went back into the kitchen and looked through some of the drawers. Did Elsa keep keys in there? He found knives, forks, serving spoons, and other kitchen paraphernalia. He closed the drawers again. He walked into the living room and over to Elsa's desk. He lifted the lid.

It was what he could have expected – a neatly organised office desk, with the usual things you might find

– files, stapler, stamps, and all the rest. Then he opened a drawer, and there they were: Elsa's keys. Two bunches of them. He picked them up and walked back to the infuriating door.

FORTY-ONE

After all his anticipation, Alex had wondered if what he would find behind the mysterious door was a cupboard but what he discovered was not mundane: it was the bedroom of a teenage girl in a house where, as far as he knew, there were none.

There was all the paraphernalia of an adolescent: photographs of a movie star, in this case, Daniel Craig; posters of a favourite singer, Ariana Grande; and heart-shaped photo frames of stars from what seemed to be boy bands, but none with a photograph of what looked like a real-life boyfriend. A teddy bear, and a lion with a ridiculously shaggy mane draped themselves across a pink, quilted bed. An Indian-style incense holder stood on the chest of drawers, and a faint smell of rosewood lingered. A laptop decorated with flowery stickers lay closed on a white desk.

Who was this girl? Elsa had not mentioned anyone, and he had not seen anyone hanging around, yet the room did not look abandoned. It gave the impression its owner had only just left. The disturbed coverlet on the bed suggested someone had been sitting on it not that long ago. But the room had been so definitely locked. Anna had never shown any desire to want to lock her bedroom, and, as far as he knew, it was not a common habit of teenage girls.

Though maybe there were a few like that. There seemed to be at least one.

When he opened the wardrobe door, he found himself looking at a fashionable array of tops and skirts, which looked as good as new. Did that mean something? Anna's clothes did not remain in a pristine state for long, and neither did his or Heather's. He inspected them more thoroughly. Had these clothes been worn at all?

A cork noticeboard was hung above the desk and he walked over to it. There was a printout from a school report card and the name on it was Rhiannon Harrison. Harrison? Elsa must have a daughter. He looked at the grades. Rhiannon did well at school. All grade A's. Definitely better than Anna. Come to think of it, looking at those dates, she must have been in the same year group as Anna. Anna hadn't mentioned a Rhiannon and there hadn't been one among her friends. Alex looked round for a photograph but could find none, which he thought unusual. Anna always had a mass of photographs of herself about her room. She was the vainest creature as Alex told her, but he knew 'pics' were a fascination of all her friends too. They took never-ending selfies, and photographs of each other, and Anna was constantly looking for something new to put on her Instagram page. Rhiannon must have a more modest temperament.

Alex's attention was drawn to a letter of admission to St Andrews University. That must be where Rhiannon was. He studied the date. That would fit; it would explain why he and Heather had not seen her around since they moved into the flat, though the indent on the bed still intrigued Alex.

But what was he doing? he asked himself. Prowling round a teenage girl's bedroom like this was a questionable thing to do. He moved towards the door but could not stop himself turning round to look again. There was something wrong in this room.

He walked back to the desk and opened a drawer, and what a thing to discover straight away, a diary. He definitely shouldn't read that. He moved it to the side of the drawer. Underneath it was a scrapbook. He supposed he should not look at that either. But he opened it and started leafing through pages. His attention was drawn to one in particular and he stopped at it. A newspaper article about a car crash. Now why would Rhiannon put something like that in her scrapbook? Then he heard a noise outside. It sounded like a car. Was that Elsa returning already? That was unexpected.

He glanced out of the window. Yes. Elsa. Perhaps she had forgotten something. He had better get out of here. It would not do to be caught in this private space.

FORTY-TWO

Heather

Heather was driving to work at the Health Centre from her parents' house. She was not well practised in this route and had not given herself as much time as she should have; she was going to be late, which annoyed her. She hadn't found any kind of even keel since the night of the fire.

She had always prided herself on at least managing to be organised in the mornings. Today she had made herself even later by not being able to find things. Where was her Health Centre identity card? Where were her car keys? And it was so much further to the Health Centre from her parents' house. Why had she never managed to persuade them to move into town? These narrow country roads were not built for the speed she needed to manage.

Coming round a corner, she found herself too much in the centre of the road, and only just avoided a headlong crash with a Volvo. She swerved in time, cursing as she did so. That did not do anything for her peace of mind. She glanced at the clock. She would be ten minutes late. She knew what reaction to expect from her supervisor. The practice manager, she of the giant shoulders and thighs, developed from compulsive gym attendance, lived for such moments. The reprimand would not be perfunctory.

When the accident occurred, it wasn't Heather's fault. She had that to console herself with. When she turned the sharp corner into the downward hill leading towards Logie, the car just moved away from her. All by itself. Didn't it? That could not have been her. She slammed her foot on the brakes in an instant but all that happened was the car slid in the opposite direction to the one she intended. And there was a car coming the other way. She had a sight of a Mini being driven by a thin young man with floppy hair and an alarmed face. He slew his car round into a spin as her Peugeot started careering towards him and when the two automobiles met there was a thunderous crash.

The shudder of it went through her. Her car bounced off the Mini and across the road into a tree where it halted in a heap. Heather had been thrown forward, sideways, and backward in the process of all of this – as far as the seat belt would allow. The front of her body was happily cushioned by the airbag that had ballooned out in front of her.

On her side, staring at the windscreen in front of her, she wondered how she had contrived to end up in such a strange position. She heard the wheels spin as the body of the car started to settle with some noisy creaks. Then eventually everything became still and silent.

Heather found herself gasping in one of her panic attacks. Her blood and breathing raced. She felt dizzy and her vision had blurred. She was stiff with tension and her body seemed to be attempting to bend over into itself, but the seat belt would not allow so much movement.

She was sideways to the world, looking at it through a cracked windscreen. She took in an impression of shattered glass outside the car and tree branches where they should not have been. She fought to calm her body down and find steady breathing but the shuddering and gasping would not allow her to wrest back control. She did manage to undo the seat belt but lay useless after that.

The side door of the car – which was now situated above her – was opened. An arm pushed through it and she looked up into the face of the same young man she had seen looking so terrified a moment before. He must have found it easier to recover from the slide of his car. He looked unharmed though there were scratches on his face and spots of blood. White and harassed it might be, but it was the most welcome face she had ever seen.

She reached up her hand as he took hold of her forearm and pulled upwards. She scrabbled for leverage with her other hand and pushed against the seat with her legs. Both hands now holding her, the man succeeded in hauling her up and out of the car. He dragged her further away onto the other side of the road, where she lay as she gathered her breathing.

But he did not let her stay there for long.

'Get up.' His voice was firm, and his strong hands and arms pulled at her again. 'We've got to get further away from your car. That engine could go on fire. Petrol's vile stuff.'

Petrol was vile stuff? Didn't she know that? That was what had destroyed her house. The thought it might destroy her too was terrifying. Frantically, she scrabbled to her feet. After an agonising scurry away from the vehicles, they lay down and tried to take in what had happened.

Heather glanced across at the Peugeot. It was just over a year old and look at it, battered, contorted, and broken. What a waste. And the Mini didn't look any better.

She looked across at her rescuer who was not someone she recognised. He looked as shocked as she felt but she had been impressed by his presence of mind. She was sure his car was a write-off as hers was, but he had shown a coolness she envied. Left to her own devices she would still be in that car which, fortunately, hadn't burst into flames.

'How did that happen?' the young man asked.

'I don't know,' Heather said.

'Your car turned into mine.'

'I don't know,' Heather said again. 'The car pulled away from me. I think something went wrong with the controls or the brakes. I think it was the brakes. They wouldn't work.'

'The brakes?'

'And it was only serviced a couple of weeks ago,' Heather said.

'Strange.'

'So what do I call you?' Heather said.

'Pete. And you are?'

'Heather. Heather Ross.'

Heather supposed they should be exchanging insurance policies and contact details – and she shouldn't be blithely admitting fault by saying something had gone wrong with her car – but her mind wouldn't settle to any of that.

She was thinking what a coincidence it was that, so soon after someone had set fire to a building she was supposed to be in, the brakes on her car had failed and she had suffered an accident which could conceivably have killed her. She told her mind to shut up. The idea that someone was trying to kill her couldn't be real.

'We ought to phone for an ambulance,' Pete said. 'You look as if you've had a bash to the head. And we ought to phone the police.'

'You don't have to involve the police just because you've had a car accident, do you?'

'One like this, yes. They'll need to clear the road so it's safe for everyone else.'

'I'm all right,' Heather said. Then she checked her limbs to make sure. 'I am all right, I'm sure.' And she did hope so.

She put her hand to the side of her head. There was a tender spot there though she hadn't been aware of anything striking her there. And when she looked at her hand, was that blood there from where she'd touched her hair? She became aware of how confused she was, and how blurry things were. Dare she get up? She put her hand out to pull herself up, then changed her mind.

'Lie quiet,' Pete said. 'I'll phone for help.'

It was good to hear a calm, assured voice taking control.

FORTY-THREE

Heather gave Black an appeasing smile but what it really meant was please go away. Heather was lying in a hospital bed and did not want to have to cope with him. She ached all over after her ordeal and could not stop her mind reliving the accident. The moment when she realised the car was out of her control – and she had no idea what was going to happen next – would not leave her.

There was a sympathetic tone to Black's voice as he said, 'I'm sorry to see you like this.'

And she could see that he was. But you're not as sorry as I am, she thought.

'How are you?' he asked.

'Battered and bruised,' Heather replied, 'but if that was the worst of it, it might not be so bad. I feel as if I'm going out of my mind with all of this.'

To which Black did not seem to be able to think of a reply.

'They're still waiting for the results of some tests,' Heather said. 'That should tell them how I really am.'

'I'm sure you'll be fine,' Black said.

You think? Heather thought. And she hoped so too, but it didn't feel as if anything was likely to go right at the moment.

'We can but hope for the best,' Black said.

'So why are you here?' Heather said. 'It was a car accident. It's got nothing to do with the fire.'

'A second accident?' Black said.

'What do you mean?' Heather said. 'Oh. I see.'

And she looked back at him fearfully.

'So I'm not having the thoughts of a crazy woman? Someone else thinks this might have been another murder attempt? I've been telling myself to get a grip and not be paranoid. Do you know that, when they asked who I wanted to be informed I was in hospital, I thought anyone – but Alex? Isn't that a dreadful thing to think about your husband?'

Heather stopped talking as she struggled with her emotions.

'But anyway…'

She started to laugh and thought to herself she must try to stop herself from becoming hysterical.

'I'm not going to allow him anywhere near me. I don't trust him. I tell myself he's not trying to murder me, but I can't persuade myself he isn't. Not that I asked for a visit from Anna either. I'm not afraid of her but she's got enough worries already without having to look out for a stupid mother who's lost control of her car.'

Then Heather stopped, afraid that nothing she was saying made sense. Black didn't say anything just allowed her to gather her thoughts.

'I'll let them get in touch with Anna when they've had the results of the tests and we know what we're dealing with,' Heather said. 'I asked them to phone my mother earlier, and she's been to visit. With Father. I haven't been deserted. My mother's been very good at calming me down and telling me she doesn't think Alex could possibly be trying to murder me. But my father just sat there in silence. He wasn't convinced. And now you turn up. Please tell me I'm only overloaded with suspicious thoughts. I did have a breakdown once. After Anna was born. I'm imagining things, aren't I?'

As Black listened, his brow became more furrowed. But he didn't speak for a while and Heather was left to try to work out why. Was he looking for the right words?

'We have to look at the facts,' he said.

'Facts?'

'I can't hide you from those.'

'What do you mean?'

'The fire was started deliberately.'

'True.'

'And your car was tampered with.'

Heather didn't want to believe that. She didn't say anything but stared.

'Neither of those facts is just in your mind,' Black said.

'Oh God.'

It would have been better if they had been. She put her hand to her mouth in case a shriek came out.

Black continued. 'Looked at on its own, the fire may not have been started in order to harm you personally, but when you link that incident to the car crash, it looks as if someone has now made two murder attempts on you.'

'You didn't say that,' Heather said. 'You can't have.'

But he had. Then the look on Black's face became uncertain as if he wasn't sure how to deal with Heather, and she realised he wondered if he should have waited before telling her that. She was still in hospital. And so he should feel sorry for saying that, she thought, even if he did have to get on with his investigation.

'Do you know who might have had the chance to tamper with your car?' Black asked.

Heather thought. 'Anyone,' she said. 'It was parked in a quiet country lane beside my mother's, which is where I'm staying at the moment. It's not even overlooked.'

'Has anybody been visiting you? Someone you know – or a stranger even?'

'No,' she said. 'There's just been me, and my mother and father. You don't suspect them?'

'Not at all,' Black said. 'If you give me your parents' address, we'll look at any cameras in the vicinity and have those checked.'

Heather had just finished writing down the address when a nurse bustled in. One look at the expression on Heather's face alarmed her.

'You've been upsetting her,' she said to Black.

'Have I?' Black said.

'He hasn't been doing anything,' Heather said. 'He's been asking questions. That's all.'

'A policeman's job,' Black said.

'Well, you'll have to finish doing it some other time,' the nurse said. 'You're tiring her out.'

'But he doesn't need to go yet,' Heather said. 'He hasn't finished, and it isn't exhausting me. Really.'

'Look, I am sorry if I've upset you,' Black said to Heather.

'I'm fetching a doctor,' the nurse said, and turned on her heel.

'Hospitals,' Black said.

There was a question Heather wanted to ask Black before he left.

'Do you suspect Alex of tampering with the car?' she said.

Black looked at her unhappily. For a moment she wondered if he was going to answer. Then he did.

'We'd be foolish to rule out the possibility,' he said. 'What do you think? Do you think he's capable of doing something like that?'

Heather was looking at Black with horror; she had come to the conclusion she could believe anything of Alex now.

FORTY-FOUR

Heather was pleased to see Stuart when he turned up at her ward. At last, someone she trusted, and he had brought with him grapes as well as his anxious smile. When he reached over to give her a kiss, she didn't want to let go of him again.

'This has been hell,' she said. 'Boy is it good to see you.'

'Are you OK?' Stuart said.

'They're still waiting for the results of some tests, but I think I'm just battered and bruised.'

'That's a relief. What happened?'

'That's a good question. The car spun away from me. And the brakes didn't work. I didn't know what was going on.'

'You still don't know why that was?'

'I was going downhill and at first I thought I must have been going too fast. But when I tried to correct it – I don't know – the steering wasn't doing what it was supposed to do, and the brakes didn't either. Then I hit the other car and everything whirled round. It was confusing. Don't ask me to explain it any more than that.'

'The other car wasn't at fault? It wasn't all because he hit you?'

'He tried to avoid me.' Her voice trailed off. She felt useless. She couldn't explain any of it. She felt the beginning of a sob and struggled to control it but failed. Stuart looked at her in alarm. She held her arms out to him and he held her and that helped a bit. The sobs began to subside.

'Oh God,' Heather said. 'The first time I had an accident was bad enough. I didn't want to go through anything like that again.'

'The fire you mean?' Stuart said.

'The fire? What? That as well. Yes.'

Stuart gave her a puzzled look.

'The other car accident I meant,' Heather said. 'This isn't my first.'

The giggle she gave surprised her. It must be nerves – and embarrassment. She dismissed it.

'Not that I make a habit of them, honestly. It's only the second. Only.'

Her voice broke into a disbelieving laugh.

'When was the other one?'

'Years ago. I don't talk about it.'

She looked away from him.

'Perhaps you should,' he said.

'Not really,' she replied, then lapsed into thought as Stuart watched her carefully.

'What happened in the other one?' he said.

Heather sighed. She hadn't wanted to tell Stuart about that, but she had already started.

'At least I understood what was happening then.' She paused. 'It was raining and had been for a while. I hit a puddle that went most of the way across the road. There's no way I could have avoided it. And the car slid away from me. All I could do was hold on to the steering wheel and hope for the best. I tried to steer but it was impossible.'

'You survived it, thank God.'

'The car was a write-off which was a pity. It was a few months old. It was my father's, and it was only insured third party, fire and theft. My father was furious.'

'I bet,' Alex said.

Though even that was the least of it as Heather knew. But she wasn't going to open up about that with Stuart. Not yet anyway.

'Things seem to happen to me,' Heather said. 'And I wonder why I'm a nervous wreck,' Heather said.

'You're not that,' Stuart said.

'Every time I look at Anna, I think she's probably the same, so I'm overprotective of her, and then that doesn't help.'

'This is a shock,' Stuart said. 'It'll take a while for it to pass.'

'I suppose,' Heather said. 'And the memories of that car pulling away from me out of control – and this one doing the same – they both go round in my head and they won't stop. I feel as if I'm going mad.'

'You're not going mad,' Stuart said. 'Give it time. It'll sink in and you won't feel so bad about things.'

'And Black. I can't stop thinking of him either. Did I tell you he visited me here?'

'Did he say why?'

'He said – oh God, he said – someone tampered with my car.'

'Black really said that?'

'Who would do such a thing?'

'Does Black suspect anybody in particular?'

'And somebody started that fire at my house.'

'So Black was right?'

'Right? Black? About what?'

'When he arrested Alex. It's a pity they let him out. Then he couldn't have messed with your car.'

'But Alex–' Heather's emotions were churning. 'Don't say that,' she said.

'If the police think he might have done it, shouldn't we?' Stuart said.

Heather stared at him with horror.

'I'll fix him,' Stuart said.

'What do you mean?' Heather said.

'I'll go round and warn him off.' Then he was on his feet with an angry look in his eye and Heather wondered what he would do if he did catch up with Alex.

As if reading Heather's thoughts, Stuart said, 'I'll just talk to him. But I'll make sure the message is clear.'

'Don't,' Heather said, though she was not sure she meant it.

She was looking at Stuart through different eyes. She'd thought he was a fly-by-night lover, and the end result of this relationship with him would be the memory of a few nights' fun, which she hadn't minded. It had been all she'd been looking for at the time. But she found herself wondering about him now.

'Alex doesn't even know about you,' she said.

'Perhaps he does,' Stuart said. 'Could that be why he tampered with your car?'

'I'm not sure Alex knows that much about cars.'

'And it's time he did know about me. And that he needs to be careful how he treats you.'

Then he left the ward – and there was a decisiveness to his movements. As he did, who should walk in but Anna, who looked at Stuart with surprise as he strode past her. Then her eyes fixed themselves on Heather and her face lit up.

'Mum,' Anna said.

'Anna,' Heather replied, and was she pleased to see her?

'Gran was in touch,' Anna said. 'Why weren't you?'

Then Anna was seated beside the bed.

'Oh that,' Heather said.

Then Anna went quiet which surprised Heather until she realised Anna was struggling to find the right thing to say, eventually coming out with, 'You look great, Mum.'

'No I don't. I look awful.'

'Yes. I mean. No. How are you, Mum? That was a horrible thing to happen to you.'

'Apart from feeling I might be on the verge of dying, I feel fine.'

Then Anna laughed and the mood improved. But the awkwardness had told Heather a lot about how bad she must look.

'I'm all right as far as I know,' Heather said. 'Stirred and shaken, of course. I should be walking out of here soon enough.'

Which was easy enough to say, not that – at the moment – Heather thought she would ever be OK again.

'I didn't want to worry you. I was going to get in touch later.'

Anna's smile in return was weak.

'You're in hospital,' she said. 'Why shouldn't I be worried? And didn't it occur to you I would want to visit?'

Heather was so pleased to see Anna, she realised she had been wrong not to contact her.

'I'm sorry,' she said. 'I should have let them get in touch. Not that I wanted you to be leaving Aberdeen again to travel so far to see me. It feels as if you hardly have the opportunity to be there.'

Then Anna asked the difficult question.

'Mum, who was that man who was walking away when I came in?'

FORTY-FIVE

Alex

Alex was visited again by Black. He had not expected to become accustomed to visits from the police, but here he was, looking into the eyes of Black again.

'I did not burn down my own house,' he told him. 'We discussed that.'

'And we need another discussion,' Black said.

Alex did not voice the reply that came to mind.

'Where were you in the evening yesterday – and overnight?'

Alex gave a rebellious look in answer.

'I do need a reply,' Black said.

'Why? What happened then?'

'Just answer the question.'

'I was minding my own business. What was everyone else doing?'

Which he regretted as soon as he'd said it, though that didn't stop his defiance.

'Look, what is this about?' he asked.

A glower was the response from Black.

'All right,' Alex said. 'I'll try to think.'

And this time he gave serious thought to what he was going to say, but he didn't think the answer would please Black.

'I was out,' he said. 'By myself.'

'Clearing your head again?'

'I went to a cinema, filled up the car with petrol, then went home.'

'And you've no witnesses for your visit to the cinema?'

'As I said, I was on my own.'

'What was the name of the cinema and the film you went to see?'

'I was trying to fill in time. I went in to see whatever was on. The Vue Cinema in the retail park in Inverness. That's where I went. The film was *David Copperfield*. I didn't like it much. It wasn't a lot like the book. But I stuck it out. Do you want a summary and critique?'

Black ignored that.

'Which petrol station did you go into?'

'Tesco's. Not far from the cinema.'

'Did you go straight home after that?'

'Yes.'

'And you've no witness for that either?'

'Obviously not,' he found himself saying, though he had been with Elsa then. Another alibi he wouldn't tell the truth about. Wasn't that useful? 'Heather's left me because of all that's been going on. You've scared her. She thinks I'm trying to murder her.'

But the appeal did not melt Black's heart and the cool assessing look he gave Alex was as annoying as the rest of the interview had been so far.

'That attitude won't help,' Black said.

'Is there anything that will?' Alex asked. 'What crime am I supposed to have committed this time? Or do you really not mean to tell me?'

'When a suspect is aggressive, it often means they're covering something up.'

'Then I'm going to have to continue to look guilty. I'm getting fed up.'

Black was silent, but Alex could see he was making calculations. Then his face softened, and he started speaking gently.

'I'm sorry to have to tell you your wife's been in a road accident,' he said.

'Heather? What? You can't be serious. Is she all right? What happened?'

Then he thought he'd better be quiet so Black could answer at least one of his questions.

'But accident isn't an accurate description, I'm afraid.'

'What do you mean by that? And how is Heather? Why aren't you telling me?'

'She's all right,' Black said. 'Fortunately she survived the attempt. She's a bit bruised. But she seems to be getting on OK.'

'Thank God for that. But "attempt" you say. What do you mean by that?'

'Oh yes, someone tried to murder her. They tampered with her car.'

Alex stared as he tried to take that in.

'But who would do that? I would? Naturally you come along here and grill me? Look, this is my wife you're talking about. For God's sake, what happened and where was this "accident"?'

Black's reply, when he made it, was deliberately neutral and unemotional, but the more ominous for that.

'The brakes were tampered with – and the steering. And she hit another vehicle on the road to Logie this morning when she was on her way to work. Fortunately, the other driver's all right as well.'

'God, that's awful,' Alex said. 'And instead of wasting your time harassing me, shouldn't you be trying to find out who actually did it? He might do it again.'

'We'll investigate every avenue,' Black replied. 'And we'll check up on everything that you've told us.'

This man was relentless, Alex thought.

'You do that. Then stop bothering me and find this man, whoever it is. Which ward is she on? I take it she's in Raigmore. I need to visit her.'

'She wouldn't welcome that,' Black said. 'She's given specific instructions you're not to be admitted. And I've put a constable outside her ward. You won't be able to get in.'

Alex felt he had had enough.

'We'll see about that,' he said. 'If anyone thinks they're going to stop me visiting Heather when she's in that state, they've another think coming.'

'There have been two murder attempts on that woman's life,' Black said.

This was ridiculous, but Alex could see protesting wasn't going to do him any good. He wondered if he could work out some way round this.

'It is your wife's wish that she be left to herself, sir,' Black said, but there was some patience in his voice. 'It often is the husband to blame in these circumstances, so we will investigate you. But my mind isn't closed.'

'Not entirely.'

'We'll examine the evidence.'

'You'll take blind guesses as far as I can see.'

'We'll look at those as well. In any case, the hospital will keep you informed about your wife's progress. You can get in touch with them any time you like, while we get on with our job and, among other things, check as much of your alibi as we can. I don't suppose you kept the cinema ticket? Or paid by card?'

Alex's heart leapt. Could he establish where he was in the evening at least? Except he had paid by cash – and he remembered putting his ticket in a bin on his way out of the cinema. But he had paid for the petrol by card.

'I should have a receipt for the petrol,' he said. But when he rummaged in his pocket, he discovered he didn't.

'Not convincing so far, sir,' Black said. 'But we can still check that payment, and the CCTV.'

'Look, it wasn't me,' Alex said. 'It wasn't. And Heather is going to be OK, isn't she?'

'She seems to be fine, sir. And, as I've said, you're welcome to get in touch with the hospital. They'll be happy to give you more details.'

'Was she on her own when it happened or what?'

But Black wasn't inclined to be any more communicative about the accident.

'Just don't go near her, sir.'

That was what he seemed to concern himself with more than anything. That Alex shouldn't have anything to do with his own wife. Visiting Heather in order to comfort her would upset her, would it? How had things come to this? Perhaps he would get more details about things from her parents. He could only hope they would have some understanding of his feelings.

After Black left, Alex was alone with his anxieties and frustration. He found himself pacing the room and muttering. When he realised what he was doing, he stopped himself. But that didn't make it any easier. Then it occurred to him what an idiot he was being, feeling so sorry for himself. He was doing what Heather frequently complained about: he was just thinking of himself. It was Heather he should be giving thought to. If someone was trying to murder her, who was it? He should be trying to work that out. He turned the idea over in his head, but there were no ready answers. And the thought occurred. If someone had tried twice to kill Heather, they would try again. And the next time, they might succeed.

FORTY-SIX

Alex was pacing yet again. The width of the lounge. Then back. And back again. He told himself to stop but didn't. Then, with a surprising effort, he managed to sit down. He stared out of the window. It was raining and raining hard. The view from the flat was uninspired at the best of times but was not improved by a downpour. He watched a car go past, then another. Nothing distracting there. Then he found himself on his feet again, renewing that steady tread. He swore to himself. He shouldn't allow things to upset him this much, but, if he wasn't disturbed by the things that were happening in his life at the moment, there was something wrong with him. His mind turned this over. He thought of the locked room in Elsa's house. What was going on there? An idea occurred. He dismissed it but it returned. He reached a decision.

He walked out of the flat and over to Elsa's house. It was locked. Of course. He turned to go back to the flat when he thought again, and he went round to the side of the house to see if there was a way in. A section was open at the top of one window and he examined it. He put his hand inside and reached down. There was a handle on the lower half of the window. If he could reach that. But he couldn't. He looked around and saw a convenient garden seat and pulled it over. He climbed onto it and reached his hand through the upper window again, then down. Now he could get at the handle. He pulled at it, opened the window, then climbed in.

He was in a corridor. All was quiet. He walked along the hallway to the living room and opened the drawer in Elsa's desk where the keys were kept. He took them and walked downstairs to the locked room.

Once inside, he stood in front of the pinboard and studied that. There was something curious about it. What was it? He thought of Anna's bedroom as it had been before she moved away to university. Shouldn't there be notes here to remind Rhiannon of this and that? Circles drawn round dates on the calendar to remind her of where she was planning to go to and when? Alex could see a report card, photos from holidays, and a souvenir of a birthday party. These were references to a past life, not one someone was in the middle of living. Weren't they? Or was he getting that wrong? His eyes flicked over the board from one item to the next, then back again. It was as if — no. Probably not. That was an odd thought. But he couldn't dismiss it. This was someone else's view of Rhiannon's life, not her own. It was a record another person had put together. Wasn't it? Or not, because how could that be? And his mind continued to ponder the life of the teenage girl displayed on this board.

He opened the desk drawer and pulled out the diary. He would read some of that this time. He flicked through it. It was not a diary crammed full of the teeming daily happenings of a teenage girl's existence. Some entries were lengthy but there were blank pages, and dates with only a note or two. There was a particularly full account of a birthday party, and he did read all of that. The description of those who attended was detailed as was the list of presents. Funny things had happened, as they would, and people had said complimentary things — and his mind turned to Anna's birthday parties. They had been similar though something had usually gone wrong too. Rhiannon did not mention anything like that in her journal.

Again, what he found himself pondering was the point of view in the diary. It was odd, not at all what he might expect from an account written by a girl for herself. It was as if it was written for someone else so that they could remember what had happened at Rhiannon's party. Perhaps Rhiannon had a dissociative way of viewing things. Was that possible?

He looked again at the list of people at the party. Going by the report card, this girl had been in the same year group as Anna, though she wasn't someone Anna had mentioned. And, not only was Anna not on the list, but he didn't recognise any of the names that were. How could she go to the same school and be in the same year as Anna and know an entirely different set of people? He looked through the names again. No. There was not one there he knew.

His gaze returned to the pinboard. Rhiannon had highly commendable grades. He examined the report sheet itself. It was strange; it was laid out entirely differently from the ones that Anna received; it was not the same report form in any way. Why was that?

He returned to the desk drawer and started looking for the scrapbook that had drawn his attention when he had been there before. Where was it? He drew it out and laid it on the desk. What had he been looking at when he was interrupted? A newspaper article, wasn't it? He turned to it. A report of a road accident. A girl had been killed. Why would Rhiannon want to keep a newspaper report of that? Was it someone she had known? The name of the girl was not mentioned. Neither was the name of the driver. The make of car was. A Vauxhall Astra. A red car. Something occurred to Alex. He looked at the date of the article. Oh no. That wasn't what it was, was it? That would take some thinking about if it was.

There was the sound of a car drawing up outside. Damn. That must be Elsa coming back. He closed the scrapbook and put it back in the drawer before pushing that shut. He glanced round the room. Had he left anything obviously disturbed? He didn't think so. He closed the door to the room and locked it, before legging it and replacing the keys. He left by the same window he had come in by.

FORTY-SEVEN

As he closed the window behind him, he heard a loud hammering. He stepped forward and peered round the corner of the building. A man was knocking energetically on the door of the flat he and Heather had been living in. Definitely not Elsa. A tall man with red hair and an angry expression. What was he doing there? It might be a good idea for Alex to stay hidden from someone in that emotional state. But Alex's curiosity was stronger than his common sense. He took the bull by the horns.

'What do you want?' he asked.

The stranger turned and faced him.

'Alex?' the man said – and the voice was not friendly.

'That's right,' Alex said, then wished he hadn't.

The man walked over to Alex and swung at him. Alex stepped back but was hit by the follow through from the man's other fist. Fortunately, it was not a successful punch even if it had been flung with meaning. The direction was poor, and it was swung from the arm only with none of the man's weight behind it. Alex blinked as he rolled with the blow and shifted his feet.

It was obvious this man had done no boxing, but Alex had, and his fists were now raised in the defensive position. It was a sport he had enjoyed participating in when younger. Even though it was not something he had kept up, he had skill, and he could feel the memories kick in. He was now on the balls of his feet, ready to attempt to move away from the blows. He felt his muscles tense as they readied themselves to give and receive blows.

There was nothing scientific in the method of the man Alex faced. He rushed forward in an intimidating manner, whirling fist after fist at Alex, who found himself struggling to ward off the blows with his arms and wishing he wasn't so out of practice. Alex's feet were dancing back, taking him further away, as the man pushed forward after him. Then Alex found he was managing better than he expected; he was blocking the punches and protecting himself well enough while the man drained himself of that initial energy. Alex readied himself for the opportunity to reply.

The man advanced once more, flailing his arms. Again, Alex was able to block the random blows before moving out of reach. Then Alex hit him with a straight left, which jerked the man's head back. Alex struck him again, before dancing further back again.

Alex found he was breathing reasonably evenly. His attempts to become fitter had reaped a reward. He noticed the man in front of him was starting to gasp. Alex hit him again before moving back. But, give him credit, he wasn't being discouraged. Alex continued to move patiently. This man would not take him.

Alex found himself starting to relax. He was feeling pleased with the way he was handling this. When he'd first seen this stranger coming for him, he had thought he was in trouble. But the man did not know how to fight, which left Alex feeling curious. What was bugging someone like this so much?

'Can we talk about this?' Alex said.

In reply, the man attempted another rush. This time he did hit Alex, jerking his head back twice, and then Alex found himself deflecting more flailing attempts with his arms before the opportunity came to shift his feet away, then land a quick left, following it up with a right that stopped his opponent in his tracks. That must have hurt, Alex thought.

When he had learned boxing in his youth, Alex had been told at the gym he had attended that he was promising. The thought occurred to him that perhaps he should have kept it up. But he didn't deceive himself. If he'd done that, he would have met up with well-trained fighters, not this.

The man came after Alex again, throwing rights and lefts. Some missed and Alex was able to stop others with his arms, before another effort managed to hit the target intended and make Alex grunt. Alex decided he'd had enough of this. He put in a straight left to soften the man up, then quickly landed his best right hook, and the man went down.

Alex had always been proud of that punch. But he knew it was not quite good enough for the ring. It didn't knock anyone out. At the gym they had wanted to work on that with punchbags and exercises with weights.

And he hadn't knocked this man out. But he was seriously discouraged. He did not get up but lay on the ground, gasping for breath. And there was a realisation in his eyes that he wasn't going to get anywhere continuing with this.

'All right,' he said. 'You've got the better of me.'

'Who are you?' Alex said. 'And why do you want to lay me out?'

'But I'm still not going to let you hurt Heather.'

'Who says I'm trying to hurt her?'

'Two murder attempts,' the man said. 'Who are you trying to kid?'

'I'm not trying to murder Heather,' Alex said.

'Somebody is – and there isn't anyone else it can be.'

'It's not me.'

'And it's not just me you're going have to convince. The police are going to have you when they can.'

'Who are you?' Alex said. 'Why are you stepping in to defend Heather?'

'You don't know?'

And it was a bit obvious.

'You're Heather's bit on the side?'

'If you want to put it that way.'

Things that should have meant something at the time started to click into place: times when Heather had hurriedly put her smart phone away when he entered a room; a strange scent that had lingered on her when she returned home – things he had dismissed. And missing time she hadn't quite managed to explain. Like on the night of the fire.

'Heather wasn't with Margaret Affleck on the night of the fire. She was with you?'

'That's right.'

Alex was even more pleased now about that right hook he'd landed.

'There always was something unconvincing about that story. But you're a brave man admitting it.'

Stuart looked up at him from his position on the ground. He fingered a bruised lip.

'Maybe,' he said. 'But don't rule out me coming at you when you're not expecting it.'

'Like just now?' Alex said.

He was tempted to laugh, but it might be a mistake to underestimate the man.

'What's your name?' he said.

'Stuart. Stuart Peattie.'

'Not a name I know. Heather's been keeping you well hidden.'

'I work at the Health Centre too.'

'It's a den of vice? Who'd have thought it? And they go in for so much virtue signalling down there.'

'You should have looked after her better.'

'Stop making excuses for yourself. So what other lover boys has Heather had?'

217

'Be careful how you speak about her.'

'Is there anyone else I should know about?'

'I wouldn't tell you if I knew.'

Alex studied him.

'So, what do you hope to accomplish now you haven't beaten me to a pulp?' Alex asked.

'Not a lot,' Stuart said. 'But you'd still better lay off Heather. If you make another attempt to finish her off, I'll kill you. And I don't care how good you are with your fists.'

And, though Stuart was still seated on the ground when he said this, Alex found himself believing him.

FORTY-EIGHT

Despite the smugness he felt, Alex knew he had been lucky. Inexpert Stuart might have been, but he'd fought with meaning. So, Stuart was Heather's 'fancy man'? At least she had found someone who had feelings for her, and, as she had someone to leave Alex for, it was no surprise she had in present circumstances, though he was still peeved about it. Obviously.

He had always been aware of the extent to which Heather had attempted to keep an eye on him. It would have been difficult not to be. And she'd done it so self-righteously. She'd questioned him about his trips away, and he knew she secretly checked his pockets – and his phone – when she had the chance, which had always irritated him. He'd always accepted it because there was nothing else he could do. He had misbehaved. Though why she continued checking quite so obviously after so many years he had never understood. And now he'd discovered she was seeing someone else. But he could hardly claim the moral high ground after his recent behaviour with Jasmine – and Elsa. Particularly as he didn't regret either encounter.

The sex had been too good. In his mind he still savoured the flavour of his romps. He thought again of Elsa, her scent, the touch of her skin, and the strength of her passion. That had been something to treasure. But what was he turning into?

His mind returned to the locked room. What had he discovered in there? He thought of the date of the crash and the make and colour of car. It had been a favourite story of her father's, that Heather had written off a much-valued car – and it had been that same year the accident in the newspaper article had happened, hadn't it? It must have been round about then anyway. He didn't remember Heather's father saying anything about the make of the vehicle, only that it was new, which had obviously irked. But what had really hurt – her father said – was the colour of it. They had discontinued that model and colour and he wasn't able to get one exactly the same to replace it. And he had been taken with that shade of red. Which was why Alex was so clear that it was red. That part of the story always struck Alex as being silly, which was probably meant to be the point of it. It was told lightly. A bit too lightly maybe. Was Heather's father glossing over something? Because Alex had certainly never been told that anyone had been killed in that accident. And someone had been in the crash reported in that newspaper.

He thought of Heather. All the time he had known her, there had been that tight ball of anxiety under the surface. It had never occurred to him before the reason for it was ominous. And there were those counselling sessions she'd received at different times. He had been told Heather was highly strung and that was the reason for them. Alex had forgiven a lot of the nagging and suspicion because of that, thinking it was his role as the man to be strong and patient.

But was there more to Heather's over-anxious behaviour than that? Had there been a fatality in that car accident of hers?

But no. That couldn't be true. If so, why not tell him?

He thought back to some of the remarks he had received from her. Yes, there could be a deep-seated guilt she needed to put onto someone else. Was that the real fault-line in their relationship? Heather had a secret to keep from him? Maybe more than one?

Heather had misbehaved with Stuart. If Heather ever did return, there would be a shift in the dynamic. He would have the upper hand. Except Alex knew he had behaved badly again. Big time. Not that it mattered, did it? Heather wasn't coming back.

Neither of them would be able to trust the other. And without that there was no relationship. So what next for him? Jasmine? Elsa?

In the meantime, there was this nagging thought that needed to be laid to rest. He needed to know the truth about that car accident of Heather's when she was young. He could check online but there was a better way than that. He could get in touch with her mother and father and ask them.

FORTY-NINE

When Alex drew up in his car outside Heather's parents' house it was with trepidation. As he pulled himself out of his car and walked up to the door, he could see curtains had twitched and someone in the house had seen him coming, which might be no bad thing though he did hope they would actually answer the door to him.

It was Heather's father, Colin Calderwood, who opened the door – with an unfriendly look. He stood there in pointed silence as he waited for Alex to state his business.

'I came to ask you something,' Alex said.

'You've some nerve.'

'You think?' Alex said. He had known Heather's parents for long enough to call on them – more than twenty years – and this was the welcome he received.

'You shouldn't be here at all,' he said. 'The police have said you're to keep away from Heather.'

'And you think that's all right, do you?' Alex said.

'It's a sensible precaution.'

'It's bloody insulting,' Alex said. 'I haven't been trying to kill Heather. And, for heaven's sake, you've known me for so long. You must know that's a load of rubbish.'

'There have been a couple of attempts on her life,' Colin told him. 'What attitude do you think they're going to take?'

'I might forgive them but I'm damned if I'm going to forgive you.'

There was an awkward silence after that, broken by Colin, when he said, 'So is that all you came to tell us?'

'Obviously not, though it was worth saying.'

'So what do you want?'

'I wanted to ask–' But Alex did not know quite how to put what he wanted to say, though, after Colin's harsh words, he didn't know why he should worry about trampling over his feelings. 'It's just – has she told you she's got another man? You know about Stuart?'

At least Colin had the good grace to look embarrassed. 'We found out recently. But then, if things have become so bad between you–'

'What can I expect?'

'Well, yes.'

And there was a judgemental look on Colin's face to go along with that. Heather had always been able to rely on support from her parents. Perhaps if they hadn't spoiled her so much, things might have turned out differently.

'And he's been round to try to beat me up,' Alex said.

Colin looked shocked at that at least.

'Has he? I didn't know anything about that.'

'I sent him away with a few bruises.'

'What did you do to him? Is he all right?'

'I did less to him than he was trying to do to me.'

And now Alex paused.

'Not that it's Stuart I wanted to talk about. Though – as we are doing that – if she needs to have someone on the side, couldn't she find anyone better than him?'

Colin tried to close the conversation.

'Can I ask you to leave now?' he said and started to shut the door.

Alex put his foot in it.

'You're not going to bash me about, are you?' Colin asked him.

'No,' Alex said. 'I didn't mean to bring all of that up. It's only – well, you ought to know about it.'

'Why are you round here bothering us?' Colin said. 'The police were clear. You're to stay away. Do I have to call them?'

Alex sighed. 'It's just—'

He'd handled this badly and he wasn't going to get anything out of Colin.

'What I wanted to ask about was – do we really need to talk on your doorstep? Couldn't I come in so we can discuss this in private?'

'You definitely can't come in.'

He was going to have to walk away with his questions unasked, Alex supposed. Then he decided he would put them to Colin anyway.

'About that car accident Heather had years ago. You know when she wrote your car off?'

'What about it? I've tried to be as patient with you as I know how but, really, I think it's time I phoned the police.'

And Colin proceeded to take his phone out of his pocket.

'No. Don't do that,' Alex said. 'That accident no one ever talks about. Don't you think it might be an idea if we did? There's been another one and there could be a link. I didn't tamper with Heather's car. I'm bound to know whether I did or not and I didn't. It hasn't occurred to you someone might be taking revenge on Heather for something she did – even if it was years ago? Can you tell me all you know about the people whose daughter was killed in that accident?'

Colin was staring at him, and Alex was trying to work out what might be going on in his head, but Colin still didn't say anything. Then Colin opened the door wide, as he stepped back and motioned Alex in.

FIFTY

Alex found himself seated in the Calderwoods' living room being treated as a guest, which was more familiar. There were nervous smiles on their faces and Alison had gone so far as to offer tea, which he refused.

When he spoke again, Colin's tone was apologetic. 'I feel bad about trying to turn you away,' he said, 'but we've been going through hell, and I didn't know what to think. The police said we shouldn't let you anywhere near Heather – and Heather's terrified of you. So it made sense, even if she isn't here at the moment. It's where she's staying.'

Then he ran out of words and Alison spoke, though she seemed to be filling the silence as much as anything.

'We've always thought highly of you, Alex. And you and Heather have been together for such a long time—'

But Alex didn't want to listen to meaningless words.

'You still haven't told me anything about the person whose child was killed,' Alex said.

'Heather didn't want you to know about the accident at all,' Colin said.

'Which is ridiculous,' Alex replied. 'Husbands and wives can't have secrets like that.'

'And you've never had any?' Colin said.

Alex winced.

'That affair of yours really hurt Heather.'

Alex thought of a few things to say in his defence but didn't.

'Which was why we told you about Heather's accident then. We wanted to tell you about the child, but Heather was desperate you shouldn't know, and we just went along with it. But we did tell you about the car crash. We hoped if you understood her a bit better you might take more care of her. Heather was besotted with you. And that accident affected her. She was a bundle of nerves after that. The only thing that settled her was you – and then you behaved like that – just after she'd had your baby.'

'If it helps, I felt like a heel.'

'You were one. And it doesn't.'

Alex noticed that reassuring air of Colin's had not lasted long. He knew Heather had been his and Alison's only, their precious baby. Alex wondered if that was really why she was such an anxious wreck at times: Colin and Alison had never let go of her.

'You both got on with things. And everything seemed to settle down OK.' Why was there something grudging in the way he said that? 'Heather always thought the world of you.'

The subtext was clear. 'Even if I didn't.'

Alex was beginning to wonder if Colin would ever get round to discussing what Alex had asked him.

'The solicitor we used at the time said it was best not to have any personal contact with the victim's parents. It wouldn't help. After the investigation and the inquest, we did send round a letter of sympathy and apology for what was an accident Heather could not have avoided. We did have compassion for them, but they didn't seem to want to meet up with us either and we didn't get in touch again after that. There was no point. What could anyone do? No one could bring the girl back to life again. And we didn't think there was any chance Heather would be forgiven for it.'

'What can you tell me about the girl's parents?'

'It was a young couple. The husband was some kind of salesman. The woman worked in a shop. I think she was a bit busy and harassed that morning. Don't ask me why she wasn't keeping her daughter closer to her than she did. I know Heather lost control of the car, but it was as much the mother's fault.'

'We never met them,' Alison said.

'Heather has never met the mother?'

'Nobody thought it wise.'

'What was the daughter's name?'

'It was a pretty name,' Alison said. 'And it must have been awful for her mother. It was dreadful for a girl to die so young.'

Then she became lost in thought.

'What was she called?' Alex asked.

'It was Rhiannon,' Alison replied.

FIFTY-ONE

After he left, Alex pondered what to do next. He should be at work. They would be thinking he had left. But his thoughts couldn't settle in that direction. He returned to the flat, where he found himself pacing yet again. He stopped doing that and stared from the window instead. But the view of tarmac and grass blurred before rampant thoughts.

It was when he'd realised the significance of the newspaper article that he'd decided it was Elsa who was trying to kill Heather. As he'd shared Elsa's bed, what kind of person did that make him?

For most of the time he had known Elsa, he hadn't given thought to her. She'd cleaned their house, and he'd been polite to her – he'd always been polite, hadn't he – but conversations had been minimal.

It had been a shock when she'd offered them a flat to stay in because it had never occurred to him that someone like Elsa would be able to do that. Though he'd always known she owned the cleaning company she worked for, which, on reflection, should have told him something.

And had it been his idea or hers they'd ended up in bed together? He was not sure. All he remembered was enjoying it. But he hadn't been stalked, had he?

He thought of the locked room, which was so much like a shrine to Elsa's dead daughter – not that he thought Rhiannon had ever even seen it. She hadn't lived long enough to reach adolescence. Elsa must have imagined that whole teenage life of Rhiannon's, and Elsa herself must have written the diary and fabricated the report cards. She'd even made up a birthday party and gone on to describe it in chilling detail. It had been her way of keeping her daughter alive. But what kind of person did that?

Elsa was obsessed. Alex wondered to what extent the fixation had taken her over. Did she see Rhiannon, hear her, and speak with her? Elsa was obviously mad, but exactly how crazy was she?

And what to do about it? He should tell the police. But tell them what? They thought he was the one trying to kill Heather so why would they believe anything he told them? He did have evidence, the locked room, but what would they think of that? Would they just see Elsa as someone mourning her daughter? And were they so blinkered about him they would think he was coming up with red herrings to draw attention away from himself?

Elsa Harrison couldn't be her real name. That would have rung alarm bells for Heather – and her parents. Unless she'd gone back to her maiden name. Certainly, the name of the girl in that article, the one who'd been killed, was Reid.

He thought of Heather again. She couldn't ever have recovered from that accident. Anxiety had never been far away from her, and it had placed barriers between them. And that must have been caused by guilt. But he'd loved her. He couldn't stand by while Elsa made more murder attempts.

He thought more about Elsa. She had not only made up a life for her daughter; she'd invented one for herself. She'd been planning this for some time; she'd bought the house in Nairn and set up the cleaning company to get close to them. How cold and calculating was that?

But what was it the police had said? They could believe Alex was trying to murder Heather because one, it would solve his financial problems, two, it would give him a way out of what they described as an acrimonious marriage, and three, it would give him the freedom to pursue his amorous inclinations. They had put forward excellent arguments for him wanting Heather dead.

Alex probed his feelings towards her. Certainly, he had loved her. But the police were right about him being in a situation where he could find motivation. And there was frustration in him. Exactly what else did he feel about Heather now? She'd been a difficult wife at times. And now, to crown it all, she'd left him for someone else.

Suddenly he felt tired. He had been through so much lately and his mind felt as if it were being worn down by having to think through so much. Which was the excuse he made to himself for the idea that occurred to him: could he do nothing and instead let Elsa succeed with her plan? Heather had given up on him; perhaps he should give up on her. But that was crazy. This was Heather he was thinking of. Were his feelings for her so little now? And was he that sort of person? Was he so callous? But, if the thought had occurred, perhaps he was.

He heard the crunch of someone's shoe in the gravel of the drive and looked out. It was Elsa.

FIFTY-TWO

Alex listened to Elsa entering her own house and hoped she didn't notice he'd been snooping around, but there was nothing to be done about it if she did. Then he heard her closing the door before walking over to the flat and knocking.

She was relaxed as she strolled in, put her arms round him and kissed him. He took a firm grip on his thoughts and emotions and returned the kiss. Until he did work out how to respond to all of this, he would have to pretend things were the same as they'd been. The look on Elsa's face was smug and irritating but he'd make sure it stayed like that – even if she was treating him like a possession. Elsa was sitting down on the sofa and patting the seat beside her. Alex sat down too and she gave him another kiss.

'A good day?' he said.

An odd question to ask someone he knew had planned two murder attempts. What was a good day to a person like that?

'I've been training a new cleaning operative,' she said.

'Since when have they been called that?' Alex said. 'What's wrong with the old-fashioned word cleaner?'

Elsa laughed. Alex wondered at how clear-eyed and innocent she looked. Was that what people who schemed to murder looked like?

'She's young and fit. She should have plenty of stamina.'

'You make her sound like a horse you're thinking of buying,' Alex said.

'Cleaning takes a lot out of you. You'd be surprised. I doubt if you've done a day's housework in your life.'

The conversation felt so ordinary. He didn't really think she was a murderer, did he?

He tried to pretend the spell was still there, the bond that exists between two people who have recently become lovers, and tried to dismiss the thought of the secret room in Elsa's house.

'Have you had a good day?' Elsa asked him. Then her brow furrowed. 'Is everything OK?'

At least he could discuss the fight. That might cover any difference she noticed in him.

'Apart from having to defend myself against an extremely angry man determined to beat me into a pulp, it was fine,' he said.

'What? You're joking?'

'Unfortunately not. It turns out Heather has a lover, a young man called Stuart. He's bought the party line I'm trying to kill Heather. And he objects. He was warning me off.'

'God. He didn't hurt you, did he? But what happened?'

'Fortunately, he doesn't know much about fighting.'

'And you do? I didn't know that.' Elsa's eyes had widened.

'I did a bit of boxing when I was younger. Enough for him anyway.'

'I'm glad of that,' Elsa said. 'You didn't get hurt, did you?'

'No.'

Then Alex shook his head as he gave more thought to that encounter. 'He did warn me off though. He really thinks I'm trying to do Heather in.'

'God, how awful.'

'Did you know there's been another murder attempt on Heather?'

Alex watched Elsa as he said this, but the surprise on Elsa's face looked real. Perhaps she was expert in dissimulation; someone who lived under a false name, particularly for the purposes she seemed to, would be good at that.

'You're joking? What happened? Is Heather OK?'

'She survived. Not that I've been to see her – and I'm not allowed to. I'm the one trying to kill her. That's what she thinks. And the police agree.'

'But why?'

And Alex explained the financial advantages as they'd been explained to him. And the other possible reasons.

'The devious police mind,' Elsa said. 'They could invent a motivation for murder that would fit anybody.'

'They have a lot of belief in mine.'

'But what happened? You still haven't told me.'

'It was a car accident near Logie. Someone tampered with the car. And I don't even know enough about cars to do that.'

'She must be going through hell,' Elsa said. 'And you must. Poor you.'

'The police have interviewed me about it. They're checking out my alibi.'

'How do they know when the car was tampered with?'

'A good question. Anyway, they wanted to know about all of my movements around then.'

'And you've got an alibi?'

'I wasn't with anyone. I was at the cinema by myself. They're going to try to verify that.'

'Will they be able to?'

'Who knows? You'd think there would be CCTV cameras around there somewhere. The problem is you never know which ones are dummy and which are real. But hopefully there were some cameras that were actually taking pictures.'

Alex looked at her. She looked so warm and real, like someone you could just throw your arms around for a hug when you were feeling low. Perhaps he was easily fooled by people. Then Elsa put her arms around him and he returned the embrace. Was he so taken with Elsa he didn't mind the fact she was trying to murder Heather? They kissed some more, then hands strayed, and clothing, as Elsa pushed, pulled and hugged him into the bedroom. And he didn't seem to mind.

Afterwards, Alex lay back and relaxed. There had been an urgent passion in him – how sick was that? But the tension that had built up in him had been massive and it had been good to let go of some of it. His body felt good with Elsa. Though his mind didn't. What else was there he had not discovered about the woman who lay in this bed beside him?

He knew her name was not her own and she had adopted the life she lived to get close to Heather to gain revenge. That was cold. And was there anything else she was hiding? What was he doing? Why was he toying with the idea of letting Elsa succeed with her plan so he could be free of Heather?

He looked at Elsa and the self-satisfied grin on her face. She reached out her hand and stroked his cheek, and he accepted this, enjoyed it.

But his head was reaching its own decision. The police might not believe anything he said, but he did need to go over and warn Heather about Elsa.

FIFTY-THREE

Heather

'Alex was over here?'

It was next morning, and Heather had been released from hospital after her test results confirmed she was fine. But she was furious when she returned to her parents and discovered that Alex had visited.

'There's not much I can do about it if Alex decides to turn up. We did tell him he wasn't welcome.'

But the look on her father's face was a guilty one and Heather wanted to know why.

'He says he's worried about you.'

That from her mother. What was this?

'You both talked to him. That means you let him in the house?'

The silence from her parents told Heather all she wanted to know.

'Why on earth did you do that?' Heather realised she was starting to shriek but continued anyway. 'He's been trying to kill me. There have been two attempts on my life. And it's Alex.'

'You can't be sure of that,' her father said – and how unbelievable was it he had said that? It must have been Alex. Who else stood to benefit?

'The police say Alex isn't to be allowed anywhere near me. Isn't that enough for you?'

'Your father did attempt to turn him away,' Heather's mother said.

'I tried to stop him at the door,' and there was a pleading tone in her father's voice.

'He told him to leave several times,' her mother added.

Then her father's stumbling voice continued. 'But it was something he was saying.'

'And what on earth could that have been?' Heather said. 'What could be more important than preventing him from trying to kill me.'

'He was asking about the parents of the child who died.'

'Child? What child?'

Heather's mind whirled around. Then it screamed to a halt, focused on something that was so resolutely dismissed from her consciousness it was nevertheless always there somewhere in the background – and here it was right in front of her, triumphant and jeering, that memory from twenty years ago. The child she'd killed. And how could Alex have possibly known about that?

'What?' she said, her voice now a mass of uncertainty. 'That girl, Rhiannon?'

'That's right,' her father said.

Good old reliable Dad. Why was he reminding her of what he shouldn't? The ghost that haunted her. But his voice was kind even if she reeled from it. Heather sat down suddenly, her arms grasping at the arms of the chair.

'Why would Alex be asking about her?' she said. 'How could he know anything about that? He was never supposed to.'

Her father and mother sat down opposite, patient if worried looks on their faces. But Heather noticed they did not answer the question.

'He said there might be a link,' Colin said. 'A child was killed in a collision with a car you were driving – and now there's been an attempt to kill you in another road accident. He was asking about the parents of the girl who was killed.'

'And your father wondered if there might be anything in it and asked him to come in to talk about it a bit more. That was all.'

Heather thought about this.

'But we've never had any communication with them,' she said, 'and they've never come anywhere near us. We don't even know where they're living these days. And why on earth would they suddenly turn up after all this time and do this? It doesn't make any sense.'

'Maybe not,' Colin said. 'But it didn't seem to be doing any harm to talk about it. It's something to consider.'

'And Alex says it's definitely not him who's trying to do these things to you,' Alison added.

'Well, he would, wouldn't he? You can't go by that.'

'And we know Alex,' her father said. 'He's never struck me as being a murderer.'

'It was your father who was always warning you about Alex,' her mother said, 'and he doesn't think Alex would go that far.'

'Can you tell by how a person strikes you?' Heather asked.

'You watch too many TV crime dramas,' her father said. 'You don't know anything about these things.'

'And it might not be possible to tell if someone's capable of murder,' her mother said, 'but I'm sure you can tell when someone isn't.'

Heather didn't think she followed the logic of that.

'But we would know if some stranger was around the place looking for opportunities, surely?' she said.

'Or not,' her father said. 'I don't know.'

And there was a weariness on his face and in his voice that communicated itself to Heather. There had been so much going on and it was wearing them all down.

'If it's not Alex – and the police don't have him in custody, do they? – then it's somebody else,' her mother said. 'And who would have a stronger motive than the parents of the child you killed?'

The circumstances were so different, but the tone in her mother's voice was the one she used when reminding Heather of the importance of working on her studies, and warning her against unsuitable boyfriends, and so much else. It was the one Heather was so used to paying attention to.

It would be nice to think it might not be Alex; it had been such a weight thinking her husband of all people might be trying to kill her. Just the thought Alex might be innocent made her feel better.

But if Rhiannon's parents were around here somewhere plotting against her, where were they? More to the point, who were they? Heather's mind flitted over all the people she knew. She wished she had met up with these people at the time. Did she even have any idea what they looked like? She remembered the photograph she'd seen of them, though, after so many years, their appearance could have changed a lot. And she didn't have a copy. Did her parents? She asked them.

But the helpless look on their faces was enough of a reply.

'Maybe the police have one,' Colin said.

The police, Heather thought. Maybe. And when she thought about it, the police needed to be told Alex had been round here, where he wasn't supposed to be.

There had been two murder attempts on her life, and it was still possible it had been him. The police should be making sure he stayed away, even if it meant posting someone here. They'd seemed to think she was safe after leaving hospital, which was why they hadn't done that already – and she hadn't followed the logic of that.

FIFTY-FOUR

When Stuart turned up, Heather was pleased. She had been feeling washed out with agonising over this and that. The hello again kiss was like a long cool drink on a very hot day somewhere near the equator – not that she'd ever been there. She was glad to see him anyway. When she pulled away from the kiss, she had another look at him.

'You're looking a bit battered, my love,' she said. 'But I suppose you would. You went over to see Alex, didn't you? Did you manage to warn him off?'

'He won't be having another go at you,' Stuart said with impressive confidence.

But he was too bruised to be convincing.

'If you hadn't rushed off like that, I would have had time to warn you,' she said. 'Alex is good with his fists. He didn't hurt you too badly, did he?'

'He didn't manage to land a punch,' Stuart said.

Which Heather knew was a lie, looking at the dents in Stuart.

'I went gently with him.'

Oh yes? she thought.

'But I was firm about him not coming anywhere near you.'

'That's why he turned up at my parents' house then, is it?' Heather said.

'What?'

'Never mind. I'm sure he'll forget about the murder attempts, dearest.' She shouldn't mock Stuart, but it was difficult with him being so much younger than her, even if that was what she liked about him.

'What was he doing over at your parents?' Stuart asked.

'He was telling them it wasn't him who's been trying to kill me.'

'Who else could it be?' Stuart asked.

Should she tell Stuart? If he meant so much to her, she ought to, and she had at least managed to tell him about the accident, if not the child she had killed.

How important was Stuart to her? Their affair seemed to have happened all by itself. She had responded to his young, hard body without thinking of anything else. And why was that? Where had she been in herself and her marriage to behave like that? And where was she now she had left her husband? What did she want for the future? Did she want something more permanent with Stuart? She had to stop and give consideration to him now. His rushing off to see to Alex had been appreciated. But it had been impulsive. There had been no maturity there. Could she discuss anything properly with him? And he probably wouldn't leave his wife for her anyway.

Then she said it.

'It could be revenge because of the child I killed.'

And why had she said it in that challenging way? She never talked about that incident like that.

'What?' Stuart said.

With his mouth open in that silly way, Stuart looked even younger than he usually did. But she supposed she ought to forgive him that impression of stupidity. She attempted to alleviate the shock.

'It was twenty years ago. I had an accident with a car. I wasn't at fault and that was official. Hazardous road conditions were to blame. It was raining, the road was covered with water, and the car sort of took off out of my control. And she was standing in the wrong place.'

'How awful for you,' Stuart said.

'And for her,' Heather said. 'I've never been able to forget what happened.'

'I suppose you wouldn't be able to.'

Heather realised that Stuart was floundering. Which was all right. Why wouldn't he?

'Do you think it's possible that someone whose child was killed in a road traffic accident would turn up twenty years later and try to get revenge by killing the driver?' she asked.

Stuart was flummoxed by that.

'I don't know,' he said. 'Maybe. Who were the parents?'

Heather could only give him their names, she knew so little else about them.

FIFTY-FIVE

Alex

Alex also went over to the Calderwoods that day, once he'd found out Heather had been released from hospital and that was where she must be. He didn't see the police car in front; he had approached the house from the rear to avoid Heather's parents; he didn't know there was a policeman on guard. All he'd been thinking was if he was ever so lucky, he would come across Heather by herself in the back garden. Not that he could be as fortunate as that, could he? Yet he knew the layout of that garden and the summer house that lay in it.

It lay in a sheltered spot right at the bottom. It was a pleasant garden laid out to shrubs and flower beds, with a sun dial, a pond, a bird table and feeder. And Heather had often talked of time she had spent in that summer house as a teenager. Whenever she had been low or had problems to work out, she retreated there. It had been a while since she had stayed with her parents, but Alex had to hope old habits died hard.

And how lucky could he be? She was there, inside, in the shade, looking out on the green splendour. It was winter, of course, and not at its best, but those neat shrubs and that well-kept leylandii hedge still made for an acceptable effort at a rural idyll.

Alex heard the rustle of a newspaper before he saw her. Oh no, he thought, it wasn't her father in there, was it? But it was Heather, leaning back on a lounger, a relaxed expression on her face. She must feel well away from the stresses they had found themselves caught up in.

'Heather,' he said.

That shattered her peace. She sat bolt upright and stared around her. When she saw him, the fear in her eyes hurt Alex.

'Heather,' he said again, and he tried to make the tone of his voice so gentle. 'It's only me. Can't we talk?'

She looked as if she might make a bolt for it or find something to throw at him. Then she relaxed and the moment when she might have shouted for help had passed.

'What are you doing here?' she asked. And her voice was normal, as if it was a casual query she might have made at any time. Which surprised him. How much were her feelings swinging around?

'I need to warn you,' he said. 'I know who's trying to kill you.'

'You do?' She stared at him as she tried to take this in. Then she reached her decision. 'You'd better come in,' she said.

And Alex stepped into the summer house and sat beside her.

'So who is it?' she asked.

'Elsa.'

'Elsa?' And Alex did not think he had ever seen Heather look so surprised.

'She's the one stalking you.'

'Elsa? But why would she do that?'

'She's the mother of the girl you killed in that road accident.'

'Elsa is? But she's – she hid that well. I thought she was just, well, the woman who cleaned our house. I don't believe you.'

'Believe it,' Alex said. 'Elsa Harrison's not her real name,' he said. 'She's that woman, Reid. The mother of that girl, Rhiannon. She's taken on a completely new identity to get close to you and take her revenge.'

'What?'

And it sounded unbelievable that the easy, light-hearted person they knew as Elsa could be doing something like that. But Alex knew it was true.

'She set fire to our house,' he said. 'And she tampered with your car. God knows what she's planning next. I had to see you and warn you that it's her.'

Heather still looked disbelieving.

'She's completely mad,' Alex said. 'There's this locked room in her house. And you should see it. She's made up a totally fictitious life for her dead daughter. And it's all over the room. She hasn't let go. She still lives with all of that. She maybe even sees her for all I know. She's not going to give up. She's off her head.'

And Alex explained about discovering and exploring that, and the things he had found inside it. Then something seemed to click in Heather, and Alex could see she had taken it all in now and was working things out properly.

'Have you told the police?' she said.

'I'm going to. I came round to warn you first. I needed to know you were safe before I did anything.'

'You haven't said anything to them yet? Don't you need to hurry up?'

Alex reached for his phone. 'I'm sorry,' he said. 'I'll phone them now. And I'm here. I'll look out for you.'

'Phone them? You don't need to do that. There's a policeman in the house who's supposed to be protecting me. I don't know how he missed you. He knows where I am. Tell him.'

'OK,' Alex said, though he didn't feel much like leaving her by herself. 'But come with me.'

But Heather didn't. He supposed she thought it would only be for a moment – which wouldn't matter, would it?

FIFTY-SIX

Elsa

Elsa had watched Heather's parents' house to try to find out what she needed to know – where Heather was – and when Heather retreated to the summer house to be by herself she realized that would be her best chance to kill her.

She thought it must be very relaxing for Heather to sit with the day's paper and look out into this green cocoon, and she resented her pleasure in it. She would make sure her peace and quiet did not last much longer. Elsa would need to use a different method this time though. It was a great pity the first fire hadn't finished Heather off – or the road accident.

There needed to be proper recompense for the death of Rhiannon. Elsa had not been able to believe the outcome of the judicial proceedings. If Heather couldn't control a car she shouldn't have been driving. And the total consequences for Heather had been she'd lost her licence for a few years. Lost her licence? Rhiannon had lost her life.

And Elsa had been so embittered by it that she had ended up not only losing her daughter but also her husband. Lindsay had tried to be patient with Elsa but he could never understand her need for revenge. It had seethed inside her; she had buried her daughter but not her memory of her and definitely not her love for her. Lindsay had said in the end he could not live with Elsa's bitterness anymore. And she didn't blame him.

Lindsay had been a good car mechanic, and she had learned a lot from him. He had been curious at the interest in cars she had acquired after Rhiannon's death, but she'd been listless for so long he thought it good she was taking an interest in anything, and he had been a patient and careful teacher.

It was when he realised what she'd been learning from him he decided to leave her. Not that he'd ever voiced the accusation in his mind. But when she knew enough to tamper with Heather's car she lost interest – and she supposed it was too obvious what was in her mind. Her first plan had been that Heather should die in a road accident as Rhiannon had.

She had taken her time over it. She wanted to know every detail of Heather's life so she could appreciate how much Heather was going to lose. And when the opportunity had arisen, she had moved to Nairn and started contriving at getting close to Heather.

The idea of justice by fire had been accidental. It had come about when she'd discovered there was a local fire-raiser, and she'd realised all she had to do was copy his methods – they had even published something about them in the local paper – then let him take the blame for the murder of Heather. And no one would suspect her, justice would be served and Elsa would finally be free.

Not that she'd been able to act for some time. Anna was as innocent of any wrongdoing as Rhiannon had been, so she had waited till Anna had left home and gone to university. And she had wanted Alex to be away so he could suffer loss in the way she had. And she'd gloated as she watched her victim go through her everyday life without guessing at the justice she would soon be facing. Then Elsa had reached her moment of decision. Let the flame of revenge burn she had thought as she had lit the fire.

When Elsa had discovered Heather hadn't been in the building, and all she had done was burn down a house, she'd been bitterly disappointed. That was why she had drawn a bunch of car keys right up the side of Alex's car. Which she was ashamed of. That had been pique and totally without subtlety. But she had her original plan to fall back on and she'd arranged the car crash without any serious difficulty. She even had Alex down as an alibi for herself for the night before the crash. It was very convenient his returning to the flat just after she'd returned from doing her work on Heather's car. So that it was even more annoying when Heather escaped the crash. But Elsa would fix things now.

She wasn't happy about the murder method she had chosen this time; she'd been reduced to looking on the internet for ideas. But it had been easy to locate a page on making a petrol bomb. Did the police know how simple that was? It was criminal of them to allow pages like that to exist on the internet. They ought to do something about it. When the time came to commit the crime, Elsa did not know about the policeman who had recently taken up guard at Heather's parents' house. It was luck she'd decided to approach the house from the rear and managed not to be spotted.

Elsa lay close to a hedgerow, hidden behind a tree, and tried to look part of the landscape as she prepared herself. Then Alex turned up. Damn, she thought, but fortunately he didn't look in her direction.

After arriving, Alex talked to Heather. It was hardly sweetness and light but Heather allowed him into the summerhouse all the same. Perhaps she should kill him as well as Heather. She had enjoyed her time with him, but that had mostly been revenge. She'd lost Lindsay because of Heather after all. Elsa had toyed with keeping Alex after it was all over. But something else occurred to her now.

The police suspected Alex of trying to kill his wife; he had even been told to stay away from her. It was good of him to turn up now to take the blame. All she had to do was wait till Alex had left and she could step forward with her bomb.

FIFTY-SEVEN

Alex

Sure enough, when Alex walked round to the front of the house, the first thing he saw was a blue, yellow, red, and white police car. There was no one in it and Alex thought if this was an attempt to give Heather police protection it was not very good – until the door of the house opened and a policeman walked towards him. At the same time another car pulled in, and Alex took in the figure of Stuart driving it. Stuart's face looked alarmed when he saw Alex, who also thought this was a complication he could do without. Stuart opened the door and started towards Alex.

'You're not supposed to be anywhere near Heather,' he was shouting. 'What are you doing here?'

'Go take a running jump,' Alex replied. 'You're not looking for another pasting, are you?'

But he thought it was probably not a good idea to say that with a policeman right beside him.

The policeman looked bemused as much as anything. Two angry men facing up to each other and one of them was Alex, the man he was supposed to be protecting Heather from.

'Calm down the two of you,' he said, 'and explain yourselves. What's this about?'

'I'm not up to anything,' Stuart said. 'I've come round to see my girlfriend. But you ought to be asking him what he's doing here. Is Heather all right? He hasn't done anything to her, has he?'

'Of course I haven't harmed Heather,' Alex said. 'I'm only here to make sure that she's safe.'

'Safe? He's likely to try to murder her again,' Stuart said.

'As if,' Alex said.

'He's violent,' Stuart said. 'He's beaten me up.'

'In self-defence,' Alex said. 'He attacked me.'

'And you don't want to go believing him,' Stuart said. 'Where's Heather? She is OK, isn't she?'

'You two have been fighting?' the policeman said. 'When was this?'

'This is a waste of time,' Alex said. 'I came round to warn Heather.'

'Warn her? Are you threatening her?' Stuart said.

'Grow up, Stuart, and start listening to what I'm trying to say.'

'Heather needs to be protected from him,' Stuart said.

'And I'm trying to tell you, constable, who Heather needs to be protected from.'

Then the front door of the house opened and Heather's father came out.

'What's all this about?' he said. 'Alex, you were told to go away.'

Heather's mother was standing beside him saying, 'Alex, it really would be a lot easier if you left.'

Then Stuart chipped in again.

'Have you not got the message yet?'

Stuart was shouting; Alex was attempting to be reasonable.

'I came round here to talk to you, constable,' he said. 'Not that I'm getting much chance. The person you need to watch out for is Elsa Harrison, our cleaner. She's the one trying to kill Heather.'

'And there's no way anyone would be stupid enough to believe that,' Stuart said. 'He's trying to divert attention from himself.'

Then Stuart was walking towards him and Alex was thinking he was going to have to be handy with his fists again when they all heard it. It was a noise like a sudden breaking of glass, and it was followed by a loud whoosh like flames bursting out.

FIFTY-EIGHT

Heather

Heather had been alarmed by everything Alex told her and was glad of the space to get her thoughts and feelings in order. She could put a face on her fears now. Elsa. Elsa was the malignant entity behind the destruction of their house and the accident to Heather's car. Heather had been fooled by her, had thought her inconsequential. But then hadn't that been what Elsa had wanted?

The guilt of what she had done had never left Heather even if she had managed to dismiss it to the back of her mind most of the time. If Elsa only knew of the agony Heather had gone through. Perhaps she could talk to Elsa and explain. It wasn't as if walking away from things had helped.

And she had blamed Alex for so much; and hadn't she driven him away? Alex's face swam before her. The typical expression on it, when she thought of it, was uncomprehending patience.

And the fact she'd been unfaithful with Stuart had nothing to do with Alex. Wasn't she trying to recover her lost youth? And wasn't that a self-indulgent waste of time? She'd always been self-absorbed and self-centred, which was in part what she'd allowed anxiety to do to her. She looked for comforts instead of facing up to things.

And she had two men now. What a muddled mess. And what a thing to do to Alex.

Alex hadn't been trying to kill her. Imagine her thinking that of him. And the way she'd treated him because of that. What must that have felt like? And she couldn't make that up to him.

But perhaps she could do something practical. She wondered what kind of time Alex was having with the police constable. He hadn't come back with him. She could at least go out front and help explain things. Perhaps he was arresting Alex for turning up here at all.

She stood up and walked to the door of the summer house. It was such a lovely view from it. Or it usually was. What was spoiling it now was the fact that Elsa was there, just in front of the doorway, and walking in her direction. And what was that in her hand? That was unbelievable. That wasn't what a petrol bomb looked like, was it?

Elsa stopped, looked down at the flaming bottle she was holding and raised it ready to throw.

FIFTY-NINE

They had gone round to the back of the garden in a rush, Alex, Stuart, the policeman, and Heather's parents. Alex somehow managed to find himself ahead of the rest, but not by much. Even Colin and Alison had found some speed at their age.

The sight that met Alex's eyes appalled him.

* * *

Heather hadn't known her reactions were so good. She was able to throw the door open with sufficient force to knock the petrol bomb from its arc and back towards Elsa.

Heather had never seen anyone burst into flames and hoped never to again.

Then the others appeared out of nowhere. The policeman was the most purposeful. When the others saw Elsa in flames they were taken aback. He had his jacket off and put it over her, trying to douse the flames.

SIXTY

Alex

It didn't feel right to stay in Elsa's flat even if they technically had tenants' rights. Alex and Heather had only come back to fetch things. Heather's parents had offered to put both of them up while they got something sorted out.

'I'm sorry,' Heather was saying, and she really did sound as if she felt she'd treated him badly – and he had to admit it was pleasant to have a contrite wife to deal with for a change. 'I should have known it wasn't you.'

And she'd said that a few times too.

'I'm sorry it took so long for me to work it out,' Alex said.

'How could you have known?'

'We should have talked more,' he said.

'It's good to hear that from you. You never want to talk about anything.'

'And it turns out you were the one who couldn't talk about things. You should have told me about Rhiannon.'

'It seems you're right,' Heather said.

'But I've been a rat to you. I should never have misbehaved with Jasmine.'

Now a harder look appeared on Heather's face.

'I agree with that,' she said.

But a guilty look followed that.

'Though I behaved as badly,' she said. 'With Stuart. And I'm sorry.'

And if Alex was being honest, he couldn't stop himself feeling for Stuart. This was a man who had been prepared to stand up for Heather against a murderous husband – and she'd dumped him. When she came to her senses she'd said. Much to Stuart's chagrin, Alex would have thought.

Though he was pleased to have Heather back, he did feel guilt. He should have helped her heal better than he had. He had never managed to get close to the part of Heather damaged by that car accident and the death of Rhiannon. Perhaps something like that could never be completely recovered from. If only she'd told him. But he should have found a way. Well, he would try to find out how to help her now. And they'd discovered they had more in common than they thought. They were both deeply flawed. Which had made them be honest with each other. Perhaps that was something that could build a bond.

And talking of bonds, they needed to do something more to help Anna and Zac. He was such an unfortunate choice of boyfriend for Anna, but he was entitled to his feelings, and there had been that suspicion of him from the police – and Heather. And how was Anna supposed to cope with everything that had been going on between him and Heather – and Jasmine and Stuart?

But what was burning in his mind was the sight he'd had of Elsa in flames; that was something he might never recover from. It was dreadful to think she was dead. And how easy would Heather find it to get over that? She was the one who had caused the bomb to burst over Elsa. But

Elsa had been trying to do that to Heather. Elsa's desire for vengeance had ended up consuming herself.

He consoled himself with the thought Heather might find strength from it; it had been a decisive act of self-preservation that might even give her the strength to overcome some of her anxieties.

Fortunately, the police didn't want to charge her with anything as they'd seen it as a simple act of self-defence. It would have complicated things if they had seen it any other way.

And at least he and Heather had been straight with each other now. Wasn't that what good relationships were based on? Not that he'd told her about him and Elsa, only Jasmine. Talking about Elsa would be difficult. He would have to think about that.

.

If you enjoyed this book, please let others know by leaving a quick review on Amazon. Also, if you spot anything untoward in the paperback, get in touch. We strive for the best quality and appreciate reader feedback.

editor@thebookfolks.com

www.thebookfolks.com

MORE FICTION BY JAMES ANDREW

The Yorkshire Murders series:

The Body Under The Sands
Death Waits For No Lady
The Riddle Of The Dunes
The Suitcase Murderer

All of these books are available free with Kindle Unlimited and in paperback.

Printed in Great Britain
by Amazon